I0659445

Compromise

A Second Chance Romantic Suspense

Marsha R West

Published by MRW Press LLC, 2021.

Table of Contents

Copyright

COMPROMISE
©2021 by Marsha R. West
Cover Art© 100 Covers
Editor Olivia Wade Alexander

PRINT AND E-VERSION published by MRW Press LLC and released November 4, 2021.
ISBN 978-0-9989415-7-8 (e-release)
ISBN 978-0-9989415-8-5 (Print)

Acknowledgments

The number of people it takes to bring a book to publication still amazes me. The small and large tweaks that happen with the passing of each new gaze upon the pages continually shapes the manuscript. Many writer friends over the years have looked at my writing and given me feedback.

Thanks to my editor Olivia Alexander. 100 Covers worked with me to develop my cover, which I love. Thanks to Susah H Vaughan for giving me the rights to her picture that was used on the cover.

Thanks to Beta Readers: Teresa Cromer, Julie Miers, and Barbara McMulllen for taking an early look at the book and giving me feedback on the book and possible covers. I really appreciate your efforts.

Big thanks to my buddies Susan H. Vaughan and Klaran Warner. I picked their brains on a couple of issues relating to small town life. They actually live in New England; I only get to visit. And a special shout out to my hair stylist Judi Perrotti for description of gray hair. I bet you'll recognize the line.

While Margie Lawson hasn't looked at any of this book, what I learned from her led to publication of my first book VERMONT ESCAPE and thus to this my ninth book. Always grateful, Margie.

None of this would be possible without the support of my wonderful husband Bob West, who shares his time so generously to edit my books, talk plot points, and make suggestions to improve the story, not to mention helping with the business end of things.

As always, any errors are my own. I hope you enjoy COMPROMISE.

Chapter One

Labor Day

"Come on, Mom. You've got to close up. You promised you'd come with us to picnic on the green."

Jessica Allen laughed at the wheedling tone in the voice of her twenty-seven year-old-daughter, Kathy. Some things never change. Kathy wore slacks in the navy blue she preferred, claiming she could pair the color with anything for a different look. In this case, she'd chosen bright yellow.

"Okay. Okay, but can you give me five minutes? Let me unpack these last two boxes. Melody sent me her latest creations." The entire family long held to the tradition of attending the Labor Day picnic held on the town green. The beautiful late summer weather blessed Tidbury, New Hampshire in the north central part of the state. Certainly beat what Jessica had grown up with in Texas when temps could hit 100 sometimes as late as into September. Jessica would've been dressed in shorts and a sleeveless top rather than the slim jeans and long-sleeved purple t-shirt she now wore.

"I know what your *give me five minutes* means, Mom. I better help, or we'll never get out of here. Despite Bobby and Bonnie demanding I drag you from this store, I guess the grands will have to wait a bit." Kathy retrieved a carved cranberry-colored candle from the box her mom had indicated. "Where do you want this?"

"Just set it on the counter, please." Then Jessica's gaze caught the object in her daughter's hands. "Oh, wait. That is beautiful, isn't it? Someone's mantle will display a one-of-a-kind treasure this Christmas."

"Mom, have you heard the news?"

"What news is that? Besides, you think I work too much." Jessica took the wine-colored candle and spun around her shop, looking for the best spot to display the creation. "Oh, this will be perfect. People will notice it first thing on entering. Guess that means it won't be around long for me to appreciate." She placed her hands on her hips and stepped back to admire the candle in its place of importance near the front door of her shop, Allen's.

Kathy took her mother's arm. "No. That you work too much is a fact and not news. This is more serious. They found Lonnie Melton this morning in his car. Dead."

"They did not."

"Afraid so, Mom."

"Did he have a heart attack?"

"It looks like he might've committed suicide."

"Lonnie? No, never. He had more zest for life than ten of us put together."

"That's what I thought, Mom, but that's the word out and about in town."

Jessica shook her head. "I can hardly believe what you've told me."

"But, Mom, if he didn't kill himself, are you saying someone may have murdered him?" Kathy barely whispered the word. "Why would anyone do that? I mean this is Tidbury. We're all good people in this town."

"Even though your Dad's family traces its roots back to the revolution here, every town has a number of folks who—" Jessica paused. "Well, who are only interested in number one. Those who will stop at nothing to get what they want. Don't let the façade fool you. Because we look like a Hallmark town, doesn't make us one."

Jessica stripped off her work apron and hung it behind the office door at the back of the shop, returning with a light denim jacket. "You're right. This can wait. Come on, let's go. I need to love on my grands. If everyone knows what happened to Lonnie, I guess this will be something of a subdued celebration." She threw on the jacket and made for the front of her shop with Kathy hurrying to catch up with her mother's switching of gears.

Again, Kathy reached out and took her mother's hand, stopping her from leaving her shop. "Mom, you need to be aware of this, too. I've already heard people speculating on who would be the best person to run for Lonnie's seat on the Tidbury Board of Selectmen."

"Oh my, Kathy, that seems terribly rushed. The poor man's not even in his grave yet. Let's mourn him first before galloping off in that direction."

Jessica shook off her daughter's grasp and scurried toward the front door. She stopped when she realized her daughter wasn't following and spun to face Kathy. "Come on."

"People are suggesting you should run."

"What? Me?" She placed both fists on her hips. "No way. No how. Why in the world would anyone suggest I run? I don't know anything about serving on the board of selectmen, which has always been men by the way, except once when a woman completed her husband's term."

"For one, because of your speech at last month's board meeting."

"Well, what can I say? Inspiration hit me in the moment, Kathy. When I heard those rumors concerning leasing part of the green for development, I knew I had to speak up." She brushed away the compliments. Hadn't been much of a choice. It wasn't that she opposed progress or hated the idea of new buildings. She opposed the location picked by the development company. And worse, they wanted to use Worley Construction. No way she'd let that happen.

"Please consider the idea."

"Jeez Louise, Kathy. This discussion has ended. I want to spend time with my grands. After the picnic, I'll go by to check if there's anything we can do for Lonnie's wife."

The Labor Day picnic was a huge success. Everyone ate a ton of food, played horseshoes, had three legged races, and generally had a great time. While they laughed and visited, still the news of Lonnie's death subdued everyone's complete enjoyment. Late in the afternoon, Jessica left the family and met up with her friend Sue Franklin to walk to Millie Melton's house.

"Thank you for coming with me, Sue." They had been friends since soon after meeting each other when Jessica moved to her husband's hometown of Tidbury after college. Unfortunately, over the years, they had made these condolence visits too many times. The people of the town were aging, and while occasionally new folks moved in, still they'd lost many old timers.

"I hate to do these visits, Jessica. It always makes me think this could be me." She stopped, one hand reaching toward her mouth as if she wished she could take back the words. "Oh, I'm sorry. I didn't stop to think. You understand exactly how she feels.

Forgive me?"

Jessica patted Sue's shoulder. "It's okay. And yes, I all too well understand what Millie's feeling. At least the shock of it. And you're right. These visits are hard because that's exactly what they make people think. While I understand something of what she may be feeling because of my shock at Ed's death, at least we didn't have to consider suicide as the cause. That would've been infinitely worse." Negligence if not something more in Ed's case. Despite not being able to come up with proof, she hadn't given up either. She knocked on the door.

After a while, Jessica knocked again.

Sue looked at her. "Do you think she's at the funeral home?"

"I wouldn't think she'd have gone yet. Guess we'll have to come back. Can't leave these casseroles on the porch. While our temperatures are moderate, they aren't cool enough to keep the food from spoiling." Checking one last time, Jessica leaned forward and squinted her eyes to peer through the cut glass panels on the door. "Oh, wait. Someone's coming." Before she finished speaking the door swung open." She jerked back.

"Good evening, Jessica. And Sue. Did you two ladies bring food for Millie?" Sheriff Gary Halbert held the door with one hand, studying them both. He wore his navy uniform pants with the sharp creases and crisp khaki shirt and kept his salt and pepper beard neatly trimmed. The closer they got to the Christmas holidays, the more Gary let his beard grow and enhanced the salt color. He played the town Santa for the Christmas Tree Lighting ceremony held on the green.

Jessica smiled at the sheriff. "We did. May we come in? Are you here on business or are you paying a condolence call?"

"Well, I guess that's something for me to know and you to find out." He stepped back and smiled. The dimples, one in each cheek, gave him a deceptively sweet appearance and one of the reasons he made such a great Santa. Nice man, but most in town knew not to mess with him. He took seriously his job of keeping the people of Tidbury safe. "You can come in. I'm leaving now. That's why I came to the door for Millie. And here she is."

Millie Melton stopped at the entry way. She looked as one might imagine-haggard, with blank eyes, and a hanky she kept twisting in her hand. "Hello, Jessica and Sue. You are kind to stop by."

Jessica stepped forward and slid one arm around Millie's waist. "We had to. Can we put these in your refrigerator? Is someone keeping up with all the food for you?"

"Yes, my niece. She left right before the sheriff arrived. She should be returning shortly."

"Millie, I'll leave you with Jessica and Sue. Think about what we've discussed, okay?"

"Sure, Gary."

"Ladies." He tipped his hat and went out on the porch.

Jessica used her hips to push the door closed behind the sheriff. "We're terribly sorry for your loss, Millie." Sue in her turn gave Millie a one-armed hug.

"It's such a shock. It's like I've been tossed upside down. My niece Sylvie is being a big help. I'd be quite lost without her."

"Let me put these in the kitchen for you. Maybe you'd like to sit down with Jessica."

"Yes, thank you."

Sue took Jessica's dish as well as her own and hastily made her way toward the kitchen.

"I don't seem to have much endurance. Come on. I'm using the informal room in the back. We did everything from watching TV to eating meals in here." She wiped at her eyes and drew in a shaky breath.

Jessica's breath hitched. The memories of her own loss, though five years past, seared still, especially because she believed the death could've been avoided if the Worley Construction Company had carefully followed the regulations. She drew in a deep breath, propelling the past to the past. Now she needed to offer what comfort she could to Millie, knowing there wasn't much she could do other than be present with her.

Sue returned and joined them. "Millie, were the sheriff and Lonnie close? We were surprised to find him here."

Jessica shot her friend a look. So not okay to go there. "Sue."

Millie shrugged. "It's okay, Jessica. I guess eventually it will come out." Having only sat on the sofa, she popped up and wandered toward the windows at the back of the room.

"What will come out, Millie?" Jessica glanced at Sue whose eyebrows shot up in question. Their friend wasn't making much sense. Losing her husband so suddenly had messed with her mind. "Millie?"

The woman turned and wandered back to them and sank onto the couch as if it took too much effort to hold herself upright. "The sheriff thinks perhaps Lonnie didn't kill himself."

Jessica leaned forward and took Millie's hand. "Oh, that's good. I'm sure you felt relief to learn he hadn't taken his own life."

Millie looked around the room until her glassy gaze found Jessica and Sue. "The sheriff thinks Lonnie may have been murdered."

"Dear God, Millie. That's horrible." Jessica straightened on the soft sofa. Perhaps not as bad as if Lonnie had killed himself. Some folks never recovered from losing a loved one to suicide.

"I'm at a total loss, Jessica. Who would want to kill Lonnie? The sheriff asked me to think of who'd want him dead, but everyone loved the man." More tears coursed down her cheeks. Millie grabbed extra tissues from the box on the coffee table to sop them up, but the tears kept flowing.

Who would want to kill Lonnie Melton? And what made the sheriff even ask that? Poor Millie. They stayed a while longer until Millie's niece arrived. Jessica and Sue walked down the steps and ambled toward the green. As if by mutual agreement, they shifted gears to discuss the subject of the committee to plan the Christmas Festival. They'd both been on the committee for several years, and this year Jessica chaired the event again. Work began during the summer, and while September had just commenced, Christmas would be here quicker than anyone could say, *Happy Holidays*.

"If you decide to run to fill Lonnie's board position, I'll step up and cover any slack on the festival," Sue said out of the blue.

Jessica glared at her friend. "What in the world is going on with everyone? Where'd this idea come from?"

"Everyone is talking about it."

"Well, not everyone. I'm not talking about it. And as I told Kathy this morning, Lonnie's poor wife hasn't had a chance to plan his funeral, much less get him buried."

Sue looped her arm through one of Jessica's and walked toward the green where streetlights lined the sidewalk and the Gazebo sparkled with tiny white lights. Various volunteers cleaned up the debris left from the picnic. "Listen, you keep up with what's on the board agenda, don't you? You have ever since Ed died."

"Yes, I have. I'll never be convinced that Worley Construction didn't bear a share of the responsibility for my husband's death."

"Well, then you've heard that Jeff Hudson, the developer, plans to use Worley Construction if the board approves his project to put that retirement center on the green."

"I had heard that, and it's one of the reasons I spoke out at the board meeting last month. I'm even more convinced it's not a project for our town. I support progress, and I can sort of understand the idea of how building a retirement facility for our aging folks, especially those who live out from town, would be beneficial. But not on our green. And that Hudson's planning to use Worley Construction? That's unacceptable."

"So you'll consider the idea of running?"

Jessica rolled her eyes at her friend with the one-track mind.

"My guess is we'll have a special election in November. It will be an easier campaign since we're not in a presidential year."

"When did you become such a smarty?" Jessica poked her friend on the arm.

"You've forgotten I majored in political science in college."

"Well, why don't *you* run?"

"Because I'm a behind-the-scenes kind of person. You make a great in-front-of-the-camera person."

"Thank goodness, here's my store. We can end this discussion."

"Have you been happy living above it, Jessica? I'm always amazed at how charming your apartment is, given its size is much, much smaller than your home at the edge of town."

Jessica looked through the window with the soft lighting shining on the new dark red candle she'd put in the place of importance. "Not my home anymore. After Ed died, I found myself rattling around the house with too many overly large rooms with too many memories of Ed. I never remembered where I'd left anything. By then Kathy was already married, and Lori would soon leave for college. This is her last year now, and who knows where she'll land. It made sense for me to move in here and let Kathy and her husband have the big house. Now they've got Bobby and Bonnie, it's perfect for them. Besides, I love the commute." A soft chuckle escaped.

"I'm glad to hear you're happy with the situation. Can you promise me you'll give serious contemplation to the idea of running?"

"Okay, I promise I'll mull over the subject." Didn't mean she'd agree.

Sue hugged her. "Great. Talk with you tomorrow. We'll make changes in the Christmas committee and plan for your campaign." She spun off down the sidewalk.

"I haven't agreed," Jessica hollered after the fleeing figure. Shaking her head, she drew the key out of her pocket, went into the store, and turned off the alarm before resetting it. Walking through the store, she passed her office to reach the stairs leading up to her apartment. At some point, climbing the stairs could become an issue. Thankfully, she had no problems with her knees. Breathing a bit fast, she let herself into the apartment and drew in a deep breath of the lavender scent she used liberally. It always brought peace.

Peace. Now why did she think of that? Because Lonnie's death made her think of Ed's death? Because of all this talk of her running for office?

She wandered into her kitchen and made a cup of hot tea using the hotspot at her sink. An indulgence for certain. She loved how it simplified her life. Dipping the tea bag up and down in her blue mug, she pondered the crazy idea of her running for the board of selectmen. Settling on the hearth, she gazed at the charming room with its wheat colored sofa and blue plaid wingback chair next to the fireplace with books filling the shelves on either side. The kitchen was open to her left and her bedroom on her right. Another small guest room was behind the kitchen. Her home. Too bad it wasn't cool enough to use the fireplace yet, but soon it would be.

Lonnie's loss from the board of selectmen meant they had one less person to speak up for maintaining the town's unique flavor. Someone besides her had to be the right person to take his place. No reason for her to consider this crazy idea. Someone else would step forward to do the job. She'd continue to monitor meetings and stay on top of the issue of saving the green, especially if any building involved Worley Construction.

Chapter Two

J eff Hudson settled against one of the high-backed white wicker chairs that lined the porch of the Mount Washington Resort. History oozed from the walls, floors, and decorations. While he loved that about the hotel, it cost more than he preferred to pay for a hang-out place when he worked a deal. In the rural state of New Hampshire, he hadn't found many options. Unfortunately for him, the local inn had not a single vacancy. The Mount Washington Resort had undergone a fairly recent renovation and was now under the Omni umbrella. Rooms and suites had been enlarged, but they'd managed to keep the historic charm of the place.

Jeff glanced around. What kept Tony who prided himself on being on time? Tony Benton and Jeff had fallen into a great working relationship. Jeff knew if something happened to him and he couldn't carry through on his company's responsibilities, Tony would. And vice versa.

Jeff sipped his black coffee laced with half and half and decided to relax and enjoy this respite from the rushed meeting schedule he usually faced. After a ton of research, Tony had come up with the idea of building their next retirement center in Tidbury. He'd found thirty families that lived around the town, all with elderly members. Once the snows set in, it became hard to make the trip to town. This would be perfect. All the tenants' needs would be within walking distance if they couldn't find it in the center itself. He and Tony hadn't quite resolved what should be a part of the center, whether it should be only residential with a restaurant or something more elaborate with a variety of services.

"Hey, Jeff. I'm late. I got caught up in drawings and lost track of the clock." His business partner and friend ran up the stairs to the wide porch running around much of the building.

"Not a problem, I've been sitting and enjoying this great view. When the leaves start to change, I bet it will be even more magnificent. You've brought your own coffee, I see. Take a seat." Jeff gestured to another of the large chairs with the soft cushions.

Tony sat next to Jeff, glancing around at the vista. He exhaled a long breath. "Boy, we don't have an opportunity to do this too often." He laughed. "I think we must be working too much."

"Well, you've got that right. Maybe come Christmas we'll take a break."

"When did we last take off for Christmas?"

Jeff rubbed a hand along his jaw. Damn, it couldn't be as long as he first thought. "Five years?"

"Yep. I think we're due."

"Well, you certainly are, Tony. I'm surprised Eva hasn't killed me."

"She enjoys the product of all our hard work. That's also why she keeps trying to set you up with someone you can settle down with and force us all to kick back."

"Eva is one determined woman, and I appreciate her concern. She'd make me happy though if she'd give it up."

"You might buy yourself a reprieve if you give us this Christmas off." Tony sipped his coffee.

"I hear ya. Right now let's talk about the Tidbury project. I drove through the town on the way here. It's quite charming. The green is much larger than you find in many towns."

"That's why I believe this will work." Tony extracted drawings from his bag, set them on the table, and secured them with his cup on one edge to keep the ends from curling.

"Hey, that's my coffee," Jeff complained when Tony snatched the cup from his hand and set it on the other end of the diagrams.

"I'll give it back. You've seen these before, but I wanted to show you a couple of the changes I'm suggesting."

"Okay. What've you got?"

"Well, I've taken out a few items I hope will make the project more acceptable to the board of selectmen and the town. I heard there was a person who spoke against the whole project at their last meeting. I thought it was smart to be prepared with alternatives. Maybe we won't have to make these changes because one of our worst critics has died."

"What?"

"Yeah. The story is a member of the board of selectmen committed suicide."

"Boy, that's rough on family members." Memories of his brother's suicide cut through his heart. Ten years ago still seemed like yesterday. Scott had never gotten a handle on his drug addiction.

"So what are these changes?"

"Originally we'd planned to have a beauty & barber shop, a dry cleaner, a trinket shop, and of course, the restaurant. If we leave in the restaurant and take out all the rest, we will be less threatening to the merchants around the green. However, if we don't have any issues on the board, we can add them back in."

"Okay, I like your suggestions, Tony. We can go with either Plan A with the additions or Plan B with only the food service offered in the center if town officials continue to raise objections to the project."

"What do you want to do now?" Tony rolled up the design papers.

"Let's take a drive through Tidbury. I'd like to become more familiar with the town. You've visited more than I, and I'd like to double-check the space on this famous green you've been carrying on about. I couldn't quite tell how much space we'd take up when I drove through on the way here."

"Let's go. Once you walk around on the green in person, you'll have no doubts about the merits of this project."

JESSICA WALKED OUT of the Congregational Church where Millie held Lonnie Melton's funeral. The whole town had been in attendance and at the gathering in the reception hall afterwards. Sheriff Halbert confirmed the rumors swirling around about how Lonnie had died, possibly poisoned. While Millie didn't have a clue why someone would kill her husband, she seemed relieved with the information he hadn't taken his own life. And while poison was most often used by women, the sheriff didn't consider his wife a suspect.

"Jessica, wait up." Mayor Rudy Lopez took Jessica's arm. "Slow down. I'd like to walk with you."

"Hi, Rudy. Lovely service, wasn't it?" She looped her arm through the mayor's.

"Yes, such a tragedy though. We've never had a murder in Tidbury, and for this to happen to Lonnie? My heart aches for Millie and for our town."

"No one holds you responsible, Rudy. We've been sheltered here in Tidbury. Out in the real world, I'm afraid this is more common."

"So, Jessica, I want to encourage you to seriously consider the idea of running for Lonnie's seat on the board."

"What? You, too?" Jessica stopped and shook her head at him before walking on. "It's beyond me why you think I can do this or why I'd want to. I stay plenty busy with the store, family, and volunteer activities."

"Doesn't Lori help out with the store?"

"Yes, she does around her college classes. And that's beside the point. I've never done anything like serving on the board."

"You were PTA president for years."

"I'm pretty certain that doesn't count, Rudy."

"You didn't sound inexperienced several weeks ago when you spoke passionately on the subject of saving the green. And we all know that Lonnie opposed any changes on the green. You'd kind of hold up that perspective on the board. Promise you'll at least consider the possibility. We're planning to call the election for Tuesday, November 5. You've got time to file and get a jump on electioneering, though I can't think anyone would run against you."

"Okay, I'll mull over this crazy idea. I'll talk with the kids and let you know. I am flattered by you thinking of me. Really." She shook her head.

They'd reached the green. The city offices were on the other side from Jessica's store, so they separated. She must be the crazy one to waste a minute on this laughable idea. She let herself into her store and glanced around. She'd have been lost without this place to work and live after Ed died.

Situated on one of the streets that surrounded the green made everything super convenient. She walked everywhere in town with the church being up on the hill two blocks and the grocery store two blocks the other way. It didn't matter what the weather. Her whole world circled around the green. And now someone intended to destroy that.

Time for a family meeting.

"YOU ARE SUCH A GOOD cook, Kathy. Your roast was the tenderest meat I've eaten in a long time."

"Gee, thanks, Mom. I wonder who taught me?" Her daughter, dressed in her traditional navy blue slacks topped this time with a white turtleneck, chuckled and rolled her eyes like she did when a teenager. "Let's move into the main room for this family meeting you've requested. Everyone bring your drinks with you. I'll put the snickerdoodle cookies on the coffee table."

Jessica carried her cup of hot tea and perched on the edge of the stuffed chair to the right of the fireplace. She pulled a tube of lipstick from the pocket of her good jeans she'd paired with another of her purple sweaters. With fresh lipstick, a woman could handle just about anything.

Bobby and Bonnie, the twins, sat on the floor close to the cookies. Didn't take too many smarts to figure out their plans.

Lori, wearing ubiquitous blue jeans and a college sweatshirt, sat in the chair across from her mom and quickly snatched a cookie. "I can read what's going on in your minds, guys, but I got mine first." The twins giggled.

Bob set his coffee on a coaster on the table. "So is this a contest to decide who can eat more snickerdoodles than anyone else?"

"Aw, Dad." Bobby took two cookies and gave one to Bonnie. "We won't eat them all."

"Better not, young man." Kathy settled next to her husband on the sofa with her cup of coffee. "Okay, Mom. You requested this family meeting. You're on."

Jessica clasped her hands around her mug of tea. Should she go through with discussing the issue with the family? She was here now. Might as well pick their brains on the matter. Maybe they would tell her the idea of her running for the board of selectmen was stupid. Not Kathy, of course, since she'd brought up the issue as soon as they'd heard of Lonnie's death. Surely Bob or Lori would have a good argument for why she shouldn't take on the task.

"Several people have suggested I run to fill Lonnie's unexpired term on the board of selectmen, and I wanted to hear what you thought of the idea."

Silence filled the room. The grands chewed on their cookies. Jessica's adult children met each other's gaze before they focused that collective attention on her.

"We think it's a super idea, Jessica." Bob picked up his coffee.

"Yeah, Mom, from when Kathy first mentioned the idea to me, I've been all for you taking this on." Lori took a bite of her cookie. "These are the best, Kathy."

"Thanks, Lori. I've made my opinion clear, Mom. The town would be lucky to have you do this, even if you don't decide to do anything but complete the one term. And maybe you'd decide you like the job."

Jessica looked at each of her kids, considering Bob her kid, too. He'd proved to be an excellent husband and father and a great handyman whenever she needed something, often thinking of tasks before she had to ask for help.

"Lori, this may impact you more than anyone else. If I run and if I win, which isn't a forgone conclusion, I may not be able to be in the store as much as normal."

"Since my classes are all online right now, I've got more freedom to schedule hours at the shop than I did when I lived at college. Worst case scenario, we can hire a part-time worker or two."

"Well, that would take care of the problem. Huh. So it looks like you're all in favor of this crazy idea?" Her family nodded. Jessica drew in a long breath and held it before slowly releasing it. "Let me consider this a bit more. I'm probably nuts for spending even a minute studying the idea. Besides, I know nothing about running a campaign."

"Not to worry. I helped elect our student government president. We had way more voters involved than we have here in Tidbury. This should be a snap. Not to mention you are good friends with the owner of our newspaper." Lori winked at her mother.

"Come on, Mom. You can do this. Sometimes we have to step out of our comfort zone to grow." Encouragement sparkled from Kathy's eyes.

"Huh. You seem to think I need to grow, is that right, Kathy?" And this would stretch her. Working behind the scenes suited her better, but maybe the time had come for her to put her money where her mouth had been for the last five years. Winning a seat on the Tidbury Board of Selectmen would put her in a position to stop Worley Construction. Jessica set her cup on the coffee table and stood. "Okay, I guess I'm in."

Her family jumped up and swarmed around for a group hug with the grands yelling, "yea," running circles around the adults, even if they didn't quite understand what the celebration was about.

"First thing is to put together a committee to help elect you, Mom," Lori said.

"I'm sure Sue will want to be on that committee. When she first mentioned my running, she indicated she'd step in if I needed to palm off anything from the Christmas Festival Committee." Humm. A tiny thrill of excitement ran across Jessica's shoulders, and she shivered. Guess they were doing this.

Chapter Three

Jeff walked all the way around the green, peeking in the various stores and going in others. Several weeks had passed since he and Tony set off to tour Tidbury. Eva, Tony's wife, had broken her ankle in a car accident, and they'd both sped back to Concord where their office was and where Tony lived with his wife and kids, who were both in college. Tony's wife would be okay, but he'd chosen to stay in Concord to help out.

The end of September brought out the leaves along with politics. The town newspaper ran a story about a woman named Jessica Allen running a campaign against a man named Palmer Northcutt for the Tidbury Board of Selectmen. Apparently, they were running to fill the unexpired term of the guy Tony had told him had committed suicide. He wondered about the man's wife. Hard times. He shook his head as he wandered on.

Jeff admired people who put themselves out on the line to run for public office. How could they stand all the constant scrutiny? And in a small town it must be more difficult because you'd run into people every way you'd turn, who knew you served on the board and would want something. He had enough of that running a development company, and he lived in a larger community, where a person could more easily blend in.

He glanced in the window of a shop named Allen's. Same name as the woman running for the board. Maybe a family member? He tried to pull open the door, but it wouldn't give. He realized it opened inward. Must be a really old building that had been grandfathered. Nowadays, doors had to open outwards for safety. Jeff gave it a shove and a gentle jingle overhead greeted him, followed by a comforting aroma. What was that?

"Hi. Come in."

An attractive woman came out from the back of the store. Her brown shoulder length hair curled slightly up on the ends and fell into her blue-green eyes. She self-consciously brushed it behind one ear.

"Can I help you with anything or are you browsing?"

Jeff jerked to attention. He'd been staring at the woman like a lovesick schoolboy. "Uh, yeah. I mean no. That's right. I'm browsing. Do you work here?"

"Yes, I do. Actually, I own the store. I'm Jessica Allen."

"Ah, the candidate."

"How do you know?" Her eyebrows raised quizzically over those arresting blue-green eyes.

"Read an article in the Gazette. Isn't that the name of your town newspaper?

She nodded. "I sometimes forget why I got into all of this. It seemed the right thing to do at the time, but campaigning is hard work. Answering all the questions for the newspaper interview. Holding campaign committee meetings. Shaking hands and shaking more hands. I mean I've lived in this town for almost thirty years. You'd think I'd know everyone, and everyone knew me. Apparently, when you become a candidate for the Tidbury Board of Selectmen, everything changes."

She stopped suddenly and laughed, a low tone that hit him in the stomach. What was that about?

"Oh my gosh. I'm sorry. What came over me? I said stuff to you I've never mentioned to my friends or family." She stretched out her arm. "Let's start again. I'm Jessica Allen and you are?"

Jeff took her hand and experienced a hard to ignore zing of electricity. "I'm Jeff Hudson. I'm the developer wanting to put a retirement center on the green."

"Oh." She dropped his hand and stepped back.

"Ah. Are you on the same side as the board member who died? Anti-development?" He folded his arms across his chest.

"No, I wouldn't say anti-development at all, Mr. Hudson. I kind of like the idea of a retirement center. I may possibly make use of it myself someday if I can't manage the stairs to my apartment." She gestured overhead. "But not, absolutely not on our green."

Her fists settled on her hips, that curved out enough to be interesting. Standing approximately five feet four, she had an athletic build. Not a stick of a girl. Jeff hated when you hugged a woman and had the sensation she might snap in two.

Jeff re-considered his combative stance which had encouraged Jessica Allen to take one, too. He uncrossed his arms. That wasn't the way to win friends and influence people. Something he prided himself on doing well.

"Ms. Allen, I apologize. We seem to have gotten off on the wrong foot. I'd like to take you for a cup of coffee so we can discuss our different perspectives. I noticed Molly's a couple of shops down the way. Could I persuade you to go there? I've heard they have excellent pie."

Several expressions flitted across Jessica Allen's open book face. That would be a disadvantage for her in politics, but that openness certainly helped him. Finally, she removed her fists from her hips and held out a hand. "All right, let's try this a third time. I'm Jessica Allen. And you are?"

Jeff eagerly took her hand in his again, hoping, wondering if he'd experience the zing again. Yep. Hmm. This negotiation would be interesting. "Jeff Hudson. Pleased to meet you. Can I take you for a cup of coffee?"

"If you make that tea, you're on. Let me grab my jacket." She stepped toward what looked like an office area, disappearing for a moment before she returned, pulling a forest green leather jacket on without waiting for assistance from him, independence in every move. "And you've heard correctly. Molly's pies are famous, not only in our area but around the state. Let's go, shall we?"

Jessica Allen led him through the door, flipping the open sign to closed and locking the door.

"Don't you have a security system?"

"Of course, but we're only walking down the street for a short while. Everything will be fine. This is Tidbury."

Jeff kept between Jessica and the road because his mom had always taught him to treat a lady that way. He lost her when he was in high school, but the lessons remained. Jessica smiled and spoke to everyone they passed. Everyone seemed to recognize her. That would augur well for her campaign.

"Here we are. Molly's. Prepare to be amazed." Jessica sailed through the door, not waiting for him to open it for her. Independent for sure.

"Hi, Molly. I've brought a guest."

"Good to see you, Jessica. Who do you have with you?"

Jessica made the introductions and added, "Mr. Hudson is with the development company that wants to put a retirement center on the green."

"Oh. Humph. I guess your money is as good as another. What would you like?"

"He'd like a piece of Molly's famous apple pie, and I would, too, with a cup of my regular tea. What are you drinking, Mr. Hudson?"

"Coffee with cream, please. As I've wandered through town, I've overheard people raving about your pies, Molly."

"You won't be disappointed. Have a seat anywhere." She jetted toward what must be the kitchen.

"This table by the window is perfect. Easy to enjoy the view of our green."

Jessica—he couldn't think of her as Ms. Allen—settled into a seat closest to the window with her back to the door. She gestured for him to join her. Ah, he could tell what her strategy was. He did have a great view of the green with its bandstand in the middle. People wandered across to reach the Post Office and town offices on the other side.

"I hope you'll be around next month to catch what happens out there. It's quite something."

Molly set Jessica's tea and his coffee on the table.

"Thanks, Molly."

"Pie will be here shortly. I'll take a fresh one out of the oven in moments."

"Tell me what happens in October?" He tipped the cream pitcher over his cup and stirred before he lifted his cup and sniffed. Nothing beat the aroma of good coffee. He blew over the top then took a sip. "Umm good."

"Everything Molly makes is the best. Folks actually travel to Tidbury from all around the state to enjoy her pies and other food. She's quite the chef."

"In October?" He cocked his head.

"Of course. The whole community comes together to raise money for our less fortunate people. You may think we're a fairly well-off little place nestled between the mountains the way we are with the super fancy Mount Washington Resort up the road a piece, but we have our share of hurting folks." She sipped her tea. "Various groups and families compete to have the best scarecrow and Halloween display. Visitors and all the town buy a ticket to be able to vote on the display they think is the best. The proceeds go to our Community Center to be shared with anyone in need."

"You sound like a socially conscious community. The kind of place we generally choose for one of our retirement centers. We checked out several locations, Jessica. May I call you Jessica?"

She nodded.

"And your town won. It's centrally located so people from all over could take advantage of the retirement center. We've looked at the Census numbers. This is an aging area of New Hampshire, with no other retirement center in this part of the state."

"I appreciate you've done your research, Jeff. May I call you Jeff?" She threw the question back at him with an arched eyebrow.

"Of course. Am I wrong or do I hear a 'but' coming?"

"I had to let it cool before cutting into this." Molly bustled up to their table. "Be careful. Hot apples will kill your tastebuds for several days." She set two plates in front of them with pieces that appeared to be the size of a quarter of the pie."

"Wow."

"I use extra-large pie plates. Enjoy." Molly hurried off to greet other guests entering the café.

Jeff cut into the steaming pie, the aroma tickling his nose and making his stomach growl. "This will count for lunch."

"It's nearly two in the afternoon. How'd you come to skip lunch?" She blew, her lips puckering in a sensual way that caught him by surprise. What was it with his reaction to this woman?

Her eyes closed, savoring the bite of pie and a small sigh escaped. He decided to sample what all the fuss was about. After blowing, he shoveled in a forkful. Oh, wow. His eyes closed, too, and his senses reveled in the sweet, tart, cinnamon flavors encased in the flaky crust.

"Incredible."

"Told you so." She pointed her fork at him and grinned. Then she scooped up another forkful of the luscious pie and popped it in her mouth, extremely satisfied with herself.

For a while they both focused on devouring the pie. After cleaning his plate entirely, Jeff moved his plate to the side and wrapped his hand around the coffee mug. He took a last sip, leaned forward, and rested his elbows on the table and his chin on his clasped hands. "Before Molly arrived with the best apple pie I've ever eaten, I believe you were about to tell me what your 'but' was."

Her eyebrows raised.

"Well, not your butt, but the but you started to tell me." He stopped and shook his head. "Help me out here before I make a worse fool of myself."

"Because I'm a kind person, I will help you out. The but is that we use the green all year long. It's the center of our town. Not only for our town. The surrounding community does, too."

"Besides the scarecrow exhibition, which does sound creative and useful, how else do you use the green?"

"More coffee, Mr. Hudson?" Molly stopped by their table. "Are you ready for more water for the pot, Jessica?"

"I'm good, Molly, thanks." Jessica poured more tea from the small pot into her cup.

"Yes, thank you, Molly. Excellent coffee and the best apple pie I've ever eaten."

Molly beamed and took their plates. "Be right back with the coffee."

Jeff studied the beautiful woman across the table from him. She appeared comfortable in her skin. Guess she'd have to be to run for a public office. "What else do you do on the green?"

"We roll pumpkins on the green. Right after Thanksgiving we decorate the smaller fir trees. A volunteer band plays carols, and we all sing along. And we drink lots of hot chocolate. A giant fir is brought in and set up near the bandstand. We have a holiday festival. Everyone participates."

The smile covering her face made him experience the event through her. It clearly brought her joy. He'd like to be the one to do that. He squirmed in his chair. Damn. He needed to get his head in the game.

"Okay, that all sounds like a movie. Tell me, does anything happen the rest of the year? What you've talked about doesn't seem to require the whole green."

"You'd be surprised. During the dead of winter, families meet up at the grandstand. We have a number of local musicians, and they often play songs there. People sing, dance, visit. Once we make it through winter, our local farmers sell their produce on the green every Wednesday and Saturday. Memorial Day brings picnics on the green, with the band playing patriotic songs and a parade that goes all around the green. Fourth of July we have, of course, more picnics and fireworks. It's spectacular.

"Then the Labor Day picnic and parade, which we recently celebrated. The green is the heart and soul of this community. So you see, you can't build a retirement center on the west end of the land." She firmed her lips as if she'd taken her best shot and hoped he'd listened. Studying him, a small frown creased her brow while she waited for his response.

"I hear you, Jessica. The green is wonderful. It's why we want to put the retirement center there. The residents won't have far to walk to access all of the opportunities scattered around the center of town. They'll be a part of your special community."

She stared at him her lips firming into a straight line. "Thanks for listening, Jeff. Guess we approach issues from different perspectives." She rose. "I've got to return to the store. Molly, thanks always. Best apple pie anywhere." Her smile lit up her face and lit up a place in Jeff. A smile like that could land him in a pile of trouble.

Molly popped over to their table and hugged Jessica. "Always happy to have you stop by." She faced Jeff. "Hope you'll come back."

"You can count on it. What do I owe you?"

"Nothing, I put it on Jessica's tab."

His mouth dropped open. "I can't let you do that."

"It's done. I don't want to be beholden to anyone. It's especially important now that I may possibly become a member of the board of selectmen. I don't want to do anything to give anyone the idea I could be swayed by someone attempting to buy my vote."

"With apple pie?"

"It's not just any apple pie. It's Molly's apple pie, and people have been known to give serious thought to harming others for the last piece." Her low laugh bubbled out again, seriously destroying his equilibrium, and that smile of hers did something to his insides.

"Then thank you for the coffee and pie. I understand how you wouldn't want to give anyone the wrong idea. Let me walk you back to the store. Another time, I'd like to take you around the green to show you where exactly we'd like to put the Center."

"Another time, I'd like to do that. I want to be sure I've weighed all the facts before I decide on an issue. If I'm elected."

He held the door for her to leave Molly's, and she tipped her head in acknowledgement, a swath of hair swinging against her cheek. They walked in a comfortable silence, passing the couple of stores between Molly's and Allen's, stopping at the door to her shop. She looked up at him. "Guess I'll run into you later."

He nodded, "I'm sure," and ambled for his car parked on the west end of the green. He'd only taken two steps when a scream spun him around and sent him charging back toward Jessica's store.

Chapter Four

Jessica could hardly find breath to scream but scream she did until warm hands clasped her shoulders, drawing her close to a strong, hard body.

"Jessica are you all right? What happened?"

She glanced behind her. Jeff. Yes, he would've been close. She drew in a shaky breath but found no words. She pointed. A dead squirrel lay five-feet inside her store with a note written in what appeared to be blood. *Don't Stop Center.*

"Jessica, have you had a chance to call the police?"

"Sheriff. No, not yet. I need to call the sheriff." She shrugged out of his hold and grasped her phone from her pocket. "Hi, Mary. Can you ask Gary to stop by my store? I've had a...a...break-in...Right now, in the last thirty minutes or so...Thanks. I'll...I'll wait outside." She disconnected. "Sheriff Gary Halbert will be here soon. He's in his office across the green."

Jeff guided her back through the door, and she dropped onto the bench outside her store, grateful that was one of the first things she'd added after buying the shop. Providing a place to rest created a more friendly environment. She wanted people to enjoy a comfortable place to stop and catch their breath. That's sure what she needed to do now.

Her gaze scanned the developer, Jeff Hudson. Handsome, for sure. Strong jaw line. Clean cut. No scruffy beard like so many men now sported. Broad shoulders. The streaks of silver adding a distinguished flare. Just under six feet she guessed.

Jeff Hudson had a lot to gain if she stopped fighting the retirement center. Would he stoop to something like this?

"Hello, Jessica." Gary stepped up on the sidewalk outside her store. "What's going on?" He glanced at Jeff.

They rose, and Jessica quickly made the introductions. "I wasn't out of the store for more than thirty or forty minutes. And, before you ask, no I didn't set the security system. We only went down the street to Molly's. When we came back, I unlocked the door and—well you look." She gestured to her store. "I'm not entering until someone else cleans it up."

Gary wasn't inside long when he returned. "Fortunately, I don't think the words are written in blood. Looks like paint to me. It appears the squirrel lost a run-in with a car, not shot which is what I thought when I first saw it. I'll clean up the mess for you. We'll analyze the note." He eyed Jeff up and down. "You're the developer who wants to put in a retirement center on the green, right?"

"That's correct."

Gary stared at Jeff long enough to make Jessica question what the sheriff had in his mind.

"Wait a minute. You don't think I did this, do you? Jessica and I have been eating pie together at Molly's. The squirrel wasn't here when we left, and I returned with her."

"That's correct, Gary." Jessica glanced between the two men. Would Jeff Hudson hire someone else to do this?

"You don't want Jessica to block the development though, right?" Gary rested his hand on the butt of his weapon.

"Well, I am hoping to convince her to support the development, but I'd never do anything like this."

"Where are you staying, Mr. Hudson?"

"I'm up at the Mount Washington Resort. No vacancy at the inn here in town."

"Can I have your contact info?"

"Of course."

"How long are you planning on staying in the Tidbury area?"

"Not more than a couple of days now. I plan to return closer to time for the board of selectmen to vote on our use of the green. Of course, if we win approval, I'll be here for longer periods of time."

"Okay, I may have more questions later, but you're free to go now." He dismissed Jeff and questioned Jessica. "Do you have a trash sack in your office I can use? I'll clean up the mess for you."

"Thank you for taking care of this, Gary. There's a sack in the trash can next to my desk. Use that." Could Jeff have somehow made this happen? While he sat eating Molly's apple pie with her? He suggested they go to Molly's. Why did the idea disappoint her the way it did?

Gary came out of her shop, and Jessica repressed a shudder at what must be in the sack.

"It looks like someone got in through that window in your storeroom. I'll send a tech to check for fingerprints. We'll try not to mess up your store too much. You better stay closed for the rest of the afternoon."

"Okay, Gary. I'm not comfortable going back inside for a while anyway." She glanced at Jeff. "The beauty of being your own boss. You can take off whenever you want. Of course, that does impact the bottom line."

Jeff nodded, like he understood. Of course, he did. He owned his own business.

"I want you to stop by my office and leave an official statement, Jessica."

"Sure." She drew in a deep breath and let it out, blowing out the stress winding her up tighter than a two-year-old fighting sleep. "I'll give you a spare key to the store, Gary." She glanced at Jeff. "We don't see eye to eye. Maybe you can find another location for your center." She nodded to the sheriff. "I'll head on over and leave the statement." Jessica set off across the green where leaves from the trees surrounding the area carpeted the grass and crunched under her feet.

After making her statement to one of Gary's deputies, Jessica walked around the edge of the green, needing to work off more of her stress. And she admitted, her fear. Hard to ignore that someone had attempted to influence her vote. She hadn't been elected yet, so what did that portend for future issues? She'd gotten into this because she didn't want Worley Construction involved in the project, more than because she out and out opposed the retirement center project. The center would bring more traffic to the town and more work for the folks of Tidbury. Surely, they could find a compromise regarding the location. She'd be darned if she'd compromise on Worley Construction. She supposed that made her an enemy of John Crowell on the board of selectmen and Tim Worley, the owner of the construction company. Well, so be it.

Jessica clutched her cell. Given the recent happening, she needed to contact her campaign committee. When she explained what had happened, her daughter Kathy insisted she come by her house and stay the night. Driving out to her old house for a meeting would be okay, but she wouldn't be staying the night. She was a big girl. While she didn't like the idea of someone entering Allen's and leaving that poor squirrel to greet her, she wouldn't allow anyone to scare her out of her shop and her home, not even for one night.

KATHY HAD PREPARED pasta with meat sauce and garlic bread for supper. Good comfort food. Despite doubts and concerns about her decision to run, Jessica had been able to enjoy the meal. Besides Kathy, Bob, and her younger daughter Lori, her friends Sue and Joe Franklin had come over to enjoy dessert and discuss the campaign.

"I hated to hear the nasty story about the poor squirrel, Jessica. Had to be upsetting. I'm so sorry."

"Thanks, Sue, but not your fault."

"Well, kind of. I was one of the first persons to suggest you should run for the board, never dreaming it would be dangerous."

"Now, Sue, calm down." Her husband Joe patted her hands clenched in her lap. "It's not dangerous to run for the board. Oh, maybe in Boston or possibly Concord, but not Tidbury." He refilled his cup from the large pot Kathy had left on the sideboard and settled himself on the sofa next to his wife. "Jessica, do you think there's a chance this Hudson fellow had anything to do with the squirrel event? I mean he'd definitely benefit if you stopped fighting his project."

"He was with me from the time we left the store until we returned, Joe. Unless he hired that done, I don't see how he could be responsible." Disappointment filled her middle at the idea he might have done that.

Everyone grew silent with their own thoughts until Bob changed the subject. "So what's the next move in the campaign?"

"Signs," Kathy spoke up. "The campaign requires signs. And what about bumper stickers?"

"I don't think we have enough time to order bumper stickers, Kathy." Bob leaned forward, resting his hands on his knees. "But we can have a sign-making party. Twenty would be enough to scatter around the town. "Will you let us put one in the back side window of your car, Jessica?"

"Oh, I don't think that's necessary. I seldom drive many places except to your house and occasionally into Concord."

"Well, if we're going through with this, I like the idea of a sign on your car. You could park it on the street in front of the shop. I bet we can find plenty of people to help knock out those signs in an afternoon." Sue seemed to have regained her enthusiasm.

"Okay, okay, we'll do signs and yes, you can make one for my car," Jessica agreed good naturedly.

"Tell me more about him." Sue met Jessica's gaze over her coffee cup.

"What? Who are you talking about?"

"You know who. The developer. I heard you shared apple pie at Molly's this afternoon before the nasty encounter with the squirrel."

"Well, we're holding our own in the top-small-town-status. The gossip mill flourishes." Jessica sipped her hot tea. She'd never been fond of coffee.

"Spoken like a true politician, evading the question," her daughter Lori teased her. "We may have created a monster." She chuckled at her own joke.

Jessica took a deep breath. Be smart to address this directly. They'd never drop it if she pretended it didn't happen. "His name is Jeff Hudson. He's staying up at the Resort." Everyone in Tidbury understood Resort meant the Omni Mount Washington Resort.

"That's pretty pricey. And why didn't he stay at The Tidbury Inn? Not good enough for him?" Sue took pride in their town and wouldn't stand for anyone appearing to snub any of the businesses. She was probably the one who should've run for board. Oh, wait, Jessica had tried to convince Sue of that, and she didn't bite.

"Calm down, Sue. The inn had no vacancies when he tried for a reservation."

Sue huffed, "Well, good." And she settled back on the sofa, cradling her cup between both hands. "So what's he like? What did you say to each other? Molly implied you seemed to be pretty chummy, and he was handsome.

What do you think? He didn't convince you to allow the retirement center to be built on the green, did he?" Sue gulped in a breath and finally stopped.

"Of course not. What he had were good points about us needing a retirement center, especially for our older population that lives outside the center of town." She chose to ignore the question concerning the man's looks. If pushed, she'd have to admit he rated high in the looks category. She loved the gray at his temples with the occasional streak throughout. The slight grooves around his mouth gave him gravitas.

"He plans to have a restaurant for the residents, but not lots of other amenities, so they'll still use our businesses. Putting the retirement center on the green meant the residents would be close enough to walk to anything they'd desire."

Jessica paused and met everyone's gaze individually. She looked down into her teacup searching for the answer and then raised her gaze. "And I gotta admit that made sense. And the town would benefit from the residents spending their money with us. But I'm still not convinced there's room for the center and all our activities. And I remain adamant against using Worley Construction. If Jeff Hudson is wedded to Worley Construction, then we'll be on opposite sides of this subject."

KATHY HAD INSISTED Bob follow Jessica back to town and accompany her into her apartment. She wanted to decline her son-in-law's company, but in reality after the squirrel event, she dreaded walking into her store by herself late at night. Not a feeling she'd ever experienced before.

Bob accompanied her upstairs to check out her apartment. "Everything looks good, Jessica. I'll lock up when I leave, and you be sure to set the alarm." He hugged her.

"Thanks, Bob. I appreciate what you're doing. How you've always taken care of me. You realize I've told Kathy if anything happens between you two, I'm keeping you." They both laughed.

"See you soon." He ran down the stairs.

Jessica stood on the landing and listened for the sound of the door closing and the lock clicking. She stepped back inside and set the alarm system.

Her family blessed her in many, many ways. Kathy and Bob and the twins and Lori. Blessed for sure, and they all lived close, unlike Sue's kids and grands that lived in Pittsburg.

Too keyed up to go to bed, Jessica sat down at her laptop and tackled the newspaper questions she hadn't yet completed. In her town, everyone paid attention to a candidate's answers in the paper. If a candidate didn't answer, the townspeople wrote off the guy as not worth their vote. Jessica had no intention of having that happen to her. Maybe her opponent, Palmer Northcutt, would take a shortcut. He'd be out, and she'd be in. Her fingers flew over the keys typing responses she hoped would win her the position on the board of selectmen. Keeping Worley from building anything else in her town made her willing to take on the fight and face any danger. A picture of the poor squirrel flashed across her mind, and a chill ran across her shoulders.

Chapter Five

John Crowell traveled to the next town over to meet with Palmer Northcutt and Tim Worley. John didn't want anyone from Tidbury seeing the three of them together. That worked against his appearance of neutrality in the board of selectmen race. Of course neutral and his name didn't fit in the same sentence. He'd already made a good chunk of change from Tim Worley's shortcuts in his various building projects. Too bad Ed Allen had fallen victim of one of those shortcuts. John needed one more vote to make the deal firm. Lonnie Melton should've agreed to go along with their plans. Too bad for him.

John had his second cup of coffee in front of him when Palmer Northcutt, a tall man with a small paunch threatening to spill over the belt of his traditional corduroy pants, entered. Palmer waved and sidled toward the table in the back of the café. He cast a giant smile at the waitress as he passed, asking her to bring him coffee. In many ways, Palmer was the perfect candidate. Good looking, over six feet, and with that great smile, he could sell a hose to a person in the middle of a hurricane. Even if he wasn't terribly smart, which made him easier to guide.

"Nice you could drop by." John didn't rise, only offered a nod and a gesture for Palmer to join him at the table.

"Here you go, sir. Would you like anything else?" The waitress set Palmer's coffee in its white mug on the table in front of him.

"Nothing and thanks for being prompt with the coffee." Palmer smiled and patted her arm. The waitress blushed and scurried away.

"Nice little spot here, John. Do I remember you saying Tim Worley would join us?"

"Yeah, he's running late. He frequently runs late. Annoying, but he has other qualities to make up for that habit." Lots of other qualities, like dollars and cents ones. He could wring more money out of a deal than anyone John had ever run across. Talk about being a master of obfuscation and misdirection. All the little places he moved a decimal here and rounded up in another place over time added up. The small things ordered but not paid for, and yet the money found its way into their pockets.

Lonnie Melton had filled an unexpired term when the former board member and John's business partner had a sudden heart attack. John had hoped to pull Lonnie into the deal, but he stubbornly refused. When it appeared he planned to talk with straight-shooting Mayor Rudy Lopez, Lonnie had to leave the picture. Such a shame he took his own life.

"Here's the deal, Palmer. I'm willing to support your candidacy with money and contacts, but you must assure me you'll support items I suggest, whatever they are.

"Your support, John, will be great, and I'm sure I can see my way clear to do what you ask. Serving on the Tidbury Board of Selectmen has been a goal of mine for a while."

John nodded, thinking how Palmer's naiveté led him to do exactly what John wanted him to do. With that smile, Palmer could lead ants into the mouth of an Anteater. "Good to hear, Palmer." He sipped his own coffee, now grown cold. He waved toward the older woman server. "I could use another cup of hot coffee."

"Of course. Be right there." And in fact, she scampered over with fresh cups for both. "Sure you don't want any pie? We've got fresh pumpkin and blueberry."

"No. We're good." John answered for both of them. He'd be sure to leave her a good tip. They'd probably meet here again, and if he made a friend of her, she'd be less likely to discuss their meetings, especially if he or Palmer of the brilliant smile asked her to forget seeing them there. That's how it worked at the other restaurant where he and Tim used to meet.

"I'll be frank, John. I'm worried about running against Jessica Allen. Her husband's family has lived here since the beginning days of the town. Of course, she's from Texas and won't ever be a real New Hampshirite, but she's well-liked."

"Yeah, but she's a woman. We've only had one other woman on the board, and she stepped in after her husband died. Most people won't be okay putting a woman on the board in her own right."

"Yeah probably so. I expect serving in this position will help my real estate business."

"Of course it will. Here comes Worley now. I'm sure I can convince him to support your candidacy, too. Hey, Tim. Good you could finally join us."

JESSICA HAD MADE IT a habit to attend the board of selectmen meetings. That's how it happened she'd spoken at the one last month, giving folks the idea she should run for the vacant seat. Normally folks weren't regularly allowed to speak. They made an exception for her because of her husband's long history with the town.

May have been one of those times it would have been better to keep her mouth shut. However, she got the board to put off deciding to award another contract to Worley Construction. She'd temporarily accomplished her goal.

Lori worked in the shop today, so Jessica and Sue could catch lunch at Molly's. Entering and scanning the tables, it looked like she arrived before her friend. Jessica smiled at the owner. "Hi, Molly. What's your special today?"

"Hello. Nice of you to come in again so soon after you were in here with that handsome man a couple of days ago. Anywhere is fine. Shall I bring you a cup of tea?"

Jessica nodded and raised a hand to sweep her hair across her face to hide the flush glowing there. Did everyone have to point out Jeff Hudson's good looks? And why did they think she needed to confirm the fact? Settling into a table next to one of the front windows, she proceeded to enjoy the view of the green and folks wandering along the sidewalk while window shopping and chatting with friends. She did love this town. Sue passed the window, stopped, and peeked in. She waved, and Jessica waived back.

"Oh, Jessica, sorry to be late. I had property to show over in a neighboring town and it took longer than I expected. My client walked through the house at least three times, top to bottom." Sue sank into the chair across from Jessica. "The good news is I'm convinced I've finally found the right one for her, and she'll buy the 150-year-old house. When we last walked through, she focused on where to place her furniture and whether she'd have to sell anything or buy anything new."

"No problem, Sue. I haven't been here long. And Congratulations. No one does a better job showing a house than you do."

"Here's your tea, Jessica. Do you want your usual coffee, Sue?"

"Yes, Molly. Thanks. What's the special?"

Jessica chuckled. "It may be a surprise. I asked, and Molly didn't tell me."

"Oh, you," chided Molly. "I'd focused on worming info from you on the handsome man you were in here with. And you were not forthcoming at all. To answer the meal question, I suggest lobster quiche with a green salad and fresh berries."

Jessica met Sue's gaze and nodded. "We're both in, Molly. Sounds scrumptious."

"I'll have it out soon, and I'll be right back with your coffee, Sue, and another pot of hot water for your tea, Jessica." The tall angular woman hurried to work on their order. To look at her, one would not believe her to be such a great chef.

Sue leaned back in her chair. "Comforting for a change to come in and have my every whim seen to."

"Oh, so Joe doesn't see to your every whim?" Jessica flashed her friend a grin then lifted her teacup.

"You know he does, but I've looked forward to this being just the two of us. You're always so busy with the campaign. I'm afraid I may have created a monster talking you into running for Lonnie's position on the board. It will be harder for us to find opportunities to do one of our ladies' lunches." Sue finger quoted her last words, laughing at their get togethers.

"Well, I may not win, Sue. So, it may not be an issue at all."

"Here's your hot coffee and more hot water." Molly hustled up to their table. "I'll be back soon with the quiche and salads."

"Thank you," Sue threw at Molly's retreating figure. "No one works faster than Molly."

"That's for sure."

"You remember we have a candidates' forum in the library tomorrow night in the conference room?"

"Yes, I've got it on my calendar. What if they ask questions I don't know the answer to?"

Sue looked at her. If she'd been standing, her fists would've been planted firmly on her hips. "You know we've gone over that before."

"Right, right. *I don't know, but I'll find out,*" she parroted her instructions.

"Yes." Sue fist pumped. "And I can't think anyone will ask more than the paper did. You answered all their questions. And you did a good job with those."

"Thanks."

"What did you think of what Palmer Northcutt said?"

"He had interesting comments."

"See, you'll be great at this. Definitely a politician's way of responding."

"Here you go, ladies. Enjoy." Molly set a plate in front of each of them with a quarter pie piece of quiche, green salad with what smelled like a tangy dressing, and fresh strawberries. "I'll be right back with a basket of muffins."

"She always outdoes herself. She could be a chef anywhere, yet she chooses to have her kitchen and restaurant here. Tidbury is lucky." Jessica cut into the quiche with her fork, blew, and then took a bite. A sigh escaped. "Oh, my yes, we are lucky. And by the way, I'm not a politician."

"Don't be cranky. Being a politician doesn't have to be a bad thing. It makes you a servant to others." Sue laughed. "At least that's what it should mean. Not suggesting you're out for anything for yourself except to make the town better."

They ate in silence for several minutes, topped off with more sighs.

"Got behind, and I forgot the muffins. How is everything?" Molly set a basket of sweet breads appearing to be mixed in flavor.

"Always excellent, Molly. Thanks. I said to Sue how fortunate we are to have you and your wonderful food in our small town."

"Ahh, aren't you sweet to say that."

"Nothing but the truth," Sue added.

"You enjoy." Molly went to assist other guests.

"Okay, so let's discuss the developer."

"You mean Jeff Hudson?"

"What other developer have you been hanging out with at Molly's. Please tell all."

Jessica stalled by sipping her tea. What could she say?

"Sue, we discussed him at Kathy's the other night."

"What's he like? Smart? Could he make conversation? Would having him hanging around for a while be an enjoyable addition to our landscape?" Sue leaned forward, holding her breath waiting for answers to her questions.

Jessica couldn't help herself, a laugh bubbled out at the way her friend got around to how good looking Jeff Hudson was again. There was no stopping her when she got a bee in her bonnet.

"Well?"

"Can't argue with any of that, Sue," Jessica conceded. "He was surprisingly nice, not know-it-all, and he seemed genuinely concerned for our elderly citizens. As I said at Kathy's, all in all, he made excellent points discussing the facility and its location on the green."

"Wow. Did he put something in your tea? I never expected to hear you say that."

"He talked. He made good arguments. And I'm a good listener. So yeah, I might possibly moderate my thinking on the idea of a retirement center. It's still a no-go if he insists on using Worley Construction."

"Did you tell him that?"

"Why would I do that? Besides, we only had one meeting. And I'm sure the other board members will have many questions for him. I'm curious how he'll handle those. Besides, maybe I won't even win the election."

"Don't you think those words, much less say them. Did you explain to him about all the activities we do on the green?"

"Of course."

"Different groups are beginning to put up the Halloween displays now. It's such a great fundraiser. Ask him to come by so you can show him a clear picture of what it's like and show him how his center will cut down on the space we have for our events."

Jessica peered through the window and nodded. "You know, Sue, that's a great idea. I'll ask him to come this weekend."

"You know how to contact him?"

"I can find out."

"YOU'LL NEVER GUESS what happened, Tony." Jeff lay his cell on top of his desk when his partner walked into their office in downtown Concord.

"If I'll never guess, you gotta tell me." Tony settled into the chair across from where Jeff stood behind his desk.

"Jessica Allen invited me to visit Tidbury this weekend. The Halloween display is up on the green. When I was in town last, nothing had been set up yet. She says it's not to be missed."

"Jessica Allen. The one who doesn't want us to build the center on the Green? That Jessica Allen?"

"Yeah, do you know any other?" Jeff settled behind his desk, picked up a pencil, and pounded out a beat.

Tony leaned forward, resting his arms on the front of Jeff's desk. "Jessica Allen has asked you out on a date. What's her plan? Make you fall in love with her or lust and convince you not to do the deal?"

"Oh Tony, Tony. Your eyes are glued to the TV way too much. And not even good shows at that. I do think she's hoping I'll recognize the green doesn't have enough space for the retirement center and all the activities they hold there."

"So, what are your plans? How will you handle her opposition?"

"I'll return and take another stab at convincing Ms. Jessica Allen we have a good plan that will help her town. You should come along. She's not like you suggested at all, though she is running for the vacant position on the board."

"Really? So she'll be in a position to vote for or against us, not only be a rabble rouser?"

"Believe that's correct. More of a reason for me to go back to visit with her. The election will be in early November, and the board is scheduled to take up our application toward the middle of November."

"Well, if it passes, we'd be ready to go right after the new year, though that's not the best time for construction. However, we can have everything lined up for the first break in the weather. We could be ready to take in residents next fall if we're lucky."

"I like the sound of that."

"You should go up and spend quality time with Ms. Allen. Sweet talk her if you can and convince her to vote for us."

"That's sleazy sounding, Tony. Besides, we have a great project, and we don't have to stoop to those tactics."

"I know. I know. That was my weak attempt to kill two birds with one stone. Get the project approved and hook you up with Ms. Allen. Wait, what does she look like? Is she pretty or an old librarian type? Apologies to librarians the world over."

"You better not let Eva hear you saying something like that."

"I did apologize, and that's no way to avoid my question. Is she pretty?"

Jeff paused a moment and decided to stick to the truth. He nodded. "Yeah, she's a beautiful woman. Around 5'4", shoulder length, thick brown hair. Trim, athletic body." He couldn't help himself. He smiled imagining his opponent, Jessica Allen.

"Hey. She's not married is she?"

"No. I understand she's a widow."

"Good. I don't mean good that her husband died, but good she's free. And you're free and have been for going on eight years since you lost Beth." Tony put a hand on Jeff's shoulder. "It's long past for you to find someone else, buddy. If it's not this woman, it's still important to begin to put yourself out there. When will you return to Tidbury?"

"Saturday. May spend the night at the Mount Washington Resort again and come back on Monday."

"Gosh man, don't I remember the town has a small inn?"

"Yes, but they had no vacancies when we visited before. That's why we ended up at the resort, nearly an hour and a half away."

"Makes sense to me to stay at the inn whenever you can. Besides that would make you more accessible to Ms. Allen."

"You may be right. I'll check it out first. Maybe they have space? You can manage everything here?"

"You bet. Go visit with Ms. Allen and work your persuasive wiles on her."

Jeff tossed the pencil at his partner, hitting him square in the chest. "You're out of control. You know that?"

Chapter Six

Jeff arrived in Tidbury on a brisk fall day. The leaves were spectacular, in their red, gold and orange, some drifting softly on the breeze. Driving by the green, he noticed what looked like statues scattered around. Jessica had mentioned the town put up displays for the two weeks leading up to Halloween. So this is what she talked about. More than he'd imagined. He glanced toward Allen's. People were going in and out and folks sat on the various benches along the street. He kept going past the green to the Tidbury Inn. A cancellation had allowed him to book a room with an attached bath. Wouldn't be the elegance of the Omni Mount Washington Resort, but it would definitely be convenient for developing a connection with candidate Jessica Allen. He needed to do everything in his power to make sure if she won, she'd be on his side.

He left his car in the parking lot adjacent to the old red brick colonial inn with black shutters. Looked like a porch had been added at an unknown time during the building's history. Climbing the front steps, he took note of comfy wicker furniture with burgundy and gold plaid cushions. Opening the door, the scent of cinnamon and fall greeted him. He did love old New England towns. One of the reasons he and Tony had chosen Tidbury for the retirement center. The town seemed self-sufficient with its various businesses, except it had no place where seniors could comfortably live when they could no longer safely live on their own.

Somehow he needed to convince Jessica Allen of the need. And her opponent, too. Though judging from the signs sprouting everywhere, she had the edge.

After checking in, he climbed the stairs to his suite with a large window looking out the front of the building toward the green. Bouncing on the bed in its separate room pleased him to realize he'd be able to get a good night's sleep. Whoever owned the inn had done a good job with modernization without losing any of its charm. It looked like they'd probably combined two bedrooms to make the generous bath and closet space. The main room had a sitting area with a sofa and a desk. This would work fine.

What first? Maybe a stroll around the town and check out the exhibit on the green before he ran down Jessica. Maybe he could start his persuasion with supper at Molly's. The thought of another meal with Jessica brought a smile to his face. Hmm. Looked to be an interesting couple of days.

It didn't take long to unpack, and then he snagged a light jacket off the back of the desk chair where he'd dropped it on entering and headed out to persuade Ms. Allen. Bounding down the stairs, he set off at a good clip. The plan to check on all the stores on the green got sidetracked by the green itself. The display drew his attention, and he stopped at what appeared to be an entrance kiosk.

"How much for a ticket?" Jeff removed his wallet from his back hip pocket.

"We don't have a set charge." The woman in a black witch's costume with green streaks on her face attempted a cackle. "It's whatever visitors want to contribute. All the money goes to our community social services. People are often more generous when you don't give them a set fee."

"I see. With no fence around the green, I guess anyone could just wander through."

"Yes, they could. You'd be surprised at how few people take advantage of the situation. Besides, this ticket gives you the ability to vote for your favorite display."

"Who's responsible for putting these together?" Jeff plunked a twenty dollar bill into the cauldron the witch guarded.

"Gosh, almost every group in town makes a display. The girl and boy scout troops, the youth group at church, the women's church circle, the knitting guild, the garden club, and practically every merchant has a display. You'll be able to vote for your favorite, and the winner is announced the night before Halloween at the bandstand. We'll have smores and popcorn. You don't want to miss out. People arrive from all over to glimpse our Halloween display."

"Thanks." Jeff wandered onto the grassy center of town. Must've been close to thirty displays, and like Jessica had told him, they spread throughout the entire area. However, it wouldn't be too hard to arrange them closer together, making plenty of room for his center. Exhibits were set up under trees, and others claimed spaces on the wide expanse of the green. They varied from the ghoulish with bloody teeth on pumpkin heads to witches on broomsticks suspended under trees and swinging in the breeze. A giant pumpkin the size of a long-haul truck tire had a whole face carved out. One display stacked up the pumpkins like a snowman. Boy, that took more than a small amount of engineering skill to keep them together.

Before he realized it, dark settled in, the streetlights winked on, and he hadn't looked for Jessica yet. He crossed the green and made for her store. The lights were still on, and he pushed open the door and was again met with the charming jingle.

"Hello. Can I help you find anything?"

The young woman who spoke resembled Jessica but wasn't she. Maybe a daughter.

"Hi. I'm Jeff Hudson, and I'm looking for Jessica Allen. She isn't working tonight?"

"I'm her daughter Lori, and you missed her by five minutes. She's picking up supper down at Molly's."

"Maybe I'll be able to catch her there."

"If you miss her, when she returns, I'll tell her you stopped by. Are you staying in town, Mr. Hudson? Can I give her a number?"

Well, Lori Allen was efficient. "That's okay. I believe she has it already." He hurried out of the store and down the short walk to Molly's. He opened the door to find most of the tables filled. Jessica sat by herself at one of them, sipping something in a cup. He walked over, surprised at the uncertainty swamping him from head to toe. Unusual to find himself uncertain with a woman, but with Jessica? Yeah, he was uncertain.

"Hi." He stopped at her table.

She glanced up. "Oh, hello. You're back. I didn't know if you'd come."

"I couldn't turn down your invitation." He smiled at her. "May I join you?"

"Oh, I'm not eating here, only picking up, but yes, you may sit. Molly's special tonight is chicken pot pie. You should order it."

"Thanks for the recommendation, Jessica. Can I get you anything, sir?" Molly had eased up behind Jeff.

"I'd like the pot pie, please and coffee with half and half if you have it."

"I'll change yours to an eat in order, Jessica. No reason for you to eat alone." Without waiting for a response, Molly waltzed away.

Jessica laughed. "You get used to being treated this way in a small town. Everyone feels obligated to mess in your life. I hope you don't mind, apparently, we'll be eating supper together."

"I don't mind at all. I stopped by your shop earlier. Your daughter told me I'd find you here."

"Oh, I'd better tell her to close up the shop and go home." She retrieved her cell from her pocket. "Hey, Lori...Yes, he found me. Molly's got us both eating here instead of doing take out...You go on and lock up and head home. Thanks. Good night, sweetie."

"Here's coffee and more hot water for your tea, Jessica. Be back with those pies soon." Molly sped away, stopping at another table on her way back to the kitchen.

"I've been wandering through the green. Those are amazing displays. Did your store enter anything?" Jeff sipped his strong coffee, made richer by the half and half. Just the way he enjoyed it. Jessica's hot tea never cut it for him.

"Actually, we do. Did you happen to notice the one with pumpkins set up like three snowmen?"

"As a matter of fact I did. Someone has great engineering chops to figure out how to keep the pumpkins balanced on each other."

Jessica smiled at him, and his heart bumped a little. Hmm. What was with that? He knew lots of pretty women, a term which certainly described Jessica. He had to admit what he experienced when he gazed in her blue-green eyes...was different, exciting, and calming all at once. Hmm. No time for an involvement now, and they lived different lives. He wasn't much for one night stands and figured she wasn't either. A guy could fantasize though, right?

"Jeff, where'd you go? I said my grandchildren Bobby and Bonnie came up with the idea of using the pumpkins to build snowmen, kind of blending the holidays you know, and my son-in-law Bob is handy and figured out how to make them stay connected."

Jeff straightened in his chair. He must look like an idiot. "Yeah, yeah, remembering how great the display looked. You have grands? You don't look old enough."

JESSICA EXPERIENCED warmth crawling up her cheeks. Come on, she could manage an off-hand compliment that probably didn't mean anything anyway. It's what everyone said. To herself she admitted how much she liked to hear those words coming from Jeff Hudson, who had claimed entirely too much of her interest. Good grief, he'd shown up in a dream last night. A bunch of craziness centered on the board, dead squirrels, and buildings falling down.

"Thanks," she finally managed. "So how long are you here for, Jeff?"

"For a while. I'm staying at the Tidbury Inn this time. Granted the Mount Washington Resort is pretty spectacular—have you been? I assume everyone living here has made the trip to check out the spectacular old hotel. But staying at the inn here is better use of my time."

He ran on like he was nervous. How odd.

"Here you go. Popping hot from the oven. Don't say I didn't warn you. If you burn your tongue on that first bite you won't taste anything for several days. Do you have everything you need?" Molly stood with a smile spread across her face, proudly admiring the work of her hands.

Jeff glanced at Jessica, his eyebrows raised in question, and she shook her head. "We're good. Thanks. Gotta tell you the aroma makes my mouth water."

"Good to hear. Blow before tasting," Molly cautioned again and then she ambled back to the kitchen, not in as much of a hurry as usual.

"She's something, isn't she?" Jeff smiled after her.

"She's the real deal, too. Jeff. She grew up working in the diner and took over after her parents retired and moved to Florida."

"Florida? Why'd they go there? Do they have family in the vicinity?"

"They couldn't manage their old two story home anymore, and hated to leave friends and Molly, but the weather helped them with their arthritis. They found a retirement center not far from the water. It even had an elevator. After that, it was a done deal." Jessica dug her spoon into the thick mixture, and steam spiraled upwards. The scents of chicken, rosemary, and thyme sent happy anticipatory signals to her stomach.

"Okay, I better do the same thing, or this will never be cooled down enough to enjoy without serious injury." Jeff plunged his spoon in, and the steam billowed forth. "So while we're waiting for this to cool, let's talk about Molly's parents, and what their options would've been had we already built our retirement center."

Jessica leaned back and crossed her arms over her chest. "You do realize I haven't been elected yet, so I have zero influence on whether you'll be allowed to build or not."

"Absolutely, but I suspect that even if you don't win the election, you can influence others." His wink made her tummy roll over.

"Thank you, I like to think that's true." She tentatively dipped her spoon and puckered her lips to blow on the food. She stopped when she caught Jeff staring at her mouth. Oh my. She couldn't eat the pie if she didn't cool it down. Guess she needed to cool down her imagination, too.

"Can I give you my pitch?"

"Of course. I think that's part of the job. Listening to everyone, and that includes developers." She hoped that didn't sound too harsh.

He first shoveled in several bites, after blowing on each one.

"She does make the best chicken pot pie. Man, I could eat this every day."

"Sorry to report it's only available one day a week. You lucked out to be here on the right day." She stirred her pie, hoping to cool it faster.

"Are you telling me she has a special every day of the week?"

"That's it exactly. Check out the sign over the register." Jessica notched her head in that direction.

"Oh, my gosh, she has meat loaf with garlic mashed potatoes. Pot roast with carrots and potatoes. I must be dreaming. Those two and this pot pie are my all-time favorites. I believe I'll enjoy staying in this town, Ms. Jessica Allen."

Jessica laughed. She couldn't help it. A big man, Jeff obviously liked to eat. "Well, you'll never be disappointed here, and at one time or another you'll run into everyone in town. Visitors, too, depending on how long they stay. The chef at the Tidbury Inn is quite good. Different kind of food, but definitely delicious."

"Looks like I'd better not skip the exercise routine, because I intend to thoroughly enjoy every single bite of this delicious food." He laughed before shoveling in another mouthful.

Jessica continued to enjoy her pot pie at a more leisurely pace. She'd eat lighter tomorrow to make up for the calories. Sometimes a splurge was called for.

Several minutes passed while they ate in silence or mostly silence, except for their moaned enjoyment of Molly's pot pie. Finally, Jeff set aside his plate. "What can I say? More than good. Maybe the best chicken pot pie I've ever eaten. Can't wait for next week."

Jessica laughed. She'd ask for a doggy bag for her left-overs. She never managed to finish one of Molly's pot pies.

Jeff wrapped both hands around his coffee mug. "So, let's talk business for a minute or so."

Jessica tilted her head acknowledging his plans.

"If my retirement center had been built on the green, Molly's parents wouldn't have had to move to Florida."

"Will your retirement center moderate our winters?" Jessica gazed at him over the rim of her teacup.

Jeff burst out in a large guffaw, making folks in the café turn and smile at them. "No, I admit the center can't do that. But being right on the green, everything would be an easy walk for her parents."

His smile did something to her middle. A surprisingly pleasant experience.

"I grant you that, Jeff. So you understand the green is where everything happens, right? You can see that for yourself with the Fall Festival spread out the way it is. We seriously need all that space for our festivals. We have an event every other month or so." She signaled Molly to bring her a to-go box.

"Have you sat down to take a look at the plans?" Jeff plopped his elbows on the table and leaned toward her.

"No, I haven't. I assume the current members of the board have though."

"Yes, they have. It's important for you—and the other guy—to look over the documents, too. Do you have any spare time tomorrow? Can you fit in a stop by the board offices across the green? I'll have space to spread them out, and you can take a good look at what I'm proposing."

"Let me talk with Lori. If she can come in for an extra shift, we can make it happen. When exactly did you have in mind?"

"I'm at your disposal and can meet you whenever. I believe you have my cell number since you invited me to visit." His smile ticked up only on one side as if he didn't want it to show.

"Yes, I do."

"You call and tell me what works best for you, and I'll be there."

"Okay, I'll do that. I think the first vote on plans for the retirement center is supposed to happen sometime in November, and they're planning to swear us in right after the election."

"You keep saying swear 'us' in. Isn't this election for the one position to fill the term of the guy who killed himself?"

"Yes, though, I've heard speculation he didn't take his own life. And I don't want to act cocky about winning, so I say *we*, meaning one or the other of us."

"Okay, I understand. I hadn't heard anything other than the selectman had taken his life. Have they decided natural causes?"

"No." Jessica looked at her hands clasped on the table in front of her, and then she glanced up. "The sheriff thinks it may be murder."

"Huh. Wasn't expecting to hear that in this small, quaint little town. Does the sheriff have any suspects?"

"Not really. Everyone loved Lonnie Melton. It's been a real blow to the community, not to mention his poor wife."

"I can imagine." Jeff's eyebrows drew together forming a deep V above his eyes. "So are you taking extra precautions?"

"Extra precautions? Why should I do that?"

"Because someone went to a lot of trouble to drop a squirrel in your shop. And you just told me the guy you're running to replace was possibly murdered. That demands you take extra precautions."

Chapter Seven

Last night Jeff had walked Jessica back to the shop and insisted on seeing her upstairs to her two bedroom apartment, walking through the whole thing, insisting on checking in closets and under the bed. She used the second bedroom as a guest room and her personal office, separate from the store office downstairs.

Weirdly unusual to have a man in her bedroom. Oh, he wasn't there for any other reason than his concern for her. Nevertheless, the bed took up a big part of her room. Kind of hard to ignore.

Jessica fixed her hot tea and toast and continued with ruminations about the night before.

After he left, though she'd reset the security alarm, she had a sense of unease she normally didn't in her apartment. Certainly not the security she'd experienced when Jeff had been there. Hmm. Not good. She was single now and had been for a while, needing to manage on her own. She'd proved to be quite capable in those five years since Ed died. The unexpectedness of his death and the lack of consensus surrounding what happened troubled her. She missed him but only cried occasionally, and mostly now sweet tears filled her eyes, not the gulping, gagging sobs of the first year or so.

She remembered Kathy's words that Ed wouldn't have wanted her to be alone. She agreed with that. Had she gone first when they were both relatively young, she'd have wanted him to find someone to share his life.

Finishing her tea and toast, she stood. This thinking wasn't getting her work done. Lori had agreed to come in and cover lunch until two. More than enough time to look at the plans with Jeff.

Jeff.

Stop this. Go down to the shop and get to work. Better open up and greet the day with hopefully lots of shoppers. With that Jessica threw a sweater around her shoulders and bolted down the stairs to the sound of knocking on the front door of her shop.

She took off the separate shop security system, twisted the lock, and threw open the door. "Welcome, welcome."

"Hope we're not too early." A woman, clearly a leaf peeper with her binoculars strung around her neck and her camera clutched in one hand, stood on the stoop.

"Of course not. I'm running a smidge late. Come right in and browse to your heart's content." Jessica went to the back of the store and flipped several switches to put more light on several of the displays.

The woman and her friend wandered the store, finally settling on one of the more expensive pottery pieces Jessica carried. The local potter was inspired and produced amazing creations.

The morning flew by with people stopping in, those merely looking and several making purchases. Fortunately, Jessica's livelihood didn't depend on how lucrative the store was. She and Ed had been successful with investments. She didn't have to be frugal, but hey, as a transplanted New Englander, she'd absorbed some of those values by osmosis. She didn't need a lot to live comfortably. Her store gave her pride and joy, the way her grands did, too. She loved that her shop brought joy to others.

Just after noon, the bell over the door tinkled again. "Hi, Mom. I'm here to spring you."

"Hi yourself. I appreciate you doing this, Lori."

"Of course. Where are you going in case someone needs to reach you?"

"I'm meeting Jeff Hudson, the developer, over at the town offices to look at his plans for the retirement center. I don't think I'll be long."

"Take however long you need. I'm planning on being here until two or so. Afterwards I've got a project for one of my classes to work on."

"Thanks again." Jessica opened the door.

"Mom."

"What?" Jessica looked back at her daughter.

"Looking good in those black jeans and that purple sweater. Any special reason you're so spiffy?"

Lori's smirk and raised eyebrows sent heat rushing into Jessica's cheeks. "Thank you, Lori. Pleased you approve. I picked up the sweater when I last visited Concord." And with that, she breezed out, hoping her daughter hadn't noticed the blush.

Jessica had taken extra care with her clothes and makeup this morning, not that she ever used much. Still...hmm. Making her way around the green to the town office, she spoke to several neighbors and fellow shop keepers. To save time, cutting across made sense, but opportunities for extra steps shouldn't be missed.

Fall decorations were scattered throughout the town. Barrels of mums in purple, orange, gold, in gorgeous, riotous colors, could be seen in front of every store and placed near many displays on the green. Bales of hay and scarecrows weren't limited to the ones on the green, and of course, pumpkins in all sizes and shapes. The variety and sizes had been one of her many surprises when she'd moved to New Hampshire after she and Ed had married. Tidbury had always had a small scarecrow display on the Green. In recent years, the number and variety of the presentations grew, and the size and variety of pumpkins boggled the mind. They showed carved pumpkins. Others stacked together to make crazy creatures. Now the smell of someone burning leaves wafted her way. Nothing like a New England fall.

What would Jeff's plans look like? Would she like them? Would it be helpful to have a retirement center in town? Probably so, but not on the green and certainly not built by Worley Construction. She steeled herself not to be swayed by the handsome developer. Handsome? Darn Lori for putting ideas in her mind. She opened the door and entered the main town offices.

"Hi there, Jessica. What brings you to the office?" Mayor Rudy Lopez stepped out from behind the desk to shake her hand.

"How are you, Rudy? Seems we're still getting a good number of tourists."

"Yep. Always happy to have that happen."

"I'm meeting Jeff Hudson to look over the plans he has for the retirement center."

"He's in the back room with drawings spread out all over."

Jessica smiled. "Have you seen Palmer Northcutt? I thought he'd want to look at the plans, too."

"Apparently it wasn't necessary for him to look. His mind is made up for the project. He's pretty close to John Crowell."

"Yep. Which is why I'm running for this position."

"I have to appear neutral, Jessica, but in my heart, I'm rooting for you."

"Thanks, Rudy."

He winked. "We Texans have to stick together."

Jessica laughed. "Well, once a Texan always a Texan, I guess, but you and I have been here a long time. What is it? Over 30 years?"

Rudy high-fived her. "About that. Once I met Livy, I was done for. Wherever she moved, I'd follow. And I don't regret one minute we've spent together here."

"Me either."

"Well, don't let me keep you from those plans. Tell me if you have a change of heart, okay?"

"I don't expect to, but I'm keeping an open mind. Except, Rudy, on our green and Worley Construction."

Rudy nodded.

"I'll talk with you after." She made her way down the short hall and eased open the door to a larger room with two long tables butted up to each other in the center. Jeff stood over the expanse. Dark blue shirt sleeves were rolled up displaying strong looking forearms. A pencil sat slanted over one ear. He seemed deep in thought.

"Hello."

He glanced up. "Oh, hi, Jessica. Good to see you. Come over here and let me show you what we're talking about."

She walked around the table and stood next to him. She'd have to put on her business hat to make heads or tails of all the squiggles. All the info tended to blend together. Focus.

"Let me show you the plans for the center itself. Next we'll look at the location issue."

"I understand what your strategy is. Pull me on board with the idea of the center and slide in the location on the green as an after-thought."

"I'm that transparent, huh?" He crossed his arms over his chest. "Guess, I'll have to up my game."

Jeff spent a good thirty minutes explaining the drawings and making sure Jessica recognized all the benefits of this homey retirement center. Yes, the building would have elevators. Yes, the dining room would be open for the town folks, the same way the Tidbury Inn restaurant was. Yes, units would be both one and two-bedroom. And yes, almost half of them would have balconies or patios.

The building would be red brick with black shutters and fit into the architecture of the town.

"To be honest, and I try always to be honest, Jeff, I'm impressed with your plans. I understand why folks would like to live here. But seriously, can't you find any other place you can build? And why use Worley Construction?"

"First things, first. Let's walk out on the green. We'll use the measure app on my cell so you can get a good picture of how much space we're talking about. After that, we'll grab lunch, and you can explain to me your issues with Worley Construction."

He gestured for her to walk out ahead of him, and she led the way. One determined man was Jeff Hudson. He and his partner developed wonderful plans. The decorations, the colors, the details he'd thought of. And their community could use this. She sighed.

"Are you all right?"

"Yep. Okay, let's do this. Show me exactly where you plan to build the center. How long would construction take? Because all that chaos will be disruptive to our use of the green." They walked west from the mayor's offices along the sidewalk.

"Six to nine months, possibly longer depending on the weather."

"Oh, that long?" Jessica stopped.

"We'll be hiring lots of local labor."

"Well, that would be good." They crossed onto the green itself. "As it is, our town folks who make their living that way, have to travel all over for work." Jeff picked up a random pumpkin. "What are you doing?"

"I'm borrowing this for a marker. I'll put it back. With three others, I'll mark out the four corners of the building, and yes, I'll return them to their correct place in their displays."

Jessica shook her head, resting her hands on her hips. Her gaze followed his movements when he gathered up three other pumpkins. After measuring, he placed one pumpkin on each of the four corners of what she guessed would be the retirement center.

"See?" Jeff walked up to her and pointed to all the area not marked off by the pumpkins. "You still have lots of green space left for all the town's festivals. I want you to walk around. Picture how you could still do your festivals and how the retirement center would fit right in."

Jessica paced the boundary of the building. It worked better for her visually and physically to check out stuff than only peer at pictures on papers laid out on a table. If she were honest, and she prided herself on her honesty, this could probably work with some rearrangement of booths and displays. Of course, it would be a mess during construction, but.... She ended up back where Jeff waited for her.

"What do you think?"

"Well, it certainly helps to look at it this way. Why don't I take you to lunch at Molly's, and we'll talk?"

"Love to. Thanks. But first let me return these pumpkins like I promised. Keeping my word is important."

"I like that quality, Mr. Hudson."

Jeff smiled, scooped up the pumpkins and took them to their displays. When he returned, they stepped into the street heading for Molly's. Out of nowhere a car whipped toward them.

"Look out," Jeff yelled, and he yanked her back. Jessica screamed, and they tumbled onto the green's soft grass. Several people rushed over to them.

"Are you okay?"

"Did you see that?"

"It looked like that car made right for them."

Jessica rolled off of Jeff and knelt beside him. His eyes were closed. "Jeff. Jeff. Are you okay?"

A bystander asked, "Are you all right?"

"Yes, but get a doctor, please."

"And the sheriff," another man said.

She slipped a finger under Jeff's nose and sighed in relief. Thank God, his breath tickled her finger, and his chest moved up and down. Moments passed, and then Jeff moaned, his eyes blinking open.

"Jeff. Are you okay? Can you talk?"

"Yeah. I'm okay." He raised a hand to the back of his head. His fingers came away bloody. He moaned again.

"Just lie there. Help is on the way."

His eyes blinked open once more, and he seemed to focus on Jessica. "Are you okay?"

"Yeah. You cushioned my fall, and I believe you may have saved my life."

Sheriff Halbert arrived at the same time as the doctor, who got busy checking out Jeff's condition. Gary took statements but then encouraged folks to leave, until only the four of them remained. Jeff sat up and made noises indicating he wanted to stand.

Doc Grayson lost the battle over checking Jeff into the clinic.

"Doc, I only lost consciousness for maybe a minute. I'm feeling lots better now. When I can put ice on this goose egg on the back of my head, I'll be fine. I did come out on the short end of the stick with that piece of granite," he said with a rueful smile.

Jessica had always enjoyed the green having several large granite boulders set around for folks to sit on or prop a foot on when tying a shoelace. Now, she questioned the idea.

"Doc, why don't you take Jeff back to the inn. I'll be along after I've talked with Jessica more."

"Listen, Sheriff Halbert, I don't want to leave Jessica alone. Let's all go back to the inn, and we'll talk."

The sheriff concurred, and they strolled at a leisurely pace to keep from making Jeff's head hurt more. When they reached the inn, Gary asked the owner, Penny Torbett if they could use the smaller of the two dining rooms. He requested an ice pack for Jeff and ordered coffee for them all. They settled at one of the tables in the empty room.

"Mr. Hudson, do you feel up to telling me what you observed this afternoon?" Gary added two spoonsful of sugar to his black coffee.

"Yes, and Jeff will do. I'd been showing Jessica where the proposed retirement center could fit on the green and how it being in that location wouldn't interrupt the activities you hold there. We were heading to Molly's to eat lunch to further discuss the situation."

He took a deep breath and blinked a couple of times, like he went over the accident in his mind's eye. Then he recounted what had happened concluding with, "I swear, it looked like the car aimed for us."

The sheriff nodded. "I found a tire track where the vehicle came up over the curb, but no skid marks indicating the driver tried to stop. You two were extremely lucky."

"Did anyone else notice the car, Gary? Facing in the other direction, I didn't catch a glimpse."

"Yes, we've got a partial license plate and a pretty fair description. A large Silver SUV with a New Hampshire license plate." He stared at Jessica. "So this is the second incident with you. First we had the squirrel and now an attempted hit and run."

Jessica shuddered. Despite clasping the mug of hot tea, which Penny knew she preferred, Jessica's fingers were icy. "Please don't say it that way."

"Jessica, how else are we to look at it? We have several witnesses that the SUV aimed right for you and Jeff here."

She looked at Jeff. "You have any enemies? Because I don't believe I do."

"I've made a few people unhappy with me over the years, when I won a bid someone else wanted, but none upset enough to want to take me out. Especially at the expense of taking out someone else at the same time." He set down the ice bag he'd been holding on his head and clasped her hand with his cold fingers. "No, Jessica, I'm afraid this is about you."

"I've got to agree with Jeff, Jessica. You say you don't have any enemies, but someone is not happy with you."

"I'm going to sound extremely paranoid, but the only issue coming to mind is the one regarding the building of the retirement center on the green. I have been outspoken against building it and against using Worley Construction." Her glance landed on Jeff and skittered away.

"Dear God, Jessica. You can't believe I had anything to do with this."

She didn't meet his gaze.

"Jessica, in this instance, it looks like Jeff is a victim as well as you."

"Thanks, Sheriff. Jessica, I'd hate if my project has somehow put your life in danger. That can't possibly be, can it?"

Chapter Eight

The incredulous tone in his partner's voice didn't surprise Jeff. "You're telling me someone tried to run you down in this sweet little town we picked for the next retirement center?"

Jeff nodded at the bizarre situation even though Tony couldn't see him. "Afraid it appears that way." He put the cell on speaker and paced his room at the inn.

"But you're physically okay?"

"Yeah, I've had to cut out jumping jacks from my workout routine, but I'm okay. So, listen, Tony. Do you think we should cancel this project and look somewhere else?"

"That seems an extreme reaction. We've already put in a lot of our time and money on the plans."

"Yes, but time and money aren't lives, Tony."

"I hear you, buddy, but let's not ditch it just yet. How's the woman running for the position on the board who's been against the project? Is she all right? When is the election? Since you seem to think she'll win, how are you coming along with convincing her to our side?"

"Hey, that's lot of questions. Give me a second, and I'll answer them all." Jeff lifted his coffee mug and took a quick swallow. He loved that his suite in the inn had a coffee pot, so he didn't have to go downstairs whenever he needed a cup, since he drank a lot of coffee. He settled at the small table in front of the window looking out over the street.

"Here goes. Jessica Allen is all right, as I said she fell on top of me. She's grown to like the idea of the retirement center. I'm still working on the idea of the location on the green. The election is the first Tuesday of November, which is only in a couple of days now. Based on rumors I'm hearing, the only way Palmer Northcutt can win is if Jessica drops out." Jeff nearly dropped his mug, sloshing coffee on the table. "My God, Tony. That's got to be what this is all about." He grabbed a tissue and hastily wiped off the spill. "The other side wants Jessica to drop out so Northcutt can win. While that's good for us because Northcutt completely supports the project, I'm not sure how good that will be for Tidbury."

"Listen, be careful, man."

After disconnecting with his partner, Jeff fixed a fresh cup of coffee. What could he do to keep Jessica safe and get his retirement center built?

"MOM, CAN I CONVINCE you to enjoy a cup of hot chocolate? The temps have dropped into the low thirties." Kathy welcomed Jessica into the home that had been hers for right at thirty years.

"Sounds lovely, Kathy. Thanks." She took off her heavy coat and hung it in the front hall closet. She'd always loved that feature of the house, lots of closets, and this one in the entry only held coats.

The front door opened, and a cold breeze blew Lori inside. "Hi, Mom, you're already here." Lori stomped her feet before taking her coat to her room. "I'll be right back."

"Here's your hot chocolate, Mom. Let's sit in the living room in front of the fireplace."

"Umm. Smells yummy, Kathy. So nice we can do this. We don't have much time to enjoy a leisurely visit anymore." Jessica settled into a plush wing-back chair and rested a foot on the stool in front. Kathy had kept lots of the charm of the old house but added wonderful updates.

"Hi guys." Lori joined them carrying her own cup of cocoa. "This is nice, right?"

"I used the exact same words." Both girls cast gazes at each other and then quickly looked away. So, was something going on here? "I love for us to have this extra time for the three of us to visit. But, Lori, aren't you on the schedule at the store this afternoon?"

"Originally, yeah, but Janell Bacon, your wonderful new hire, asked me to trade with her."

"Mom, Lori and I wanted to talk with you."

So, her daughters were ganging up on her. They did that on occasion. What had put a burr under their saddle this time? "Okay. If you want to talk, you don't have to bribe me with hot chocolate. You can stop by the store anytime and almost always find me there."

"We know, but we wanted more privacy than at the store." Lori appeared nervous, taking a couple jerky gulps of the hot chocolate, getting a small white mustache from the whipped cream.

"Sis, use your napkin." Kathy gestured to the space right below her own nose.

"How are you always able to drink this stuff and not get it all over?" Lori chuckled.

"I sip and not gulp."

The girls had always been like that. Back and forth teasing. Jessica carefully sipped her cocoa. The whipped cream made a great variation over marshmallows. Took more time to fix than the white puffy pillows which you just plopped on top, but the cream? Yeah. Special indeed.

"Okay, let's do this." Kathy set her cup on a coaster on the coffee table. "Mom, Lori and I think you should leave the campaign."

"What? What's going on? The idea to run came from you in the first place. Then we all discussed the option, and we all agreed I should do this. You helped set up the campaign."

"But, Mom, that was before the squirrel in the store," Lori said.

"And before someone tried to run down you and Jeff Hudson with a car." Kathy rubbed her hand over her eyes. "That really scared us, Mom."

Jessica set down her cup. "Thank you. I understand this is because you care, and I appreciate that. But, girls, your father and I taught you once you start something, you need to complete the job. When it's difficult, it's especially important to tough it out. I owe it to your father's memory to make sure Worley Construction does not build this retirement center."

"So, have you decided that the center will be okay on the green?"

"I'm not completely in agreement, but I'm not adamantly against it, Kathy. I can understand how having a retirement center somewhere near the center of town would be good for the town and for the folks who'd live there. My main reason for running is to keep Worley Construction from doing any more work for the town. And I'm sticking with that." She stood. "Now I'm going out to shake hands with folks. I want to win next Tuesday."

Her daughters looked at each other. An expression passed between them. "Okay, Mom, if you're determined, we'll support you in every way, right, Lori?"

Lori nodded. "But you have to promise to be careful."

"Of course. And girls, thanks for caring. I'll pick up my coat and find my own way out." She kissed both girls on the cheek. "Talk with you soon."

After getting her coat and scarf from the closet, she set out to walk back to town. The wind had picked up, and she pulled on her gloves. This would have to be a brisk walk. She hadn't meant to worry her kids, and hated that she had, but she couldn't back down. Some things were bigger than individuals. She needed to make sure Worley Construction didn't injure anyone else in one of their buildings.

Walking briskly, she reached town in right at twenty minutes. After shaking hands with everyone she found in all the stores surrounding the green, Jessica made her way back to her store. Janell had become a great asset, and she assured Jessica she could handle the rest of the evening. Good news because the chat with her daughters drained her emotionally, and all the conversations with town folks left her physically exhausted. People's positive response to her campaign buoyed her, but now all she wanted was to settle in front of her fireplace with a cup of tea and a book she'd been meaning to read.

ELECTION DAY DAWNED clear and crisp. The main thing on the ballot was to fill the unexpired term. Jessica and her team, consisting of her kids and best friends Sue and Joe Franklin, made sure all her supporters got out to vote. By the end of the day when the results were tallied, Mayor Rudy Lopez declared Jessica the winner. Northcutt grudgingly conceded. And the celebrations began. Kathy held the election party at her house. Everyone in town showed up to congratulate Jessica with lots of chatter and laughter filling the packed house.

"Hi there. Let me add my congratulations to all the others." The warm tones of the voice sent tingles through Jessica's middle. She pivoted to find Jeff Hudson standing nearby.

"Hi, yourself."

"I hope it's okay I came. I saw signs inviting everyone. It kind of looks like everyone has come." Jeff glanced around the crowded house.

"Of course, it's fine for you to come. No lasting effects from the accident?"

"No, I'm good. No headaches or dizziness, which would've concerned the doc if that happened. Guess my head is harder than your granite."

Jessica chuckled at his sense of humor.

"Listen, will you have supper with me tomorrow at the Tidbury Inn? I'd like to discuss a couple of things with you. We've both been busy, and I haven't seen much of you in a while."

Jessica hoped the dim light kept him from noticing the flush climbing her face. "I'd love that. When did you have in mind?"

"Does eight p.m. work for you? I'll come by the store, and we'll walk to the inn together."

"You don't have to do that."

"Oh, yeah, I do. My mother would come back and haunt me."

He smiled, and she couldn't help herself. She smiled back. "Well, that sounds like it should work fine."

"I'll let you return to your party now, and I'll meet you tomorrow evening." Jeff made his way to the front of the house, nodding to people he passed.

"Mom, I like him. I think he likes you." Kathy slipped an arm around her mother's waist.

"Don't be silly. He's focused on his business."

"He's taking you to the Tidbury Inn and not Molly's. Definitely a step up, Mom. What do you plan to wear?"

"Oh, honey, I haven't given it a thought."

"You must. And, Mom, don't wear your regular jeans. Not your good ones either. Pull out those lovely black wool pants. And wear the teal sweater. And those boots with the heels. Spiff up a bit. You can do it, Mom." And with that, Kathy wandered back to the party.

Oh my. She wished Kathy hadn't gone there because now all that swirled in her head were questions about the various options hanging in her closet appropriate for her not quite date tomorrow night, because it wasn't a date. Or was it? And did she want it to be a date?

She heaved out a long sigh, very much afraid she did want it to be a date. And she couldn't figure what to make of her ambivalence.

"YOU LOOK GORGEOUS, Jessica." Jeff stood inside her store, staring as she walked from the back, her coat thrown over one arm. She'd taken Kathy's advice and had spiffed up. Guess Jeff approved of her spiffiness.

"Thank you." She handed him her coat, and he helped her into it, squeezing her shoulders once before moving to the door. "Thanks for working tonight, Janell. Close up at nine."

"Sure, Jessica. Have fun."

"This sure is a busy little town." Jeff kept her on the inside as they made their way toward the Tidbury Inn.

"Yes, we have folks coming through all times of year, though fall with the changing leaves brings our largest number of visitors. Now while the leaves are mostly gone, people keep coming. A magazine issue featured an article about our green with all our yearly activities, and people have shown up in droves. Certainly good for business."

"Congratulations, Jessica. We're excited you won." Passing them on the sidewalk, an older woman paused to pat Jessica on the shoulder.

"Thank you, Mrs. Cook."

"The consensus today seems to be everyone is happy you won. Seventy-six percent to twenty-four is a significant win." He led her up the stairs of the inn and inside toward the dining room.

"Good evening, Mr. Hudson. We've got a special table for you by the window. Congratulations, Jessica." Penny Torbett, the inn owner greeted them.

"Thank you." Jessica smiled, and Penny left them with menus.

"I'm flattered you agreed to come out with me tonight. You're something of a celebrity now, you know."

Jessica laughed. "Oh, this is a tiny fishbowl, and the notoriety will pass quickly. We've all known each other forever."

The server came and took their drink orders. Jessica requested a Merlot, and Jeff ordered a bourbon on the rocks.

"I never learned to drink hard liquor."

"A friend in college introduced me to this, and I've stuck with it." He perused the menu. "What do you recommend? I'm sure you've eaten here often."

"Actually, probably less than four times over the years. We don't eat out much, and we usually end up at Molly's. However, I have recommendations from folks who frequently eat here. The pot roast and fresh veggies are outstanding."

He glanced at the menu once more. "Okay, you've sold me. I'm ordering the pot roast. And you?"

"The other thing I've heard is excellent is the grilled pork chop with local veggies."

Jeff gave their orders and sipped his bourbon. "Let's take care of business first, shall we?"

First? What did that mean? "Of course."

"When are you sworn in?"

"Next week. My first meeting will be when we hear the report on your project. The vote is scheduled for a meeting the first of December."

"Jessica, can you tell me more specifics about why you don't want us to use Worley Construction?"

"My husband Ed worked as a compliance officer, inspecting job sites, and he saw lots of issues with Worley's work. He refused to sign the certificate of occupancy documents to allow him to move into a particular building. Worley told him he'd addressed the problems and for him to come check it out again. The last time Ed went out to check on the building, a piece of concrete broke off and fell on him. He died on the spot. No one could figure why the piece of concrete would break off the way it did. I've always believed someone tinkered with it and then toppled it over on my husband."

"Did you report those suspicions to Sheriff Halbert?"

"Of course. I also provided him with Ed's write ups on the project. But Gary couldn't find anything in the box to count as proof of what happened in the building. And the afternoon Ed was killed, no one else was around. He'd gone to the building by himself."

"I'm sorry, Jessica, for your loss and for all the uncertainty. In our case, Worley Construction had the best bid for our project."

"I don't doubt that, but he cuts corners. I'm convinced he does. I've never been able to catch him at it. I think that's what Ed did."

JEFF'S GAZE FELL ON the wine glass part way to her lips. Those lips slightly parted. Did she realize how beautiful she was? He guessed not. "What if we could get out of using Worley Construction?"

"What? Can you promise that?"

"I can't promise, Jessica, but I will ask our lawyers to get working on the possibility."

She nodded, took a sip of her wine, and set the glass on the white tablecloth. "That would mean a great deal to me, Jeff. Of course, I can't promise you how I'll vote. I'll read all the papers and documents and listen to the presentation. I can see how having a retirement center would be beneficial to our town. I'm not entirely convinced of the location. Let's say I'm still willing to consider the possibility."

"Good to hear. A fair hearing is all we want. Okay, enough of business. Tell me about you."

She nervously grasped her glass and took a hasty sip. "There's nothing to say. I'm afraid I'm an ordinary middle-aged woman."

"Hardly. You saw a problem and set out to tackle it. Put yourself out there. Do you realize how few people reflect for even a minute on running for office? Much less actually run. That takes a gutsy person."

"Well, thank you. That's kind of you to say." She glanced at diners in the room aware of the sounds of utensils and the chatter of others surrounding them. Facing him, she said, "Tell me your story. How'd you get into this development business?"

"I'm the son of a developer. I went to work with my father while in my senior year of college. Dad wanted me to join his firm, but my grandmother died in surprising circumstances at a retirement center that we considered to be excellent. They put up a good front but cut back on services to save a buck. When I realized what happened, I swore I'd do whatever I could to make sure that didn't happen to anyone else's grandmother. So Tony Benton, my business partner and I specialize in retirement centers. We've done them in several cities and towns in New Hampshire, Vermont, and have recently branched out to Massachusetts."

"Sounds like you're doing important work. I bet your grandmother would be proud of you. Was your father disappointed you didn't go into business with him?"

"Yeah. Strained our relationship for a couple of years. As Tony and I became more successful, Dad forgave me."

"Where does your family live?"

"Dad's in Boston. My mother died when I was in high school."

"I'm sorry, Jeff."

"Thanks. Long ago now."

"The business is in Concord, right?"

"Yeah, Tony and I liked a smaller fishbowl than Boston."

She laughed, a low sexy sound. Hmm. He didn't need or want that complication in his life right now. But she was beautiful. And so courageous. He admired her for taking on the system.

"So, you've lived here all your life?" Jeff sipped his bourbon.

"Since college. Ed and I met at Texas Christian University and got married in Fort Worth, Texas, where my family lived, but we moved up here where his family has been for generations. My parents died almost ten years ago. My older sister Maddy still lives there, and I return to Fort Worth once a year. She has her own family, and they come up almost every summer to escape the Texas heat. They rent a house and stay for several weeks. We have a super time. She was excited to hear I'd run for the open position on the board and won."

"Have you always lived above the shop? That's kind of the in-thing now in development. It's called mixed-use in cities. Helps to cut down on folks having to climb in their car every time they want to go anywhere." He paused and laughed at himself. "Guess I should give you a chance to answer my question."

Her smile indicated she didn't mind. "I'm surprised to hear our arrangement is so hip. Lots of older towns have this arrangement. What's that saying *everything old is new again*? I'd say we fit right in."

The server appeared with their food, Jeff refilled her wine glass and then sampled his meal. "Umm. You were right. The pot roast is the best. It falls apart with my fork, and the taste makes me think I'd enjoy seconds."

"Well, their desserts are quite wonderful, too, so you may want to leave room for their coconut cake. It's as good as Molly's apple pie, simply different."

"Thanks for the heads up. I will eat accordingly. How is yours?"

"My porkchops are amazingly tender, and the seasonings are perfect."

"So, I never gave you a chance to answer my question. Have you always lived above the shop?"

Jessica took a sip of the wine and set her glass on the table. "No, we didn't raise the family there. The place where we had the election night party? That's the family home. My husband Ed's family lived there. It's over one hundred fifty years old. Of course, we made changes over the years."

"Why did you leave?"

"I had bought the store prior to Ed's death but being in the house afterwards hurt too much. Lori had started college and was mostly out of the house. Kathy and Bob had a much smaller place with the twins. I wanted to give them the house, but they insisted on paying me. So I remodeled the upstairs apartment and moved above the store. I realize the stairs might become an issue at a future date. If that happens, I'll deal with it then. We could probably remodel and set up a bedroom in the back on the ground floor, or I could put in an elevator."

"It certainly makes commuting easy." He gestured to the server for another bourbon.

Her warm chuckle bubbled out. "That it does."

He picked up the wine bottle to refill her glass, but she inserted her hand between his and the top. "No more please or my stairs will do me in."

"I'd never let that happen, and I'll be sure to return you safely all the way up to your door. Besides aren't we eating dessert in a bit? You'll be fine."

Jessica removed her hand. "All right, but you've been warned."

The coconut cake with cream cheese icing proved to be as good as Jessica had promised, and it was close to ten-thirty when they reached the front door of the shop. Jessica unlocked the door, flicked on a tiffany lamp sitting near the entrance, and turned off the security system.

"Is this the main security system?"

"This only serves the store. I have a separate one to get into the apartment."

"And can you operate this one from upstairs and down here?"

"Yes, it cost more to set it up this way. Kathy, Bob, and Lori insisted on the arrangement."

"Given what all's been going on, the extra security seems smart."

"Yeah, I agree."

"Let's look more at the stairs. Maybe there's something we can do.

She walked through her shop and Jeff followed her.

"I didn't pay attention when I came up before, but yeah, they seem overly steep." Jeff looked behind the stairs and around the back part of the store. "Have you ever considered remodeling these to take out a couple of inches of that incline? I believe you've got the space for that." He climbed the stairs. "You'd be amazed at what a minor change could make."

"Is that possible? No, I never investigated the idea of changing the slant of the stairs. They just are what they are, which is very steep." She exhaled as if she'd been holding her breath all the way to the top. "So, I didn't fall down. Of course, I didn't finish that third glass of wine." She chuckled.

"Could I come in for a cup of coffee?" Pushy perhaps, but he didn't want the evening with this intriguing woman to end. Unusual to be sure.

She cocked her head at him as if she were weighing the wisdom of letting him in. Finally, she blinked as if coming out of a trance. "Of course. It's small you know, but l love it."

Jessica unlocked the door and deactivated the apartment alarm system. The smell of fall greeted him. Cinnamon and a hint of lavender maybe? Definitely welcoming.

She flipped on lights. "Let me take your coat." He shed his overcoat, and she draped it over a hall coat tree. He helped her remove her black wool coat, and she did the same thing with it.

He hadn't paid much attention when he walked through after the incident where the car tried to run over them. Now he took note of more details. Her apartment wasn't large, but it warmly welcomed with its soft early American style.

She moved into the kitchen area. "Would you like a cup of coffee?"

Jeff nodded.

"I have one of those instant coffee pots with the little pods. It won't take a moment. While I don't drink coffee, many of my friends do, and everyone in the family does." She inserted a pod and added water. "How do you take it?"

"Do you happen to have any half and half? I hate to ask. I confess it sounds sissy. Someone hooked me on it a couple of years ago, and I admit I'm spoiled."

"As a matter of fact, I do." She poured the half and half into a small pitcher and set it and his mug on a tray. "I'm not a tea snob. I use a special instant hot water spigot." After plunking a tea bag in her mug, she put the mug under the instant hot spigot. "Perfect tea in an instant. And I admit to being spoiled by the instant gratification of the hot water spigot even faster than the pod coffee." She carried the tray into the living room where she set it on the coffee table in front of an old fireplace.

"I guess we're both spoiled then." Jeff settled into a plaid wingback chair to the right of the fireplace.

"Real wood?" He nodded his head toward the hearth, helped himself to the cream pitcher for his coffee, picked up his cup, and sipped. "Umm good. Is that a hint of hazelnut?"

She settled on the ivory covered sofa. It helped lighten up the room.

"Yes. If I have to drink coffee, it's what I prefer. I don't add cream or sugar. I'm happiest with my tea." She raised her hand and placed her lips on the edge of the cup.

Jeff didn't move his gaze from her face.

"Oh, this is good." Jessica set the cup on the table. "The fireplace originally burned real wood. We converted it to gas when we did the remodel. I didn't want to haul wood up those stairs and carry the ashes down. Besides, this seemed safer, too."

"Makes sense to me." He finished his coffee and rose. "Listen, I should head back to the inn. He walked toward the door. Jessica followed behind him. He pivoted and she nearly ran into him. He reached out to steady her and gazed into her blue-green eyes and fought a desire to kiss her. Staring at her lips he leaned toward her. She seemed to lean toward him.

He drew in a deep breath and let it out. Couldn't do that. But boy did he want to. He couldn't wait to complete this project to pursue the attraction they both seemed to feel. He drew back at the same instant she did. A lovely flush rising on her cheeks. Oh, yes, he definitely wanted to pursue this woman.

"Don't forget your coat. You'll need it on the walk to the inn."

"Thanks." He slung on the coat. "Good night, Jessica."

"Good night, Jeff. Thank you for dinner. I enjoyed our evening."

"My pleasure. And I hope we can do it again sometime soon."

He went through the door. She stood on the landing. He could feel, her gaze following him down the stairs, and then she moved inside and closed the door to her apartment. The lock clicked with the locking message following him to the front of the store. He stepped outside to the sound of tumblers falling, and the security system setting brought him a sense of relief about her safety.

Standing outside Allen's for a moment, Jeff wondered what he'd been doing. Jessica lived here in Tidbury. Tidbury which tied up her whole adult life, and now she'd been elected to be a part of the town government. What could possibly come of this...this thing he sensed developing between them? And oh yes, it wasn't only on his side. The blushes told him that. Pulling on his gloves, he strolled in the direction of the Tidbury Inn, which did indeed have wonderful meals. He'd caught one or two meals in the dining room before. What made tonight's especially great? Unless it was because of the person sitting across from him. He was in for a world of hurt here. He'd never looked at a woman since his wife died eight years ago. And now Jessica. Could it be worse timing? Or location? Why couldn't he feel this way about someone in Concord? On top of it all, he faced complications with the retirement center and the added worry for her safety. Not what you'd expect in a small New Hampshire town.

He shoved aside the Jessica issue and made his way to his room in the inn, determined to get a good night's sleep. Tomorrow was another day.

Chapter Nine

What had she been thinking? "What were you thinking?" she asked herself. "You came close to kissing the man." Her words echoed her thoughts. Maybe not thinking. Maybe it was all about feeling. She couldn't deny something drew her to Jeff Hudson. But how silly in the extreme. He lived in Concord. Her life was here. Apart from that, he'd planned to use Worley Construction to build his retirement center. Yes, it appeared he'd found a way for the center to fit on the green and still leave room for all of their seasonal activities there. Yes, he said he'd look into the possibility of not using Worley Construction. Guess she'd wait to see if he could pull it off.

Oh, my gosh. She dropped onto the sofa. Yesterday she'd read over the training materials for board of selectmen. One of the sections concerned conflict of interest. She couldn't vote on the issue of the retirement center if she and Jeff had a relationship.

Relationship. They had no relationship, did they? Yes, he'd bought her meal tonight. Maybe she should've insisted on paying her share. She'd raised the issue over the pie at Molly's. Why hadn't she this time?

The most important thing was to make sure Worley Construction didn't continue to do work in the town. And, if she had her way, they'd have to go out of business. Jessica didn't want another woman in another town to lose her husband the way she had. And if it meant she had to let go any possibility of a relationship with Jeff? So be it. Not that a possibility of a relationship existed in the first place.

Well, what a depressing thought. She dropped her head back on the sofa. What was the matter with her? In under five minutes, she'd bounced around like a ping pong ball on steroids from one thought or emotion to another. And they'd been at opposite ends of the spectrum. She was a mess.

"HEY, LORI. BREAKFAST is ready." Kathy set a plate with the scrambled eggs, bacon, and toast on a placemat on the counter. I remembered you were going in early to open up the store."

"Thanks." Lori sat at the bar and picked up the coffee laced with cream and sugar.

"I don't think you can call that stuff you're drinking coffee, sis."

"To each his own, Kathy. I don't make fun of how you put the cinnamon in your coffee."

"So, Lori, do you think something is troubling Mom?"

"She never takes a morning off, and she's done that a couple of times now. Do you think it's because of getting elected?" Lori bit into a piece of the bacon.

"Did you see her at the election party talking with Jeff Hudson, the man who wants to build the retirement center?"

"I saw her talking to a man I didn't recognize. Could that be who you mean?"

Kathy dithered whether to mention anything to Lori, but she was twenty and had always had a good head on her shoulders. She set her cup on the counter and leaned toward her sister. "So what do you think? Are they perhaps interested in each other? They've hung out together for a couple meals. He even took her to supper at the Tidbury Inn."

Lori paused with a forkful of eggs in front of her mouth. "Does that appear to you to be a positive or a negative?" She proceeded to finish the eggs.

"Seriously? I don't know. I think he lives in Concord. If something developed, where would they live?"

"Hmm. If she moved there, do you think she'd keep the store? Gosh she'd have to hire more people to work there. I wouldn't be able to cover her hours and mine, and me finish up college next May."

"No you couldn't. I think we should bring up the topic of this man and see what she says. I mean what does she know about him?"

"Kathy, would you mind if Mom found someone else?"

"No, it might be uncomfortable at first, but mainly I want her to be happy. But Hudson's life is in Concord."

"Listen, I'm heading to the store after I finish eating this yummy breakfast. By the way, thanks for cooking, Sis. Why don't I ask Mom to stop by the house for tea? I'll tell her we'll make final plans for the Thanksgiving meal."

"There's not too much to that. We always have the same thing. Tell her I'm making a new dessert and want her opinion."

"Okay. Do you have something in mind?"

"No. Guess I better find a new something to bake so it doesn't look too cooked up." She paused. "Pun intended."

"Oh, you are bad. Dad is the only one who could get away with those."

Lori walked back to her room and returned with her coat, gloves, and hat for the walk to the store. "I'll call you to confirm she's coming."

"Great. Love you, kid."

Lori rolled her eyes at her sister and spun around, heading for the front door.

"HERE'S YOUR TEA, MOM." Kathy handed her mother a teacup. "Lori's got her coffee and mine. I'll bring the apple walnut cake I experimented with this afternoon. You take a seat in front of the fire."

"Thanks for setting up this time to chat, Kathy. I happy we could find another time together again. We all live such busy lives. Be sure to thank Bob for me for keeping the twins. Not that I don't adore the little darlings." Jessica settled into the stuffed chair that had been in the family for years, now recovered in a cheery white and navy plaid.

"Hurry and tell me what you think of the cake, Mom." Kathy stared at her mother when she took a bite of the cake.

"Umm, this is good, Kathy. Did you use whole milk or canned cream?" She cut another bite.

"No, that's the weird thing, it has eggs, butter, sugar, flour, apples, and spices. A heavy batter to mix, let me tell you." Kathy flung her hand up and down to release the tightness still in her hand from the task.

"What do you think, Lori?" her mother asked.

"What's not to like? It's got apples, cinnamon, flour, and sugar." They all laughed.

"So, Mom, how are things going with the retirement center on the green? Are you still adamant against having it there?" Kathy asked.

"Yeah, Mom, tell us about the center. Have you had many meetings concerning the situation?"

Jessica noticed her daughters kept sending side glances at each other. Had they hatched something and gotten her out to the house under false pretenses, like they'd done when they wanted to convince her to get out of the race?

"I thought you invited me here to sample this new cake recipe, which is yummy and maybe finalize plans for Thanksgiving, which is next week."

"Well, sure, but we'll probably have what we always have, right?"

"Right, Mom. We've got it set now. Since we lost Dad, Bob makes the turkey and everything else is the same." Lori looked at her sister under her eyelashes. "So tell us what's going on with the center."

Yep, they were up to something. Best to play along. "I have talked with Jeff Hudson a couple of times. He showed me his plans, which are quite complete. It's not tacky at all and would fit in with the rest of the town architecture, and I hate to admit this, but I appreciate how the retirement center would benefit the community. Instead of having to move away from family to find a safe place to live, our elderly would be right here. Hey, that could be me in a few years if I come to struggle with the stairs."

"What's the situation with losing space from the green?" Lori set her empty plate on the coffee table.

"Well, Jeff creatively used pumpkins to mark off the space. He showed me he had space to build his center, and we'd still have room for all our activities. I think it will work."

"Jeff?" Kathy set her plate on the table.

"How many times have you met with him, Mom? I've heard you went on a date with him to eat dinner at the Tidbury Inn. Is that right? We'd appreciate you keeping us up to speed if you've decided to date someone." The words spewed from her younger daughter at a pace Jessica's brain could hardly follow.

"Wow. So, that's the purpose behind this little get-together. What made you think something was going on between Jeff and me?"

Both her daughters looked at each other and spoke at the same time.

"People have seen you together."

"One night pretty late at the Tidbury Inn," Kathy added.

Jessica set her teacup on the table and dropped her head into her hands. After a moment, she stood and reached out a hand to both her daughters.

"Girls, I wouldn't do anything that would upset you. There's nothing between Jeff Hudson and me." Would she like there to be? Maybe. "Yes. We've eaten a few meals together, and then the SUV tried to hit us. I think folks have put us together in their minds. I won't do anything to mess up our family."

"Mom, it's not that we wouldn't be okay if you found someone. It's this man. We don't know much about him. He doesn't live here."

"Lori, that sounds more parochial than I'm comfortable with, even for our small town." Kathy set down her cake plate. "I would hate for you to move to Concord, Mom, but we want you to be happy. We just hope to be in on what's going on with you." Kathy rose and drew her mother into a hug. Lori joined in, and it became a three-way. "We love you, Mom. Please keep us in the loop."

Jessica stepped back. "I can promise to do that. There isn't any there-there, as the saying goes. But thanks for being concerned about me. I don't imagine I'll be seeing a lot more of Mr. Hudson. Keeping my distance will be important so I don't have a conflict of interest or appear to have a conflict when I vote on the retirement center issue the first part of December."

"We love you, Mom." Lori echoed her sister.

"So now, I'm heading back to the store, but I'll stop by Molly's to pick up chicken potpie for supper. I'll have enough left over for tomorrow's supper, too." She shrugged into her coat and then pulled the car keys from a pocket. "I didn't walk because it is super cold out, and darkness falls like flipping a switch at this time of year."

"Walking is healthy, Mom, and I'm proud you do it so often, but I'm relieved you'll be in the car this evening. Wait a minute, I want to send a couple of pieces of the cake with you." Kathy dashed into the kitchen and returned with a plate covered with aluminum foil.

"Thanks. I'll have to freeze it, or the scales will hate me."

"Don't forget to call when you get home, okay?"

Jessica laughed at her younger daughter. "Yes, ma'am." She kissed both girls on the cheek and scooted down the front stairs to her car, a small four-wheel drive, much needed in the mountains of New Hampshire during the winter. They'd had several light snows, and the weather station had forecast a big storm for the area.

She steered her SUV away from the house she'd moved to as a young bride. Where she'd brought home both baby girls. Lots of memories wrapped up in that house. Kathy and Bob's work on the house made it emotionally easier for her to visit. Much was the same, but much was different. The short trip had no streetlights to enlighten her path, and the road curved back and forth. Now the snow fell in earnest. Giant fluffy flakes, beautiful if you were inside to enjoy. Not so much while driving. Guess the storm arrived earlier than expected. Her hands encased in gloves clutched the steering wheel tighter.

Rounding the next curve, bright lights flashed, blinding her. The vehicle approached way faster than safe for these roads. And oh, my gosh, he seemed to be heading for her. The vehicle crossed the center line and careened right at her. Jessica yanked hard on the wheel and the car/truck, whatever, whizzed by. She couldn't right the SUV, and her car plunged off the side of the road. She screamed, and everything went dark.

"MOM SHOULD'VE CALLED by now, Lori. Even stopping at Molly's, she should've been home and should've called." Kathy picked up her cell and tapped her mother's name and waited. "Mom's not answering her cell either." Kathy shook her head.

"I'll call Molly's to make sure she stopped by there." After a quick conversation, Lori disconnected. Her eyes, wide in her white face, Lori's voice shook. "Kathy, Mom never got there."

"Okay, I'm calling Sheriff Halbert. Gary will find her." After a quick call, Kathy disconnected. "Gary requested we stay put. He's going after her." Kathy and her sister alternated pacing back and forth in front of the fireplace.

Bob returned with the twins from his parent's home northwest of Tidbury. "Rough roads out there. We hadn't left my mom's long when the snow fall increased making visibility difficult. I was anxious for us to safely reach home." He stared at the two women clinging to each other's hand. "What's the matter?"

Kathy told them their concern and Bob quickly fed the twins and got them tucked into bed. When he returned he asked, "Anything from the sheriff?"

Kathy shook her head. "And Mom's still not answering her cell."

Bob put his arm around Kathy, and she leaned into her husband. "Didn't you notice her car or anything when you came?"

"No, but I came from the other direction and not the main road into Tidbury."

Kathy's cell sent out its recognizable song of "Everything's Coming Up Roses" from Gypsy, a musical she'd done in high school. She snatched it from the coffee table and looked at the screen. "Hello, Gary. Did you find, Mom? Is she all right?" She paused while she listened then let out a long sigh. She nodded toward Lori and Bob. A big smile spread across her face. "He's got her. Mom was in a wreck. He's taking her to the clinic." She spoke into her cell. "We'll meet you at the clinic. Thanks, Gary." She disconnected and returned the phone to her jeans pocket. "Bob, stay with the kids while Lori and I go to the clinic to check on Mom. I'll call you after we arrive to bring you up to speed when we find out what's what."

"Of course, hon. The twins and I will be fine here. You drive carefully now. It's bad out there." He helped Kathy and Lori into their coats.

They plopped their hats on their heads, threw scarves around their necks, and drew on their gloves before setting out.

"Did Gary say anything else, Kathy?" Lori climbed into the SUV.

"She made it half-way between here and the green and appears to have lost control of the car and careened off the road. No signs of why that happened."

"You don't think she had a stroke or a heart attack, do you? I mean, at fifty-three, isn't she too young for those things? But how else to explain her losing control of the car? She's an expert at driving on snow."

"I don't know, Lori. No one in our family tree has those health issues. We're lucky; amazingly almost everyone has mercifully died of old age."

"Oh, my gosh. Look, Lori." Kathy slowed down driving by their mom's car."

"Okay, well, now I'm terrified. The front fender is a mess." Lori looked in the side view mirror as Kathy continued driving, but faster now.

"Please, God, let Mom be all right," Kathy whispered.

"Amen." Lori put her hand on Kathy's shoulder.

Kathy parked in the clinic lot, and she and Lori tramped through the snow toward the entrance where Gary met them.

"Hey, girls. You made good time. Speeding as usual, Kathy, even in this weather?"

Nice to be teased by someone who knew you as well as Gary Halbert did. And if he were teasing, things must not be too bad. "How is she, Gary?"

"Let me find the doctor. My badge hasn't convinced him to share too much with me. Wait here." He went down a hall.

Kathy clasped Lori's hand, and they huddled together. In only minutes Gary came back, followed by a woman in a white coat.

"This is Dr. Grayson. Doctor, this is Kathy Shepherd and her sister Lori Allen. Can you tell us how their mother is?"

Dr. Grayson looked at the girls and at the Sheriff.

"Go ahead and speak in front of the sheriff, Dr. Grayson."

"Well, your mother is extremely lucky. The tree stopped her from plunging down the incline. She's got a minor concussion and moving will hurt for a while. Amazingly nothing's broken. All the air bags did their job."

Kathy drew Lori into a long hug. "Thank God." She smiled at Gary and the doctor. "Can we take her home?"

"No. We'll keep her overnight, but I hope to release her at noon tomorrow."

"Can we go into her room?"

"Sure. Come on back. She may be dozing, but don't let that alarm you."

"May I come, too, Dr. Grayson? If she's awake, I'd love to ask her a couple of questions."

Dr. Grayson glanced at Kathy and Lori, and they both nodded. They all followed the doctor back down the hall and into an area with several curtained off areas. Dr. Grayson tugged back a curtain, and Jessica, her eyes closed, lay on the bed, so white it was hard to tell where the sheet ended, and her face began.

"Oh." Kathy breathed a long sigh. "Mom, can you hear us?"

JESSICA MOANED. SHE must've had a bad dream. It seemed so real but couldn't be. She shivered. Lots of bright lights.

"Mom, can you wake up?" Lori spoke.

Jessica struggled to open her eyes. She must've stayed up too late and Lori had come to wake her to come down to the store. Oh, what's that bright light? She squinted.

"Lori, did I oversleep?" Her voice didn't sound strong. What was the matter? And there's Kathy, and what's Gary doing here in her bedroom? Who's the woman in the white coat?

White coat? Doctor. "What's going on? Where am I?"

"Ms. Allen, I'm Dr. Grayson. You're at the clinic. You've been in an accident. You have a concussion, but you'll be all right."

Jessica raised a hand to her head and found a bandage.

"Jessica, it's Gary Halbert. Can I ask you a couple of questions?"

She nodded and then moaned. "Not a good plan to move my head too fast."

"Can you tell me what you remember? How did you end up off the road?"

"Truck. Maybe a truck or something. Came right for me. Must have lost control."

Both her daughters gasped. Gary took a note pad out of his pocket and wrote something. Maybe she was dreaming. She wished she were dreaming because maybe her body wouldn't ache with every breath she took.

"Could you identify the truck, Jessica?"

"Truck? Did I say truck? I don't know. All I remember were blinding bright lights that seemed to be coming straight for me. I jerked the wheel to avoid running into the guy..." She couldn't keep her lips from trembling, reliving that agonizing moment she realized she'd lost control of her SUV and... "But I..."

Kathy patted her mother's hand. "It's okay. Mom. You will be okay."

"Why don't we let our patient catch up on her rest. You can check in with us in the morning." Dr. Grayson made gestures to herd them from the room.

Her daughters nodded and both leaned over and kissed her.

"See you in the morning, Mom." Kathy and Lori spoke simultaneously.

"I'll make sure to have your car towed into the garage, Jessica, and I'll talk with you more tomorrow. Take it easy."

Dr. Grayson ushered out her guests. Jessica brushed at the tears sneaking out of her eyes and trickling down her cheek onto her neck. She used the sheet to wipe at them. No point crying now. She was going to be okay. Everyone said so.

But she was scared. The third time something bad had happened to her. Not her normal life. Had she made a mistake running for office? Had that decision led to all the accidents? She and Ed had always taught the girls by words and actions to stand up for what was right. Especially when it became difficult. But this was beyond difficult. This had become dangerous.

Chapter Ten

The small town grapevine worked well in Tidbury. By the next day, the story spread all over everywhere that Jessica Allen had an accident running her car off the road. Jeff heard the story repeated several times, each with extra pieces of information. Immediately upon hearing the stories, Jeff tried to contact her on her cell, but she didn't answer. He made his way to the sheriff's office to learn what he could about her situation.

"Sheriff Halbert, do you have a minute?"

"Sure. Come on in." The sheriff indicated a chair in front of his desk. "What can I do for you?"

"I'm hoping you can tell me the truth of the rumors I'm hearing concerning Jessica Allen. Did someone run her off the road last night?"

"Well, I think I can confirm she had an accident. I found marks on the road indicating something happened making her brake suddenly. Could've been a deer or moose. Could've been the snow, which fell pretty heavy, but still."

"Or could've been another vehicle?"

"That's what she's claiming."

"How is she? Where is she?"

"I'm not at liberty to discuss her health, but by now she should be set up at her daughter's house. She spent the night at the clinic."

"Okay. Sheriff, are you concerned we have a pattern of harassment where she's concerned? A dead squirrel. An SUV truck aimed at us when we started to cross the street. Something causing her to wreck. Seems like a pattern."

"I can assure you we're taking seriously what seem to be threats aimed at Jessica."

Jeff nodded. "Okay. If there's any way I can help, let me know." He stood and shook hands with the sheriff.

Standing on the street in front of the sheriff's office, he decided he needed to pay Ms. Allen a visit. He walked back to the Tidbury Inn where he'd parked his SUV, climbed in, and traveled to Kathy Shepherd's house. He regretted if his and Tony's plans to build the retirement center on the green caused all the attacks on her.

After the ten minute drive, he parked in front of Kathy's house. He hurried up the stairs and used the door knocker. In only moments, he heard steps inside, and then the door swung open.

"I'm Jeff Hudson."

"Yes, I remember you, Mr. Hudson. I'm Kathy Shepherd. You came to the party celebrating Mom's election. Come in."

"Thank you. I'm hoping to visit with your mother. I understand she's staying here."

"Yes, she is. Have a seat in the living room, and I'll check with her."

"I appreciate that."

"Would you like a cup of coffee?"

"I don't want to put you to any trouble."

"No problem. We always have a pot on. I'll bring you a cup."

Jeff moseyed into the main gathering room with the giant fireplace, trying to imagine Jessica being a young mom and raising her daughters with her husband here. Hmm. Her husband died five years ago. Some people moved on after two years. Others took ten years. Others never moved on. Had Jessica moved on a little? At all? How far had she traveled down this path? Was he nuts to consider something with her? They lived different lives in different locations. She had deep roots in Tidbury. Concord had been good to him. If his decision to build a retirement center in this town somehow put her in danger...well, he'd be hard pressed to live with himself.

"Hi, Jeff."

He wheeled around to find Kathy helping Jessica into the room. She wore hunter green sweats, but he guessed she wouldn't be exercising anytime soon. "Hi. Are you up to coming in here?"

"I welcome the excuse to move. It's not comfortable, but the longer I don't move, when I have to it's brutal."

"You have a seat on the sofa, Mom. I'm getting Mr. Hudson a coffee, and I'll bring you a hot tea."

"Thank you." Jessica settled on the sofa. "Kathy has been doing a thorough job of spoiling me. I thought I'd be fine back at my place above the store, but the stairs proved to be a bit of a challenge. She insisted I come here, but I hate I'm putting her out." She paused. "Gosh, I've kind of rambled on. Sorry. You're my first visitor."

"It's good to find you're able to be up and around. I wasn't sure. I talked with Gary Halbert, but he wouldn't tell me how you were, so I decided to come check for myself. Do you feel like telling me what happened? Stories going around include sightings of Big Foot."

She chuckled and then moaned. "Oh my, no more funny stories, please."

"Sorry."

"Here's a cup of coffee, Mr. Hudson."

"Please call me Jeff."

"Of course, Jeff." Kathy smiled her mother's smile. "I've brought out cream and sugar not knowing how you drink coffee. You can fix it how you like." She set down the tray, took a teacup and saucer, and handed it to her mother. "Here you go, Mom. I'm getting to work on lunch. You enjoy."

"You see? She's spoiling me. I could easily fall into the habit of sitting in this lovely room and letting her spoil me." She sipped her tea.

Jeff added cream to his coffee. "I'm certain it wouldn't take too long before you'd find that boring. You seem like a doer to me." He sipped his coffee. "Oh, this is good."

"Kathy is a good cook."

"Did she learn that from you?"

"Yes, and her father. Ed and I both cooked. Both girls enjoy cooking."

"And do you still cook?"

"I make a couple of special things, but you can find quite excellent, premade foods at the market, so I'm afraid I've grown to be a lazy cook. Do you cook, Jeff?" She cocked her head at him like she was deciding whether he did or not.

"Yes, I do, and I enjoy cooking. I've missed doing that while I've been here, but at home in Concord, I cook several times a week." He set down his cup. "Can you tell me how the accident happened?"

She sipped her tea and rested the saucer and cup in her lap, one hand on the teacup and one on the saucer. "It wasn't an accident. I entered that sharp curve about halfway between Kathy's and town, and all of a sudden, bright lights blinded me. They kept coming closer and closer, not staying in their lane. I hit the brakes but realized that wasn't the best idea when the wheels lost traction. I jerked the steering wheel but couldn't straighten out the car. I went off the road, and the other vehicle whooshed by." Her hand trembled as she raised the cup to take a sip.

Jeff ran a hand over his face, imagining what nearly happened to Jessica, a person he realized he'd come to care for. "I hate this happened to you. Are you able to describe the vehicle at all?"

"No. The brightness of the lights hurt my eyes something fierce. Those blue/white glaring lights ought to be outlawed. I told Gary all of that when he came by the clinic this morning. I'm not sure he believed me."

"I'm sure he did. I do. I hope he can find who's targeting you. I hate that I might've caused this."

She set down her cup. "What do you mean? How?"

"If I hadn't wanted to build the retirement center, you wouldn't have had to oppose it and attract such animosity that someone has attacked you." He leaned forward. "You know I'd never do something like this."

"I ADMIT, I'VE WONDERED, Jeff. I mean you look around and ask who profits from a situation. If I'm out of the picture, well, that helps you."

"Oh, Jessica."

"But we've talked a lot. You've explained in detail your goals for the property. I agree your project would benefit the town without negatively impacting our ability to host all our events on the green throughout the year."

The frown lines between his eyebrows smoothed out. "That's a relief."

"And if you hadn't come to town to build on the green, another Worley Construction project would've come up, and I'd have opposed it." She sipped her tea and held out her cup. "Can you take this please."

Jeff hopped up from the chair and took the cup and saucer and set it on the tray. He sat on the sofa next to her and took one of her hands in one of his.

Oh my. Butterflies did their thing in her stomach. She hadn't experienced that in a long time.

"I'm relieved you're all right. I want to find who's doing this and make them stop. It's all so wrong." His hand squeezed hers.

She patted the top of his hand. "Thank you for caring, Jeff. We'll get through this."

His gaze settled on her lips, and he leaned toward her. And she responded. The twins burst into the room as their lips were about to make contact.

"Gram, Gram, who is this?"

Jessica drew back and smiled at Jeff and then the twins. "He's a...a friend."

"We have unfinished business." Jeff stood. "How long do you think you'll stay here at your daughter's?"

"I hope to move home the day after tomorrow. Probably could tomorrow, but better safe than sorry. Want to make sure I can manage the stairs."

"I'll check on you after you return there, and in the meantime, call if you need or want anything."

"I will. Thanks for coming by."

"Ah, this is where you got to." Kathy entered the room.

"Hey, Mom." The twins spoke in unison.

"You're supposed to be setting the table." Kathy stood with both hands on her hips and pretended to scowl at her kids. They weren't fooled, laughed, and scampered away. "Would you like to stay for lunch, Jeff?"

"No, thank you. I'd love to another time, though. Jessica, while you're safe here at Kathy's, I'll head back to Concord for a couple of days, but I'll return to help keep an eye on you when you move home."

"Thank you." She could hardly meet his gaze because of the heat climbing in her cheeks.

"Thanks for that great coffee, Kathy." He nodded to Jessica. "See you soon." And with that, he slung into his coat, and left.

"So, what's the blush about, Mom? It certainly takes care of those pale cheeks you had. By the way, I like him. Back to the kitchen for me. Holler if you need anything."

Jessica settled back onto the sofa. Oh my. She and Jeff had come close to kissing for the third time. Wasn't the third time supposed to be the charm? What should she make of that? Excited. Scared. Hopeful. Did a chance for them to have a relationship exist? No. Probably not. What a shame. It had been a while since she'd been admired by a man. It wasn't like she required a man to reinforce her self-esteem, but she appreciated his admiration. She'd be fine on her own; she had been for five years. Well, for at least three when she started to turn the corner and accept her new normal. Now, she'd concentrate on getting back to a hundred percent and being the best selectman-selectwoman, the town had ever had. She'd look for extra help at the shop to make it easier for her to concentrate on the business of the town.

Chapter Eleven

John Crowell waited impatiently for Tim Worley to show up at their favorite coffee shop the next town over. He liked not recognizing folks or being recognized, which would happen if they held their meetings back in Tidbury, where everyone knew everyone and everything going on with them. The downside of a small town.

He sipped his milky white coffee with two spoons of sugar. Disappointing as hell that Jessica Allen had won the election. More disappointing Worley hadn't been able to take out the new member of the board. John had been on the board longer than anyone else. He'd been able to convince everyone else to continue to use Worley Construction for projects. Tim took his shortcuts, and they both ended up with extra dollars. No harm, no foul. All those regulations were for sissies. But not now.

The door opened and Tim Worley hurried in, brushing snow from his overcoat. "Man, it's getting nasty out there. Glad my truck has four-wheel drive. I don't want to be stuck in this town. Not that I don't enjoy the coconut pie they have here." He placed his order with the gray-headed waitress. "Thanks, babe."

"You seem to be cheery for a person who didn't successfully take care of our problem."

Tim frowned. "I did the best I could. Jessica Allen isn't often by herself. Other folks surround her. I messed up trying to get her when she and Hudson were together. I didn't realize they were, or I wouldn't have tried anything. Don't want to bump off a potential client."

"What went wrong the other evening?"

"I—Thanks, babe. Looks good. No cream." The waitress set his pie and coffee on the table and moved away. "Listen, I didn't want to smash up my truck because that would be hard to explain. I veered a moment too soon, or she'd have missed the tree and plunged off into the ravine. Still her car suffered damage, and she was shaken up. I put the fear in her."

John shook his head. "So, what's plan B or will this be C?"

"Maybe burn down her shop with her in it."

"Tim, have you lost your mind? Her shop is in the middle of other stores. I don't think you can target her shop without destroying others."

"Well, I could grab one of her daughters or grandkids. Instead of asking for money, she'd have to agree to support our work.

"So what do we do with the kid? Keep him hidden for as long as we need her to agree to do what we want? Nah. That would never work, Tim. Why don't you shoot her? Or kidnap her and lose her somewhere up the coast. Take her up into Maine and throw her off one of those rocky coast areas. You can find many dangerous sites that would lend themselves. I've read plenty of stories of people slipping to their deaths."

"Okay. I'll research that idea. She won't be up and around for a while, and Thanksgiving is next week. Maybe I can work something out after that."

"You have plans for the holiday?" John wasn't familiar with Tim's private life. They weren't friends, merely business associates.

"Oh yeah. Big family. We all get together. Everyone cooks. The grands and cousins all play outside in the snow. They sit at smaller tables and all the adults are at two long oak tables with tons of dishes. Lots of laughing and good eating, I can tell you. What do you do?"

"We'll go visit my wife's family in Massachusetts. Be gone the entire week. If you could dispatch our problem while I'm gone, that would be perfect."

"It will definitely happen before that meeting where they have to vote. I think they hear the first presentation right after the Thanksgiving holiday, but the final vote is in December. So, I'll make sure she's out of the way by then. Don't you worry, John. We have a good deal going here, and we will for a long time." He stopped to eat several big bites of his pie. "Too bad Northcutt lost."

"Yep. That's why your efforts are crucial to us being able to continue the way we've been doing." John drained his cup and stood. "If we don't run into each other before, Happy Thanksgiving." John walked toward the door, buttoning up his coat and pulling on his gloves. Nasty out for sure. He sure hoped Tim could handle his part of the deal. He slipped on the snow freezing on the sidewalk. Better take his time getting home.

JEFF PACED IN HIS OFFICE in downtown Concord. He loved the old building that housed their offices. He expected Tony to arrive momentarily. They hadn't talked in person in over a month because he'd spent so much time in Tidbury.

"Hey, Jeff. I know, I'm late. Not my fault. Eva kept me discussing Thanksgiving. We have more people coming than expected. She wants me to rent another long table. You and your dad are coming, right?"

"Wouldn't miss it." If he were honest, he'd like to spend the holiday with Jessica. But didn't look like that could be worked out. Jeff rose and crossed to the round table in one corner of his office. "Have a seat. Let's talk about how we can get out of the contract with Worley Construction. What are the lawyers saying?"

"I don't think you'll be happy to hear this report. Andrew Mulligan who's the top in his field on this kind of thing says we can't get out of the contract unless we can show malfeasance on at least one or more of their projects. Situations where they intentionally cut corners. And it's hard to prove intentionality."

"You're right. I hate to hear that. I told Jessica we'd be able to break out of the contract. She's adamantly opposed to not only us but anyone using them. Thinks they cut corners and don't follow regulations, and that's why her husband died."

"Hard to argue against emotion. Can we find out if that's true, or just the whining of a suffering spouse?"

"Her husband was the inspector, and he kicked up static about the work they'd done on that building on the edge of town. Sheriff Halbert told me he looked but couldn't find proof. Lonnie Melton, the guy whose place Jessica has taken on the board, believed Ed, Jessica's husband. Melton had told everyone he wouldn't vote for this project."

"Well, it's one contract. No one would do anything to hurt someone over one contract, would they?"

"I don't know, Tony, but Jessica has certainly been harassed once and attacked twice. She seems to be well-liked in the town. I mean she overwhelmingly won her race."

"What does the sheriff say?" Tony crossed his leg over his knee and his foot jiggled.

"He doesn't say anything that I've heard. The only evidence we have is for the incident that involved me. He couldn't tell anything from where Jessica went off the road. The ME found poison in Lonnie Melton's tox screen, but so far Sheriff Halbert has no suspects."

"Listen, Jeff, maybe you were right, and we should bail on this project. If we don't do the project, we don't have to use Worley Construction. I'd hate if our actions were responsible in any way for someone getting hurt or killed."

"I appreciate your sentiments. They are mine, too, but it's such a great project for the area. I hate to give up. Let's keep open our options, Tony. We'd take a hit financially for sure if we break the contract, and they sue."

"Yeah, I know."

"Let's hold off for a while until we're both ready at the same time to pull the plug. After Thanksgiving, I'll return to Tidbury to determine whether Jessica is still in any danger. I don't like bullies and hate to back down, but I don't want to take a chance with her life."

Tony uncrossed his leg, rested his arms on the table, and leaned toward Jeff. "Talk with me about Jessica. You've spent lots of time with her and stayed in Tidbury more than is your usual pattern on one of these projects."

Jeff shifted in his chair. He picked up his pen and rolled it back and forth making a clicking sound.

"Jeff, did you not understand what I asked? Do you have feelings for this woman?"

Jeff ran a hand through his hair, and slowly nodded. "Yeah, I believe I do."

"Well, it's taken you long enough to find someone after Beth. I'm happy for you, buddy." He stretched out his arm to give Jeff a high-five.

Jeff shook his head and didn't meet his friend's palm. "Don't get too excited yet. We've got issues."

"What issues? If you care for each other, you figure it out. Look at Eva and me. Religious and political differences, and yet we're still together."

"I don't have a clue how she feels."

"Well, you better find out."

"Yeah, you're right. I better find out. Thanks, Tony."

Chapter Twelve

Jessica hadn't moved back to her apartment yet. Both daughters insisted she stay through Thanksgiving, and she agreed. This was one of her favorite holidays. Even before she'd lost Ed, a hint of bittersweetness always underlay the enjoyment of family, good food, and laughter. Different family members passed on and left empty places at the table. Her family had chosen to honor those people by continuing to make whatever that family member had brought.

Ed's Aunt Viv made a scrumptious shoe peg corn casserole with cream cheese. Lori especially loved it, and now she made that dish. Another aunt had made a sweet potato casserole sweet enough it could count for dessert. Kathy made that because she wasn't fond of pumpkin pie, which Jessica now made ever since her mom had died.

"Bob, that turkey sure smells yummy." Jessica put an arm around her son-in-law.

"Not sure I'll ever challenge one of Ed's turkeys, Jessica, but I keep trying."

She smiled and went back to cutting up the celery and onion for the dressing. Her jobs were always the pumpkin pies, cranberries, and the dressing. Other people brought all the rest. Besides the turkey, these were her favorite dishes anyway. As a younger woman, she'd always sensed pressure to eat at least a bite of everything anyone brought, but that led to a dreadful result on the scale the next day. Several years ago, she'd hit on the plan to sniff and ooh and ahh over all the dishes but eat only what she wanted.

"When are we planning on eating?" Kathy set her mother's cranberries in a special bowl on the dining room table which had been expanded to seat fourteen people. Jessica's good friends Sue and Joe Franklin were joining them today because both their kids were eating with the in-laws. Sometimes over the years, the families had celebrated the holiday together.

"The turkey will be done in an hour. I'll pull it out, and we'll let it settle. Jessica, you can put in the dressing. What's that take?"

"Forty-five minutes. When it's almost ready, we can warm up anything like the green bean casserole, the mac and cheese Sue is bringing, and the corn which Lori has already made."

"Looks like three pm then."

"Yes," Jessica raised her arm and wiped at her right eye where a tear gathered from cutting up onions for the dressing. "But I think Sue and Joe are coming at two to give us a better chance to visit. I do like eating later. Facing only one giant meal instead of a giant meal at noon followed by a later meal of everything again at five or six is much kinder to my waistline."

"I agree, Mom." Lori reached her hand for a sausage ball. "Besides, it leaves more opportunities to snack." She ambled out of the kitchen. Her chore completed.

"What's Jeff Hudson doing today?" Kathy worked with her mom to set the table with the best silver. They only used it for special meals. It had belonged to Jessica's mother.

Jessica took care folding the burgundy, gold, and forest green cloth napkins for each place. Without meeting her daughter's gaze she said, "I believe he told me he and his father would spend the holiday with his partner Tony and his family in Concord. I think they are close, like Sue and me."

"When is he returning?"

"I'm not sure. He indicated in a couple of days."

"Well, he'll contact you when he gets here, right?"

"Maybe, I don't know, Kathy."

"Well, you want him to, right?"

"What is this, twenty questions? I'm going in search of the special runner for the table." She set the last fork on top of the last napkin and whirled away from her daughter. What was going on with Kathy? Did she think she could play matchmaker or something? Dear heavens. Jessica wanted things to go back to the old normal. But the old normal stretched back to before Ed died, and that she couldn't have. She'd done a good job building a new normal. Did she want another relationship? She wasn't ready to answer that question, but cartwheels tumbled in her tummy every time they'd nearly kissed.

From the linen closet, Jessica retrieved the extra-long runner used at Thanksgiving with the table opened to its fullest length. Colorful leaves were stitched on top of a woven ivory cloth. She returned, determined not to let her daughter get under her skin. "Here's the table runner." She and Kathy arranged it by bunching it in a couple of places to give an artistic twist.

The doorbell rang. "I'll answer it." Jessica hurried toward the front door and away from her daughter. "Hi, Sue, Joe. Come in. Come in."

Sue and Joe entered, bringing the cold air with them. "Boy, that wind is something. We nearly froze walking in from our car." Joe helped Sue off with her coat.

"Did you bring the mac and cheese? The kids will be disappointed if you didn't."

"Kids? What are you talking about? I'd be disappointed." Joe winked.

"You take the dish to the kitchen, and I'll hang your coats up here in this closet." Jessica juggled the coats and then hurried to the kitchen to find everyone greeting and hugging. She did love the Thanksgiving family gathering.

After the scrumptious meal, where everyone ate more than they probably should've, including Jessica because the corn casserole tempted her, and she didn't resist. The women settled in the main room in front of the fireplace. The men took the twins outside. Too much time inside and the kids' energy exploded, sometimes not in a good way.

"You must be disappointed not to be with your kids this year, but I'm sure happy you can be with us." Jessica took Sue's hand and squeezed it.

"Always feels like home here with you and your kids. I've missed our regular chats. How do you like serving on the board? I found the swearing-in ceremony to be pretty exciting. When's the decision made on the retirement center on the green? Is that a done deal?"

Finally her friend stopped, and a smile spread wide across Jessica's face. She loved Sue, especially when words spewed from her mouth faster than a skier going downhill.

"I looked over the plans at the city offices, and I admit they impressed me." Jessica nibbled on a cookie. "Not sure where I'm putting this."

The women's laughter filled the room, mixing with the wonderful scents of cinnamon and turkey. "We should probably be out with the kids, burning off these extra calories," Lori said. "But tomorrow will be good enough."

"So, what about the green?" Sue reminded them.

"Probably more important to find out why Mom keeps getting attacked." Kathy wiggled her toes encased in Christmas socks.

"Oh, let's not go into that, Kathy. This is a joyful time. No negative thoughts allowed." Jessica dismissively waved her hand at her daughter.

"Jessica, I think she's right. I'm concerned for you. Do you have any idea who's behind these threats?" Sue sided with Kathy.

"No, not really." Jessica shook her head.

"I thought it must be Jeff Hudson, the developer, because he'd benefit the most if Mom stopped opposing the project, but they were together for two of the events. You don't think it's him do you, Mom?" Lori's hands cuddled a cup of coffee.

Jessica wished Lori hadn't brought up Jeff. "No, I don't. I admit I wondered at first, but the more I got to know him—I mean got familiar with his plans—well, I don't oppose the retirement center any more. Jeff showed me how it can fit on the green and still leave us plenty of space for all our festivals."

"Well, that's a relief. Joe liked the idea of having an alternative to moving all the way to Concord to find a place to retire if the time comes where we can't keep up our large house. I worried we'd find ourselves at cross purposes."

"The bottom line is I still don't want them to use Worley Construction. Jeff expressed his determination to get out of his contract with them. If he can do that, I can vote for the project. Otherwise, I'm afraid I won't be supporting the town moving forward on the center."

"I think you should keep that quiet, Mom. That info paints a great big X on your back. You won't be safe."

Jessica huffed at Lori. "Speaks my daughter whose nose is always in a mystery novel. Real life isn't like in a book, hon."

"But maybe she's right, Jessica. When are you moving back to the apartment? Do you think you'll be safe there?"

"Oh, I'm sure I'll be fine, Sue. You're all making too much of a couple of unrelated incidents egged on by my adventure-reading daughter." Jessica scowled at Lori. They needed to change this subject.

"I'll relax if nothing else happens. And if something does, I will insist you move in here permanently. This whole thing makes me angry we encouraged you to run for office." Kathy rose. "I'm getting more coffee." She left the main room.

"Sorry, Mom. We worry about you. I'll go calm her down." Lori followed her sister.

Jessica let out a long sigh.

Sue patted her hand. "It's because they love you, Jessica. We all do and want you to be all right. So tell me what's going on with Jeff."

"Not you, too." Jessica laughed. "The problem of a small town. Everyone knows everything you do."

"I did hear stories about something that looked like a romantic dinner for two at the Tidbury Inn not long ago."

"It wasn't a romantic dinner. I'd call it a business dinner. It's when he told me he'd try to break the contract with Worley Construction."

"Kathy told me she and the twins walked in on what appeared to be you and Jeff heading toward a kiss."

Jessica dropped her head into her hands. What to do?

"Even if you want to deny the reality, the blush speaks for itself."

"WHAT A GREAT MEAL, Eva. Appreciate you having me." Phillip Hudson, Jeff's father, pulled on his coat.

"We're always glad when you can join us, Phil." Eva tied his scarf around his neck.

"Jeff, I'm heading on out. I'll be in touch."

"Sure, Dad."

"Thanks again, Eva." Phil slipped through the front door.

"Thanks for the to-go box, Eva." Jeff shrugged into his coat.

"You're always welcome here." His hostess sent a gracious smile in his direction.

"Jeff and I will walk around for a bit, hon, and I'll be back to help you with cleaning."

"Bundle up. I've heard the wind howling." Eva headed back toward the kitchen.

"We're going for a walk?" Jeff glanced at his friend.

"Yeah, I wanted to follow up with where you thought we were with the Tidbury Retirement Center project." He closed the door behind them.

"We're still on go. We have a public presentation scheduled for next week. I hate we don't seem to be able to terminate the contract with Worley Construction. For one, I think Jessica will probably vote against us. For another, if the project is approved, it will mean a great deal more work to stay on top of Worley Construction and make sure they don't do their usual cutting corners with our project."

"What does that do to you and Jessica? Whoa. That's a wind." Tony twisted his scarf tighter.

"Yeah another cold front has blown through. What are you talking about? There is no Jessica and me."

"Don't give me that. I've seen how your eyes light up when you talk about her. I heard the worry in your voice when you told me about the incidents. There's definitely something there."

Jeff shrugged. Hard to deny how the woman made him feel. She'd tipped his world upside down. "Tony, I've always been sure about my plans and what I needed to do to accomplish them. Now, I'm not so sure. Jessica's roots are planted in Tidbury. Our work is here in Concord. I love our partnership. We do worthwhile work. I can't figure this out." He scuffed his boots along the snow-covered sidewalk.

"You want to know what I think?"

Jeff glanced at him. "Do I?"

"I'm telling you anyway. Go talk with her. In fact, take her up to the Mount Washington Resort for supper. Maybe spend the night. See what develops. You've been working hard. You deserve a couple of days off. She probably does, too. Why can't you do those together?"

"I like the idea, Tony. But not sure I can pull this off. The resort never has openings last minute. What makes you think she'll go? And to spend the night?" Jeff realized his heart rate had kicked up at the idea of spending the night with Jessica.

"Promise me you'll take a stab at making it happen. You'll both be happier."

They angled back toward Tony's house. "Give it a shot. If you don't ask, you preclude the possibility of hearing a yes."

Jeff punched Tony on the arm. "Okay, I'll take a chance. Thanks again for today. I'll head back to Tidbury and see what happens."

"It's not a long drive from Concord, Jeff. You could commute if you had to."

"Guess I ought to consider those ideas, Tony. You enjoy the rest of the weekend. I'll check in with you Monday." Jeff climbed into his SUV parked at the curb, adjusted the temperature upward, and drove away toward his condo. If he'd be spending more time in Tidbury, he needed to take care of business so he could be away for longer at a time. And he needed to decide if he should pursue Jessica. Being with her made him a better person, able to conquer all kinds of mountains.

But she'd be so angry with him if he ultimately used Worley Construction for the project. Would she forgive him? Could he push past that with her? He darn sure wanted to try. He parked in the garage under his condo and walked up the steps. He unlocked the door, tapped the off button on his security system, and hung his coat in the front hall closet. Two bedrooms were plenty for him.

What if Jessica moved in with him? Would they have enough space? Now, they each lived in a two bedroom apartment. Together they might require more. And the big stumbling block was she lived above her shop. In Tidbury. Would she want to leave Tidbury, even part-time?

"Hey, Bud, you are getting way ahead of yourself." And now he talked out loud to himself. He sat at his desk and studied the contract with Worley Construction. If their lawyers suspected they couldn't terminate it without paying a huge penalty, they probably couldn't. He pounded his hand on the desk and thrust away the papers in front of him. How could anything work with Jessica and him if he were stuck with Worley Construction? Jeff rose from the desk, restacked the papers, and paced to the large front window overlooking the street. Okay, he'd take a stab at it anyway. He owed it to himself and to Jessica to give them a chance to find some way they could be happy.

Chapter Thirteen

Friday morning after Thanksgiving, Jessica left Kathy's, drove home in her repaired car, and resettled at her upstairs apartment over the shop. Bob and Kathy both went with her to make sure she got in okay. Jessica had given Janell the morning off and left the shop closed. Yes, odd to do on Black Friday, but really, sometimes everyone needed a break. She washed a load of clothes in the morning, opened Allen's at one that afternoon, and people flocked in.

She sold enough in the afternoon and early evening to make up for being closed Friday morning. Getting settled back in her apartment made her feel in control once more. She'd be in the shop Saturday all day and Buddy Stanley, the high school senior she'd hired to mostly do the heavy lifting for her, would cover Sunday from eleven on.

Back to real life. What a relief.

She received an email with the agenda for the Tuesday board meeting. She'd do her homework and be prepared. Other than the issue of the retirement center, other items on the agenda were just routine. Next year's budget had been approved last month prior to her swearing in. And she'd been okay with how the tax dollars were divvied up.

Sunday evening sitting in front of her computer in her apartment, she studied the documents Jeff submitted to Rudy Lopez, the chair of the board of selectmen. Nowhere did Jeff indicate what construction company he'd use. Guess she'd have to ask that at the meeting and get it on the record. Darn, she hated to be confrontational. The doorbell rang, and she jumped. Not used to being home. She checked the camera Bob had installed. Jeff stood outside the shop, pacing back and forth beating his hands on his arms. Not like she could leave him outside to freeze. She clicked off the alarm, unlocked the apartment door, and stepped out on the landing.

Jeff pushed open the door. "Hi." He looked up at her. "May I come up?"

"Of course."

He closed the door. She stepped into the apartment and reset the shop alarm.

His footsteps echoed up the stairs, bringing him into her home. "How about hot chocolate? Or tea, or coffee? Seems like something hot is in order." She relocked the apartment door. Something she never used to do.

"Hot chocolate sounds great." He removed his coat and placed it on the hall tree where Jessica's coat also hung. "Is this okay?"

"Sure. We tried to add closet space when we remodeled but couldn't find an area for a front hall closet. I don't have lots of visitors up here. Mostly, I meet with people in the shop or at Molly's. Though in the future, I'll plan on eating at the Tidbury Inn more often. I enjoyed it the other evening."

"Happy to hear that. I did too."

"Would you like whipped cream?"

"I wouldn't say no." His grin kicked up more on one side than the other.

She plopped a significant scoop on top of his drink and passed the cup to him.

"That smells really, really, good. Do you have a special recipe?" He sipped. "Oh, yeah. The taste matches the good smell."

Jessica smiled. "Good to hear you're enjoying the cocoa. Let me start the fire, and we can sit in front of its warmth." She clicked a button, and the flames sprang up, bringing dancing colors of yellow, orange, and an occasional blue. So comforting on such a frigid night. "How did your Thanksgiving celebration turn out?" She settled on the sofa and drew one jean-clad leg up underneath.

"We had a great time. Dad and I went to Tony and Eva's, who had both their family members and lots of excellent food. Good times. How did your family celebration go?"

"We had a lovely day at Kathy and Bob's with Lori, Bobby, and Bonnie. Sue and Joe Franklin came over, too." She laughed. "Not sure why the twins never seem to run down. When one starts to wear out, the other one kicks on, and we're off to the races again. Whew! But Kathy and Bob manage them well. Of course, it helps having Lori there."

"Has Lori figured out what she'll do after she graduates? Will she stay in the area?"

"She wants to teach. My guess is she won't be staying here. Our one small elementary school probably won't offer her enough opportunities. She's always been exceptionally good with kids, camp counseling, and stuff like that. So I wasn't surprised when she announced she wanted to be a teacher. Do you have children, Jeff?"

He shook his head. "We never had a chance. When the cancer struck, we focused all our attention and efforts on getting Beth the best treatment and doing everything we could to beat the disease. Lots of progress in cancer research, but not enough for us. I lost her eight years ago after a valiant and long fight." He sipped his cocoa.

"I'm sorry, Jeff. I didn't realize. How difficult for you both. Losing Ed suddenly tore me from my moorings but seeing your loved one slip away must be gut-wrenching."

He nodded. "That's about right. I leaned on Tony during the years we fought the cancer. After Beth died, I threw myself into work, trying to make up to Tony for him carrying the heavier load during her illness. The business never missed a lick, and we kept growing."

Jessica sipped her chocolate, licking her lips to catch the whipped cream that wanted to stick there. Should she mention business? Yeah, better to hit it head on. Neither of them needed any surprises. "When I read over the papers for the meeting Tuesday night, Jeff, I didn't find any mention of who you'd be using for a contractor."

"No, it wasn't required by the town." He set his cup on the coffee table and faced her on the sofa. "I'm sorry, Jessica. I haven't been able to find a way out of the contract with Worley Construction. I keep hoping but, at this point, I can't promise you anything."

Jessica set her cup on the table, rose, and walked behind the sofa, gazing out the window. Disappointment swamped her, making a gaping hole in her middle.

"But, Jessica," Jeff rose and crossed to her, turning her to face him, "I promise you I will personally monitor the company's work. I guarantee, they will meet all standards. Besides hiring a separate inspector to be on site, I'll find a place to rent. I can live here and commute into the city, so I can keep a close eye on the work, too."

"I appreciate your good intentions, but how will you make that work, Jeff? You'll make a ninety minute trip back and forth every day?"

"Lots of work I'll do from here. Tony can run the office in Concord. We can talk, use FaceTime, Zoom, or whatever to keep in touch. I can make it work." His hands slid from her shoulders down to her hands, which he clasped. "Just give me a chance. Let us build the retirement center, and I promise we'll build to meet or exceed all the standards. You'll be proud."

"I don't know, Jeff. I'll consider your proposal."

"The sooner you can come forward to say you're not blocking the project, the sooner you'll be safe." He dropped her hands and stepped back. "Damn, I'm sorry. That sounded like a threat. I'm not threatening you. I'm not behind any of this, but I am convinced the attacks against you are because of this project, and I hate that."

Jessica sighed. Where did that leave her? "Thanks for stopping by." She walked to his coat and lifted it.

"Here's your coat and what's your hurry?" His smile rueful.

"Sorry, but it's been an exhausting day, and I have to open the store in the morning. Jeff, I do appreciate your honesty. I would've hated for you to tell me you'd gotten out of the contract, when the likelihood of breaking it was slim."

Jeff slipped into his coat. "I'm sorry, Jessica. I haven't given up all hope, but it's not looking good. If there's anything else I can do to reassure you, let me know. Otherwise, I guess I'll see you Tuesday evening at the meeting." He walked out and closed the door.

When Jessica heard the shop door open and close, she set the downstairs alarm system, went back in the apartment, and set that alarm. She picked up both their cups and took them to the kitchen, running water in each before putting them in the dishwasher. Drinking hot chocolate with whipped cream was supposed to make everything better. Not sure it worked this time.

WALKING FROM JESSICA'S to the Tidbury Inn, Jeff retrieved his cell phone from his pocket and placed a call to Tony. Not many people on the street at this hour. Stores were all closed. He didn't have to worry anyone would overhear his conversation.

"Hey, Tony."

"Did you tell her? What'd she say?"

"Yeah, I did. She was disappointed, Tony. I promised her I'd stay here and oversee the work, to make sure the company didn't cut any corners."

"What? How will you do that from here?"

"I'll find a place to live in Tidbury until the center is completed. I can commute back and forth. You run the Concord office. We'll talk on the phone, Skype, FaceTime, or Zoom. Whatever it takes."

"Wow. You must care for her a great deal to do that." He chuckled. "Well, and our company to make sure the deal goes through."

"Yes, to both of those, but Tony I'm unclear if my offer will be enough for her to vote for our project. While she's only one person, she's respected in this community. I have little doubt she could sway enough others on the board for us to lose the project."

"Guess we'll have to wait until Tuesday night for the resolution. I'm working on another deal over in Jackson. It looks like it could be a similar project to the one in Tidbury. I'll email you the info I've gathered."

"Great. I'll take a look at what you've got."

"Sounds good. Remember to cut yourself some slack, Jeff. You've done everything you can. If the deal doesn't make, we'll lose money, but it won't be the end of the world."

"Thanks, Tony. Be in touch." Jeff disconnected and put his phone in his pocket. He climbed the steps to the Tidbury Inn and went inside. The inn was a great place to stay on a temporary basis, but if he'd be here for however long the build took, he needed something with more space. Seems like he remembered hearing Jessica's friend Sue Franklin worked in real estate. If the board approved the project Tuesday night, he'd contact her.

The entry was only dimly lit, but light blobs sat on every step of the stairs, increasing the safety. He liked that. He'd double check they had that kind of stair lighting at the retirement center. He let himself into his room and switched on the lamp. After hanging his coat in the closet, he poured himself a bourbon, settling in front of the window overlooking the green. The green, the center of Tidbury. Their retirement center would be a great new addition to this town. The bronze liquid burned going down, not quenching his sadness at his inability to give Jessica what she wanted.

THE NEXT MORNING FLEW by, with a surprising number of customers and good sales. Janell came in right after lunch, and Jessica went out for a much needed energizing walk. After getting into her coat, mittens, and scarf, she set out, walking toward Kathy's. It made for a good destination. After a quick visit, she'd grab a cup of hot tea, use the bathroom, and head back. The walk would provide a good opportunity for dithering, to figure out what to do. If she had more time, maybe she'd be able to find proof of the shortcuts Worley Construction took on projects. It couldn't have been the only instance on that one building that got Ed killed, could it? It couldn't have been an accident.

Careful to step off the road whenever she heard a car behind her, Jessica trudged along, her breath making puffs of white. She'd have walked facing the traffic on the other side of the road, but the drifts were larger over there.

Yes, she needed to buy time so she could keep up her research. Could she find a way to postpone Tuesday's action? She'd served as Parliamentarian for the girl's school PTA and bet she had an old copy of Robert's Rules of Order. Or maybe do an online search. If a strategy existed, she'd find that strategy. And postponing the vote would give her a chance to find proof Worley Construction cut corners. Maybe she wouldn't find enough for a conviction, but the bad PR would hurt the company. She hated if her actions would also hurt Jeff and Tony's company. They'd probably lose money. She'd hate it if it meant Tidbury never got a retirement center, but she had to keep her eye on the goal, stopping Worley Construction.

By the time she got to Kathy's, Jessica had resolved that this was the best course of action. She had to find the right parliamentary maneuver, and she needed to convince one other member to vote with her besides Rudy Lopez, the mayor who would go along with her.

Stomping the snow off her boots, she knocked on the front door.

"Mom, come in. You don't have to knock. Come on in."

"I appreciate that, Kathy, but I wouldn't want to walk in on anything." She chuckled and wiggled her eyebrows up and down. Blood rushed to her daughter's face.

"Mo-om."

Jessica smiled. Such fun to still be able to pull the two-syllable word from her daughter. "Kathy, I want to go through one of the boxes in the garage. I'm looking for my old copy of Roberts Rules of Order or any of the training pages from when I worked with the PTA."

"Sure, Mom. Help yourself. Those five boxes are in the back left corner of the garage with *MOM* written in block letters. I'll fix us cups of fresh hot chocolate. You'll be crying out for this hot yumminess when you come back in."

"Great, thanks. I think I'll recognize the right box. Back in a bit." Jessica went down the back steps to reach the garage. Built on a hill, the garage sat on a lower level than the rest of the two story house.

Jessica flipped on the lights and made her way to the section Kathy mentioned. Sure enough. Here were her five boxes. Odd that was all that remained of her years living in her old home. Of course, she'd taken many things with her to the apartment over the store and given away many others. She rubbed her hands together. Her excellent gloves didn't provide enough protection in the unheated garage, despite no windchill to lower the temperature. If she worked in here long, she'd be frigid in no time.

Maybe it would've been smarter to drink the cocoa and to warm up after her walk before searching in the ice cold garage. Finding what she needed to stop Worley Construction drove her to continue. At the point she thought she couldn't work in the garage for a moment longer, she found the right box holding her old PTA materials with the parliamentary materials she wanted. Why had she saved this stuff? Of course, it might be beneficial she had. Now for the house and Kathy's hot chocolate.

"Gosh, Mom, I was about to send out a Saint Bernard. I worried you'd frozen into a solid block in the garage." She set a large cup of hot chocolate with two marshmallows on the coffee table in front of the hearth. "Take off your coat and sit by the fire. You'll be warm in no time. I love the brown and black combination." She eyed her mother's jeans and sweater outfit.

"Thanks." Jessica sipped the cocoa and caressed the cup with both hands. "Oh, this is wonderful." She closed her eyes and sighed. "Such a comfort."

"Did you find whatever you were looking for?" Kathy, dressed in dark blue jeans and a red wool sweater, settled on the sofa.

"I've figured out how to stop the retirement center project, or at least delay our decision."

"But I thought you'd decided you liked the project and that being built on the far end of the green would leave plenty of room for our festivals."

"Kathy, I do think that, but Jeff is having trouble getting out of the contract with Worley Construction."

"Are you sure?"

"Yes. He came by my place last night to give me the news. He held out only a sliver of hope. He was upset, but, Kathy, I can't let Worley succeed in building another dangerous building in our town."

"Jeff came by your apartment?"

"Yes, he did." Jessica hurried on to explain to Kathy how she needed something to slow down the action of the board of selectmen and hoped to find it in her parliamentary procedure notes.

"Humm." Kathy sipped her cocoa. "What you're looking for is a motion to postpone. I bet you can find the votes for that."

"Of course, wonder why I didn't remember the word. Thanks. You've made my research easier. I want to make sure I'm comfortable with all the ins and outs."

"How does your determination to kill the project affect your relationship with Jeff?"

"Oh, Kathy, we don't have a relationship. Could we have? Maybe, but I have to stop Tim Worley, I can't compromise on that issue. If Jeff gets hurt by my actions, I'm sorry."

Chapter Fourteen

Jessica had done her homework and understood exactly how to use the motion to postpone. She'd had a couple of private conversations with Rudy Lopez, the mayor, and Ralph McGinley. Ralph and her late husband Ed had gone to high school together. They had a tight connection. Rudy and Ralph both listened to her and recognized the necessity to slow down the project. If they went along, and the building had problems and elderly people were harmed...well, it didn't bear thinking.

Everyone wouldn't be happy. She hated what she was doing to Jeff and his partner Tony, but she owed it to the town and to Ed's memory to make sure the Worley Construction Company harmed no one else.

Janell agreed to work the late shift and to close up the shop. Jessica walked into the meeting room next to the town offices. Tension made her stomach hurt and her hands tremble. The Board sat behind an eight-foot table with the town people sitting on chairs in front of them. A speaker's stand in the center faced the board. They didn't have microphones because everyone could be heard in the small space.

The members greeted one another and took their seats. More town people attended the meeting than usual. Rudy called the meeting to order, and two members of the town's boy scout troop led the group in the Pledge of Allegiance. After approving the minutes from the last meeting, they took up the next item on the agenda: the retirement center on the green. Jeff came forward and made his presentation. He had pictures of other centers his company had developed.

Rudy asked for questions, and Jessica raised her hand.

"Yes, Jessica?" Rudy called on her.

Boy she hated to do this. Her stomach cramped, but she persevered. "Thanks for the clear presentation, Mr. Hudson. I do have one question."

She paused, and the world stopped. The silence in the room deafening. She swallowed. Now's the time.

"What's your question, Ms. Allen?"

You'd never guess from Jeff's tone they practically had a relationship. Lucky they hadn't kissed yet. Talk about complicating the situation.

"Mr. Hudson, have you selected a construction company to build the center?"

Jeff paused, studying each member of the board, stopping on her. "We have a contract with Worley Construction."

"Have you heard concerns expressed regarding the work of this company?" Jessica pressed the subject.

"Not until after we'd signed the contract."

"But you have heard concerns now?"

"Yes."

"And what were those concerns?"

"Well, I hate to repeat what I've heard because it's hearsay."

"We're not in a court, Mr. Hudson. Did you hear they cut corners, and their work doesn't always meet standards?"

"Rudy, are you running this meeting or is Ms. Allen?" John Crowell blustered and pounded his hand on the table. "You can't sit quiet and let her smear a company that does business with the town."

Surprised she'd gotten away with as much as she had, Jessica nodded. "I don't have any more questions, Rudy."

"Thank you. Does anyone else have questions?" Rudy glanced at the members to his left and right. No one said anything, and heads shook. "Mr. Hudson. You may sit down. Well, are we ready to vote on the motion to approve Mr. Hudson's project to build a retirement center on the west side of the green?"

"Rudy, pardon me, I have a motion."

"Yes, Jessica?"

"I move we postpone this decision until our next meeting, so we can determine if we want to have the center built by Worley Construction."

Ralph McGinley spoke up, "I second that motion." Jessica barely tipped her head in his direction acknowledging his support.

"All right now, we have another motion on the floor, and it takes precedence. Any discussion?" Rudy followed procedure while Jessica held her breath. John Crowell scowled at his buddy Stan Henson. Jessica was certain they would vote together, but her side should prevail.

"Hearing none, all in favor raise your hand."

Jessica, Ralph, and Rudy raised their hands.

"All opposed raise your hand."

John and Stan raised their hands.

"The Motion passes. We'll postpone this motion and take it up at our next meeting."

"You will regret taking this action, Jessica Allen. My lawyers will sue you for libel." Tim Worley jumped up, pushing his chair over and raised his fist, shaking it at her. The crowd rumblings grew loud. He shoved his way out of the building.

Rudy pounded his gavel. "Order. Order. We will have order, or we will clear the room.

John Crowell stood. "You'll regret this decision, Jessica Allen. This is a good project for our town and will bring in more people and money." He stomped out of the meeting.

Rudy pounded his gavel again. "Since we still have a quorum, let's finish our agenda. With the holidays approaching, I'm sure we all have many things to do to prepare." The other items were quickly dispatched, and the meeting adjourned.

Jessica shook hands with Ralph and Rudy. She tried to talk with Stan, but he veered away from her and walked out.

"You did well, Jessica. Maybe with more time, this will work out the way you'd like. But to be truthful with you, if you can't find evidence, I'll vote for the project. It's a good one for the town." Rudy patted her on the shoulder, and she nodded.

"Jessica, can I talk with you?" Jeff stood behind Rudy.

"Of course. Ralph, Rudy, we'll visit soon." The two men walked away, and Jessica focused on Jeff. "I'm sorry we had to go down this road. I couldn't let Worley win the bid tonight."

"I understand. I won't lie and tell you I'm not disappointed. I had hoped my assurance of staying on top of the company would be enough."

"Jeff, I appreciated the effort, but practically, I couldn't figure how you could be here twenty-four-seven, which is what it would take. You have other responsibilities, and I couldn't compromise with anyone else's life."

"I get it, Jessica. I don't understand what you've accomplished by postponing the inevitable. If we do the project, we'll likely have to use Worley Construction. Without real proof of malfeasance, our attorney's word, on their part, we're stuck with them."

"I bought us time, Jeff. Hopefully, during this period, something will happen that will let you find a way to end the contract. I hope I've been clear my opposition doesn't relate to you, your company, or the project itself. You convinced me it would be beneficial for the town to have the retirement center."

"Yeah."

"I guess you'll be heading back to Concord now."

He nodded.

"Why don't you return for the Christmas Festival beginning the 18th of December. It runs for the weeks leading up to Christmas and through New Year's Eve. The town and the green are all decked out, and we have all kinds of activities and competitions."

"Like what?"

"Snowman making and gingerbread house decorating competitions to name two. All kinds of booths are set up on the green. Hot chocolate, cookies, and hot pretzels, and so much more. You can decorate an ornament and hang it on our tree that stands right next to the bandstand where we sing Christmas carols. Of course, we have a special tree lighting ceremony. It's quite spectacular."

"This little town does all of that?"

"And more. Please say you'll come back. Bring Tony and his wife."

"I'll talk with them. It does sound fun."

"Will you leave in the morning?"

"Yeah, I've been gone longer than I planned already." He helped Jessica on with her coat and then buttoned up his own.

"How would you have managed if I'd agreed to the deal with you keeping an eye on the project?"

"I planned to rent a house and alternate between staying here and Concord."

"Thank you, Jeff. I appreciate your willingness to do that, but since we've delayed the decision, we've got more of an opportunity to hopefully find evidence."

"Shoving back the beginning of the build will give us better weather to work in, but it will also make it less likely we'll open in the fall. We'll see how it all works out. Let me walk you back to the store."

"Thanks." Jessica hadn't expected winning to leave her feeling empty inside, and she didn't say much on the way to her apartment.

"Jessica, what will you do now? Both Worley and Crowell threatened you in the meeting. I'm worried about your safety. I'll check with our lawyers if the attacks on you can be tied to the company if that will give us any more leverage for breaking the contract."

"I'll be fine. Everyone looks out for everyone else in Tidbury. Sometimes you hate everyone knowing your business, but it's a good thing. And it's because everyone is concerned for our town. Our family."

"Can I come in tonight?"

"Of course, and I bet I can find a cup of coffee for you." She unlocked the door, flipped on the Tiffany lamp, and shut off the security system. She relocked the door and reset the alarm.

Jeff followed her up the stairs, and Jessica sensed him behind her. "Actually, I'm relieved you wanted to come home with me. I admit it unnerved me to hear Tim Worley say I'd be sorry, and Crowell say I'd regret this decision. I shudder to think what they might mean by those words." She unlocked the door to the apartment and turned off the separate alarm.

"I like your system here. It gives me confidence. Are you connected to the sheriff's office?"

"No. We're not that hi-tech here in Tidbury, but the alarm is super loud. My biggest concern is if it went off, it could cause Mr. Jones in the store next door to have a stroke or heart attack."

Jeff laughed, and she joined him. "Let me serve you that coffee I promised." She slipped into the kitchen. He hung his coat on the hall tree by the front door.

Jessica returned with his coffee and her tea. They settled on the sofa in front of the fire. They both spoke at the same time.

"I'm sorry. You go first." Jessica sipped her tea.

"I should say ladies first, but I've set my mind on saying this, and if I don't do it now, I might not have a chance later."

"What is it?"

"I like you, Jessica, and I'd like to see more of you."

"Well, we do see each other."

"But for business. I'd like to see you when it's not on the subject of business."

"Oh." She set her cup on the table, clasping her hands together. "But aren't you returning to Concord tomorrow?"

"Yes, but it's less than ninety minutes away. I can easily come up on a weekend or you can come to Concord. I'd like to show you the town I know and love. And I want us to go to the Mount Washington Resort. It's one of my favorite places." He took her hand. "I love the history of the place. I want to share that with you."

Jessica met his gaze and smiled. "That sounds like fun. I haven't been there in years. Weekends are normally busy for me, but I can probably ask Janell to cover a Saturday."

"We'll plan on a trip soon. I'll check when they have available reservations for dinner. We can go out early and enjoy the remarkable old building. I mentioned I love history, right?"

Jessica laughed. "You did at that."

Jeff stood and pulled her to her feet. "I'm heading back to the inn. Best to get an early start in the morning."

"Of course. I don't want to keep you." Warmth filled her face at her lie. She admitted to herself she wished Jeff would stay. She liked him a lot, maybe more than liked, but gosh, did that mean she wanted to sleep with him? She'd never slept with anyone but Ed.

She'd begun an internal lecture on the benefits of being cautious when Jeff tipped her chin and leaned forward. Oh, he was about to kiss her. She didn't draw back. She leaned into him, and the kiss was at first tentative and sweet. But oh, did he know how to kiss, and their tongues began that age old duel. It was entirely possible her heart might explode through her chest.

Slowly Jeff drew back but kept his hands on her upper arms. "Well, Ms. Jessica Allen. What about that?" He drew in a deep breath. "Following up on that kiss is required, and I look forward to the experience." He skimmed his hands down her arms to clasp her hands. "You'll lock up when I leave?"

"Of course."

They walked hand in hand to the landing. Jeff kissed her on her cheek. "I'll call you soon. Take care of yourself."

Jessica watched him lope down the stairs and to the front of the store. He paused at the door and waved to her. She nodded; a Texas-size smile spreading across her face. She set the alarm, went into the apartment, and spun around. She felt absolutely giddy, happy, attractive. Not an issue she'd ever given much attention to, but after fifty a woman had to. The mirror beside the apartment door showed sprinklings of gray among the light brown. She'd never colored it because her mother hadn't. Blessedly, lines were at a minimum, crinkles at the corners of her eyes, but none on her forehead, and the smile lines around her mouth were less than one might expect. She'd never been much of a sun worshiper despite growing up in Texas.

No telling where this thing with Jeff might go. She had a bazillion questions, but no answers. For now, she'd hold those in her heart. No reason to share her doubts with anyone. A giant task faced her. Find something on Worley Construction to shut down the business. And time was a wastin'.

Chapter Fifteen

John Crowell sipped his coffee and toyed with the chocolate cake he'd ordered from the café in the neighboring town. Tim Worley hadn't arrived yet. Not anything unusual for him. Damn the man for sounding off at the board meeting, but he hadn't been much better himself. He wanted to wring Jessica Allen's neck. Because her dead husband's family had been leaders in this town since its founding didn't mean she could mess with his plans. Too bad she won the election. He could've manipulated Palmer Northcutt with his eyes closed.

The door opened and Tim hurried in, brushing snow from his shoulders. "Man, it's rough out there. Not certain the roads will be open much longer." One hand rattled the change in his pocket, a nervous habit that set John's teeth on edge.

"Coffee and apple pie, Babe," Tim told the waitress, who rushed off to do his bidding. "Are you sure we needed to meet?"

"You think we should ignore your outburst at the meeting the other night? I'd like us not to have to mess with Jessica Allen because she's a royal pain in my keister, but we can't announce it at a board meeting. That was too stupid for words."

"So, what do we do now?"

"I told you before. We should disappear the woman before the issue comes up at the next board meeting. You were supposed to do that before this meeting."

"Jeez, John. You really mean get rid of her? You talked about that before, but I thought you were kind of kidding."

"How successful have you been at making her change her mind, Tim? You've tried scare tactics, and nothing works. So I haven't changed my mind. She'll never forgive or forget what happened to her nosy husband."

"Guess you're right. How do you think we should make this happen?"

"Well, up to now, you haven't accomplished the task of with getting her to back off. I figure it's time to hire it done. Hate to spend the money, which will come out of your share, by the way, if we have to go in that direction. But we'll never push this project through if she remains on the board. And I want you to get this job."

"I agree, John. We should be able to pull in a hefty pile of dough. We can find a dozen or more ways we can cut corners on this one."

"We're agreed. I'll make it happen. In the meantime, keep your trap shut. Don't do anything else to call attention to yourself. When it happens, I don't want them coming to look for you. I'll key you in on the time to make sure you have an alibi. Both of us should have one. Solid, no way they can pin anything on us."

"Okay, if you think you can handle it, John. I kind of liked the idea of taking her to Maine and dumping her into the ocean from one of the rocky cliffs. That was going to be my next thing to try. But if you're going to handle it, that's fine with me. I'm heading out." He rose and shrugged into his coat.

"Yeah. I'll drink another cup of coffee to go with my cake here, and then I'll follow you." John signaled the waitress and settled back on the bench as Tim walked out of the café.

"LEAVE YOUR CAR AND let Bob drive you back to the shop, Mom. The roads are treacherous. Or better yet, you can stay here."

"I've got good snow tires, Kathy, and I've been driving on this stuff for thirty years now. I've got this. I will take the thermos of coffee you prepared with me, and I've always got extra blankets in case something happens. Anyway, we're only talking right at a mile. I drove because I didn't want to walk in the forecast blizzard. Unfortunately, the storm came in way earlier than expected."

"Here's your coffee. I know it's not your choice, but it will do in a pinch. And call me when you're safe in the apartment. If I don't hear in a reasonable time, I'm calling the sheriff."

Jessica couldn't stop the giggle from bubbling out at the idea of Kathy calling on the sheriff to ride to the rescue like in some western movie. "Thanks for the thermos, and I'm sure I'll be fine, Kathy. I won't take any chances. I appreciate you're worrying because you love me. I love you, too. Tell Lori not to come in to work tomorrow. Depending on what the weather does, I may not open in the morning, but I'll be able to handle customers if anyone is willing to brave the cold temps." She tugged her white wool knit cap down over her ears, pushed her hands into heavy leather gloves after zipping up her puff coat. Smart she'd worn boots when she left the shop. She hugged Kathy longer than usual and made her way outside. The wind bit into her exposed skin. It wouldn't take long for her cheeks to be rosy from the cold. Cautiously stepping down the stairs, she trudged through the drifts already piling up, though she hadn't been at Kathy's long.

The wind made opening the car door a challenge. Straining her arm muscles, she kept the door open long enough for her to scramble inside the car. As she dragged in her left leg, the door blew closed, barely missing her. The car had grown cold, and she didn't have far enough to go to reach her home for the heater to warm up the car. The downside of driving short distances. After turning on the ignition, she cranked up the heat anyway and punched the buttons for the seat warmers. Such a brilliant invention. Warmth enveloped her in an instant, and she wiggled her bottom against the car seat. If she'd walked from town, she'd be forced to stay at her daughter's. Not a dreadful occurrence but getting home to her own place seemed important. They'd probably all be hunkered down for two or three days. The possibility of losing power seemed likely. Her store and apartment had a generator. She'd be all right once she got there. One of the additions they'd done in the renovation she'd been grateful for a couple of times. It only took one week-long power outage to make the expense worthwhile. The refrigerator and the HVAC kept working. But first, she had to make it to town, the store, and her apartment.

Carefully looking both ways, Jessica left Kathy's and drove out on tires seeming to float above the road, she had so little traction. Wow, possibly the worst road conditions she'd ever driven in. She hoped not to need the emergency coffee, and she fully expected to get safely to her warm apartment, but the trip would definitely take longer than usual. She couldn't risk skidding. The image of the fire glowing in the hearth with the warmth streaming out, and her sitting with a cup of hot tea made her smile. She could hardly wait.

Lights in the rearview mirror blinded her for a moment. Looked like she wasn't the only idiot out on the road. She struggled again to keep the car from sliding. Her fingers in gloved hands tensed on the steering wheel. Why hadn't she agreed to stay with Kathy and Lori? Would've been way smarter. Not her best thinking. Periodically, her car slid, the tires not gripping. Each corrective action she took, led to the car moving another direction, and not the way she intended. Each slip and slide had her heart jumping out of her chest. Her fingers tightened on the steering wheel when the car, truck, whatever behind got closer and closer. Surely he didn't want to pass. On such a narrow road, if another vehicle came toward them, they would have no space for error. Jessica took her foot off the gas and gently tapped the brake. Maybe the red lights would remind him to back off. Her windshield wipers had trouble keeping up with the snow as it poured from the clouds in giant flakes she would've appreciated in any other situation but now made visibility difficult.

She was close to town, maybe a quarter of a mile and drew in a deep breath before tipping her head left and right to lessen the tension in her neck. The truck, dark in color, slowed down. Thank goodness. She only had a little farther to go before she made it home. And that's all she wanted to do. Arrive safely home. Between the lights in the rear view mirror and her own lights reflecting off the snow, sparkles bounced around in her eyes, the rainbow reflections making her struggle to see.

Clunk. Her car jerked; her head jerked. The truck had plowed into her bumper. What was the matter with him? Had he lost control of his vehicle? Did his brakes go out?

Clunk. Again. Harder this time, sending her car into a skid followed by a 360 degrees spin, pulling an imitation of a tilt-a-whirl at an amusement park. Her heart battered to get out of her chest when the car careened across the road. A scream tore from her throat as the car left the ground and sailed into the air before plunging into a ditch. Everything went dark.

"OH," JESSICA MOANED. Cold. So cold. Why was she cold? Prying her eyes open took effort, but she did it. What was that? Could a large tree branch break through the passenger side front windshield? She must be dreaming. Her hand reached out, expecting it to sail through the air. The sharp bark of a real tree limb scraped her fingers, drawing blood and surprising her. Wow. The branch had crashed right through, all right. She'd be dead if it had come through the driver's side. Shuddering shook her body, and it wasn't from the cold. Or only partly. She carefully swiveled her head to the left and then to the right. Yes, everything seemed connected. Based on how much she ached everywhere, she was alive. A good place to start. Vapor puffed from her mouth.

The airbag had deployed and deflated.

What time was it? Had she lost her phone? No. Thank goodness. She grabbed for it still sitting in the cup holder. Looking a second time, she was amazed to find an hour had passed since she left Kathy's. Her daughter must be worried sick. Would she have called the sheriff? Jessica should call anyway. Carefully she grasped her phone, removed one glove to type in Gary Halbert's number. However, her fingers, numb from the cold, wouldn't work correctly. She couldn't get a connection. Should she stay in her SUV? With the hole in the windshield, the car didn't provide much shelter from the cold. Could she climb out? Should she? Less than a quarter of a mile wasn't far. But in this blizzard? Staying on the road would make the trek doable, but....

"Gut up, Jessica." Her words though not loud, spurred her on. She could do this. Walking would help her stay warm. It wasn't far, but the conditions were horrific. Before she made any attempt at getting back to town, she drank half the thermos of hot coffee. Grimacing at the bitterness. How could people drink it? Especially with nothing in it. However, the warmth traveled right down to her toes, making her sigh. The caffeine gave her a jolt of energy she needed.

Taking a deep breath, she unhooked her seat belt, which fortunately wasn't jammed, clasped her hand on the car door handle, and shoved. Nothing happened. Oh, no. She had to make it work. She shoved with her shoulder again. Still nothing. Would the car start? She could roll down the window and crawl out that way. She twisted the key still in the ignition. The car turned over, sputtered, and died. What now?

All of a sudden, she remembered the emergency tool she'd gotten to use to break out the window if she ever lost control of the car and ended up in a lake. She kept it in the center glove box. It took her a couple of times to pry open the box, and she rummaged around searching for the instrument. The box contained too much junk. Finally her gloved fingers connected with the tool. Thank God. Now she needed to break the window. Could she do it? Guess she'd find out how good the tool was.

She positioned the tool in the corner of the window and hit it hard, and yes, the window cracked, and she carefully pressed it out.

Could she crawl out? Remaining in the car and waiting to be rescued didn't seem right. She twisted around to reach the spare blanket she kept in the back seat and tossed it out the window. Next went her small shoulder bag she carried everywhere, followed by the thermos. Her cell went into her coat pocket, and after a struggle she closed the zipper to keep the phone secure.

The only thing left was her. Go out head-first or feet-first? Feet-first. Shifting her weight, she curled up her legs close to her chest then thrust them through the opened window. This would be the world's hardest sit up. She wriggled and wriggled, scooting her bottom closer to the door and extended her legs farther through the window. Next she grasped the top of the window for leverage. Maybe she should've taken off her coat first, but the idea of doing that in the deep freeze temps hadn't entered her mind, and it was too late now. She'd wedged herself half in the car and half out. This had to work. She had no other options.

The good thing was, nothing seemed to be broken, or she wouldn't be able to play this contortionist game. With one last giant effort, she thrust herself through. Yikes. Despite the several layers of clothes on, she probably skinned her back sliding through the opening. Whoa. She spread eagled on her stomach when she landed on the blanket, protecting her from cutting herself on the broken out glass, which made a crunching sound as she landed. Dragging in a deep breath, she struggled to her knees and stumbled to her feet. Okay. She lifted the thermos and stuffed it in the other coat pocket. Her shoulder bag slung over her head, with the strap crossing her body. Next she picked up the navy blanket, shook it out several times to remove the snow and glass, and draped it around her shoulders for extra warmth.

Now she only had to trek into town. Only. She stumbled up the incline to the road. Her breath came in big gulps and vapor billowed out in front of her face. "I can do this. I can do this. I can do this," she whispered like *The Little Engine That Could*, a book her daughters had loved when they were kids, and she'd read to the twins.

No cars passed on the road. What did she expect? Only she and the crazy truck driver who made her lose control of her car were stupid enough to be out in this storm. She'd never hear the end of this from Kathy. How many times would she utter the words, *I told you so*? And rightfully, so. This was stupid. She'd never live this down. On the other hand, she was alive. What happened to the truck and the driver? Why didn't they stop to help? Everybody stopped to help someone in distress. That's the way people behaved in rural areas.

The wind howled, like something from a scary movie. The snow blew straight at her, making her cheeks sting. The cold slithered right through the scarf she'd wound around her neck and lower face. The fingers of both hands burned from the cold. What would it be like if she didn't have on the gloves? She folded her hands into fists and pulled them up into the sleeves of her coat.

One foot in front of the other. That's all it took. One foot in front of the other, and she'd make her way home. Home. Her eyes watered, making it hard to see. The moisture trickling down her face froze. So not good. Shivers shook her whole body. Snow had slithered inside her boots during one of the tumbles, and she trudged forward on feet with giant blocks of ice attached. It took all her determination to pick up one foot and set it in front of the other. Hard to balance on the numbness her feet had become, and she lost her footing, tumbling onto the road and rolling into the ditch. She landed on her back staring at the bare branches while cold, icy snow pelted her face. She lay there a moment struggling to get her breath. Could she do this? But she had to. She had family she wanted to get back to. Closing her eyes she drew from some internal well of strength, forced herself to roll over, and pushed up on her hands and knees. Then began another precarious climb up the incline. Taking deep breaths she drew in much needed oxygen, but the cold seared her throat and lungs like a menthol cough drop.

After each fall, the struggle grew harder to get her feet back under her body. She had to keep going. If she didn't, she'd freeze out in this storm. She trudged for what seemed like ages but must not have been because she hadn't made it to town yet. Suddenly up ahead, lights flashed in front of her. She moved to the side of the road facing the traffic. Help. Finally help. Pulling one hand from under the blanket she waved. The vehicle slowed to a stop not far from her, and the door opened.

A man got out and slipped and skidded toward her.

"Jeff." No one had ever looked as good to her as Jeff Hudson did to her at that moment.

"Jessica. Jessica." His arms clasped her close. "Are you all right?" He set her away enough to look at her and with a gentle touch knocked the ice from her cheeks.

She nodded. "Y-yes. Now, I am."

He settled an arm around her shoulders and guided her toward the passenger side of his SUV. "Let me help you inside where you can warm up." He boosted her into the car. She couldn't find the muscles to pull up her legs to climb in on her own.

"Th-thanks." She barely pushed the words past her trembling lips.

Jeff hooked the seatbelt for her. A good thing, her fingers wouldn't have managed the task. He went around the front and climbed in, closing out the cold. He flicked the blower on high.

"Oh, that feels wonderful." She held out her hands in front of the vent where warm air streamed forth, rubbing her gloved hands to encourage the feeling to return. Return of feeling to her fingers brought pain, and tears stung her eyes. "Oh, my. That hurts."

Jeff concentrated on turning his car and heading back to town. She let out a deep sigh when he accomplished the tricky maneuver on the narrow road. All the questions bubbling around in her mind, she kept to herself, not wanting to distract him. Why was Jeff here? What happened to the sheriff?

"Kathy. I better call Kathy. I'm sure she's worried sick." Jessica fumbled with getting her phone out of the zippered pocket. Though warmer, her fingers still wouldn't work. Tears of frustration formed in her eyes. "I-I can't dig it out."

"Hang on, Jessica. Use mine. Can you remember the number?"

She smiled. "Kathy's had the same number since she turned sixteen and worked at the local pizza shop. It's the only number I have off the top of my head."

"Tell me, and I'll put the call through."

Jessica repeated the numbers, and Jeff used the voice activated system to call her daughter who picked up almost instantly. "Who's this?"

"Kathy...it's mom. Yes, I'm...I'm sorry...yes, I should've listened to you. I'm okay...Jeff Hudson found me...Did you call Shariff Halbert?....Oh. I understand...I guess I'm going home." She cut her gaze at Jeff. He nodded. "Yes, I'm going home. Yes. I'll talk with you later." She disconnected.

"Kathy told me a big traffic accident happened out on the freeway, and that's where Sheriff Halbert is." She rubbed her hands together to keep the warmth moving. "How come you're here?"

"I'd arrived in town right before the full brunt of the storm set in."

Jeff's wipers struggled to keep the snow from piling on the windshield and sticking. That would be bad. He wouldn't be able to see. They still could end up in a wreck beside the road. Jessica shivered.

"I stopped by the sheriff's office to check on how everything was in town at the same moment Kathy's call came through saying she hadn't heard from you. I told the deputy I'd go look for you. By the way, there's hot tea in that thermos."

"Oh, good. Thank you." After a couple of unsuccessful attempts, she unscrewed the cap and poured the steaming brew into the attached cup and eagerly sipped. "This is sooo good. Thank you."

"When you're ready, can you tell me what happened?" Jeff's gaze cut in her direction.

Jessica finished her cup and put the cap back on the thermos. "To begin with, I'm incredibly pig-headed. Kathy told me to stay at her house, and I insisted on getting out in this mess and driving home. I will always regret my decision."

After a long breath, she began her story. "While it was bad out, I've been driving in this for thirty years and expected I'd be fine. And I would've been if that truck hadn't come up behind me."

"A truck?"

"Yeah. He rammed my bumper. I guessed he'd lost his brakes, but then he dropped back. And I breathed a sigh of relief. But the relief didn't last long because the driver sped up and rammed me again. That's when I lost control and spun around. Like completely around." Her voice trembled when the pictures replayed in her head, making her dizzy. "My car sailed off on the other side of the road. Everything went black. When I came to, I found a tree limb stuck through my passenger side window."

"Wouldn't the car start?"

"No. The engine sputtered, and then it died. Staying in the car seemed a way to make sure I froze to death. A giant tree limb had gouged a huge opening in my windshield on the passenger side. Oh, I think maybe I said that already. Anyway, I'm not much for sitting around, waiting to be rescued." She glanced at him and extended her arm to stroke his. "Not that I wasn't relieved for you to arrive. I am grateful. A quarter of a mile is not long except when you're trudging through a blizzard."

Ahead on the road Tidbury appeared through the snow. "Thank goodness. What a beautiful sight."

In moments, Jeff angled his SUV into a spot in front of her shop. He hopped out and came around to help her out. Her legs gave out when she tried to stand. Jeff scooped her up and carried her to the front door where snow had drifted. He lowered her but kept his arm around her.

"Can you find the key?"

"Yes. But keep holding me while I dig it out of my bag. My balance is off." After a few moments of frustration, she gave up. "Oh, I can't do this either. Will you please? She shoved her bag at him. After he retrieved her key, he returned it to her.

She fiddled with the key to get it to unlock. "I can't make this work. Can you try?"

Jeff worked with the key, but the lock stubbornly resisted. "It's not unlocking. Has this happened before?

"A couple of years ago a doozy of a cold front blew through with temps dropping to zero for several days, and the lock froze up." She looked at Jeff. "I can't get inside. Out on the road, I kept imagining being in my safe, warm apartment, sipping tea. And now I can't get into my own home." Tears of frustration welled in her eyes.

Jeff pulled her in for a hug. "It will be all right. Let's go back to the car to drive to the inn. Normally we'd walk from here, but not in this weather. You'll have to stay there. Probably better for you to be around others anyway until we're certain you're all right."

Jessica didn't argue, a testament to how shaken up she was. She nodded and pivoted toward Jeff's SUV. "Okay."

Jeff traveled the two blocks in the blinding snow but passed no other cars on the street and no one walking. He stopped the car in front of the inn. "Okay, you'll feel better once you're inside warm and dry." After helping her out, they lurched up the front steps, and he opened the front door, using both hands to shove it closed against the wind.

"I was expecting you earlier, Mr. Hudson, so your suite is ready." Penny Torbett, owner, manager, and head chef of the Tidbury Inn greeted them.

"What can I do for you Jessica? You don't look too good if you don't mind my saying so. Do you want a cup of hot tea?"

"Jessica had an accident returning from her daughter's house. I found her and brought her back to town."

"I'd love a cup of your special blend, Penny. The lock in the front door of my store is frozen shut, and the key wouldn't work. Jeff suggested he bring me here. Do you have a spare room I can crash in until this weather breaks, and I can go back to my apartment above the shop?"

"You're welcome to rest in the parlor, Jessica, but we're all filled up. We had a couple of extra folks caught in the storm show up, and they took my last rooms."

"Oh." What in the world could she do now?

"We'll figure out something. At least the electricity has only flickered twice. We have a generator for the inn if we lose power, but we'll have to be careful and conserve so it will last as long as necessary."

"Penny, can you find any dry clothes for Jessica? We'll go up to my suite. Can you fix us hot tea, hot soup, and a couple of sandwiches?"

"Sure, Mr. Hudson. And I'm sure I've got something that will work for you, Jessica. I'll bring it upstairs."

Jessica looked at them both. "I can't go up to Jeff's room."

"It's important you climb out of those wet clothes and into dry ones. Then you need warm food in you." Penny brushed aside Jessica's words and walked from the main room to the back part of the inn where her personal quarters were.

"Come on, Jessica, let me help you up these stairs. This is temporary until it's safe to return to your place." He took her elbow and guided her toward the stairs.

"Okay." What else could she do?

She clasped one hand on the railing and limped up the stairs with his arm around her waist.

Jeff let them into his suite.

"Oh, you've got the room with the fireplace."

"Yes, and I'll light it in just a moment." He guided her to a comfy chair and then flicked the switch which started the fire.

"Yes." She sighed and rested her head on the back of the chair.

A knock at the door drew Jeff there. He swung it open.

"I've found dry clothes for Jessica. And I'll put that food together right away." Penny pivoted to go.

"Penny, thank you," Jessica called out to her.

"You're welcome. Do you want me to find the doctor to check on you?"

"No, thanks. I'm sure she's tied up with the accident. I don't think anything is broken. Ibuprophen will knock out most of the soreness."

"I'll have that food ready for you soon." Penny waved a hand over her shoulder and eased out of the room.

Jeff closed the door and carried the clothes to Jessica. "Can you manage getting into these by yourself?"

Heat rushed through her body at the idea of Jeff helping her undress. She looked away. "I'll manage."

"Well, I'll head down to pick up our food and give you a chance to change. I'm sure you'll be more comfortable once you're out of those wet clothes."

Jessica nodded. Jeff walked out the door and closed it quietly behind him.

She drew in a deep breath. Somehow she needed to do this on her own while Jeff was out of the room. Wouldn't do to be half clothed when he returned. Her body grew hotter. What was the matter with her? Jessica took off her coat and hung it on the coat tree. What did Penny bring her to put on? Anything warm and dry would be welcome.

Ah, drawstring warm-ups and a giant sweatshirt. This would be perfect. Penny had remembered socks, too. Never mattered how many layers she wore, if her feet got cold, so did the rest of her. Moving quickly, which wasn't quick at all because her fingers still weren't working well, she dragged off her clothes and climbed into the soft fluffy outfit Penny provided. Jessica settled on the hearth and let the warmth crawl up her back. Ahhh.

A quick tap followed Jeff's words, "You decent?"

"Yes, come in."

Jeff opened the door.

"Not fashionable but warm and dry. Do you have hot tea?"

"Yes, and hot tomato soup and grilled cheese sandwiches. Penny did us up proud." He glanced at Jessica. "And not only with the clothes." He set the tray with the containers on the coffee table in front of the fire. "This seems to be the best place to eat."

She scooted over to make room for him on the hearth, and he settled next to her. She realized the touch of his shoulder gave her a sense of security. Ever since the election and all the incidents, her sense of peace had vanished. She wrapped her hands around the mug of soup. The warmth slipped from her finger to her hands up her arms. Ahh, wonderful. She drank half the soup before she paused to set down the mug. The tangy touch of hot spice perfect. Next she sampled the grilled cheese. "Oh my, this melts in my mouth. Comfort food doesn't get any better than this."

Jeff laughed. "Sounds like you'll survive after all."

"I think so. I've got aches and pains making themselves known, but yeah, I think I'll be okay. And Jeff, if you hadn't come, I'm not sure I would've been."

He slipped an arm around her shoulder. "I'm relieved I found you, but I bet you'd have made it to town. Judging by your handling of Worley, you're not someone who easily gives up."

She smiled and leaned into him. His strength and warmth gave her courage, which she seemed to crave right now. "My family has accused me of being stubborn."

"Eat the rest of the soup while it's still hot."

She'd eaten the last bite of her grilled cheese and swallowed the last of the soup when her cell beeped. Pulling it from the pocket of her sweatpants, she looked at the name. "It's Kathy. Hey sweetie. No.... Well, we're at the Tidbury Inn. The lock froze up at the store...Yes it did it once before.... Jeff brought me here to the inn. Penny supplied me with warm dry clothes, and she made scrumptious tomato soup and her special grilled cheese sandwiches. So, I guess I'm here until the storm breaks. You're okay?...Good. Yes, I'll keep you posted." She disconnected. "Kathy says the blizzard has gotten worse than expected, and now they're saying we could be socked in for a couple of days." She glanced at him and away. "I'm afraid you may be stuck with me for a while."

"There's not any place I'd rather be, and I had no plans to leave you alone after the ordeal you went through. You're better off here with others than at your apartment anyway."

She sighed and leaned into him more. Such a comfort. "Thank you. It seems since you found me, those are the only words in my vocabulary."

"You're welcome. I'll take those wet clothes down to Penny and ask her to wash and dry them for you. Tomorrow will go better if you're in your own clothes."

"That's thoughtful of you."

"I'm a thoughtful kind of a guy. My dad insisted on it and made sure I knew how to treat a lady." He leaned close and kissed her forehead. "I'll take our dishes downstairs, too, and bring back another pot of hot tea. I can make coffee in here, but you're a hot tea gal. Penny will provide that."

"Thanks for remembering my preference. When it's cold like this, I live in a teacup. Except I really appreciated the hot coffee I drank in my car before starting the trek here."

Jeff scooped up her wet clothes and the tray and headed out the door.

My goodness. Now what? If she'd been able to enter her shop and her apartment, would he have stayed with her there? She didn't want to be alone right now. She wrapped her arms around her middle and leaned closer to the warmth of the fireplace. The pictures of her trip from Kathy's toward town played out in her mind. The truck lights coming up behind blinding her. The shock of him running into her. And the second time. She shivered. Had he intentionally run into her? She was beginning to feel like a cat with nine lives, and some of her nine lives were getting used up in these near misses.

A tap at the door heralded Jeff's entrance. He carried a carafe and a plate. She drew in a deep breath, recognizing the special blend of tea Penny used. Jeff kicked the door closed and set everything on the coffee table. "Penny threw in her snickerdoodles. I thought you wouldn't mind."

"Oh, my goodness, no. Her snickerdoodles are known far and wide. Seriously, folks travel to Tidbury for them."

"How do you drink this?"

"Just plain black tea."

"Can you manage the carafe?"

"I think so. Would you like a cup?"

"No thanks. I'm sticking with my coffee." He fixed his coffee using the in room unit and then settled on the hearth next to her and reached for a cookie. He took a bite and his eyebrows rose. "You weren't kidding. How have I missed them when I've stayed here before?"

"I don't know, but you've always been pretty busy when you've been here, working to convince a certain board of selectmen candidate to support your project." She took a bite of the cookie. "Yes. These are scrumptious. Lots of folks swear by sugar cookies for the approaching holidays, but I've always been a snickerdoodle person. My mom made incredibly good ones. They melted in your mouth with the perfect amount of cinnamon and sugar. I think Penny uses Mom's recipe." She took another bite. "Yeah, these remind me of Mom's."

JOHN CROWELL GLANCED at his cell. Tim Worley's name showed up. "Why are you calling, Tim?"

"I fixed her."

"What do you mean you fixed her? If you mean Jessica, I told you I'd take care of the problem when we both had an alibi."

"Driving back into town, I recognized her in the SUV in front of me. What are the odds of me finding her out in the middle of a blizzard? I couldn't figure how she happened to be there, but I took it as an omen and grabbed an opportunity too good to pass up."

"What specifically did you do? And when? It's important for us to both have alibies."

"I rammed her SUV and ran her off the road. Wow. I must've hit her in the exact right spot, because she spun around completely before sailing off the road and ending up in the ditch off to the side."

"Are you sure she's dead?"

"I climbed out of my truck and trudged over and took a better look. She sat slumped over the steering wheel, and a tree had poked through the windshield. The airbags deployed but didn't appear to do her much good. She should freeze to death, and it will look like a natural accident. I reversed and drove back the way I'd come and checked into the small motel in the next town over. Everyone's snowed in. Who knows when they'll find her?"

"Good job, Tim, and our problems are behind us. Okay, we'll talk again after the blizzard's over." John disconnected and smiled. Yes, now their problem in the shape of Jessica Allen existed no more. A great Christmas gift.

Chapter Sixteen

Jeff held the Ibuprophen bottle in one hand and a glass of water in the other. "Here you go, Jessica. This will make a difference. It's important to stay ahead of the pain curve."

"Oh, I'll be okay." Jessica hated to take medicine.

"Yes, you will be okay, but aches and pains in unfamiliar places will rise up to gobble you whole. I recommend being proactive." He shook the bottle. "These will take off the edge."

"So, you're a doctor, now?" She grinned at him. He did seem to think of everything.

"No, but I am experienced with a couple of fender benders and various sports accidents. The Ibuprophen always makes a difference."

"Well, I admit to twinges here and there, and I don't look forward to them getting worse." She took the bottle, shook out two pills, and popped them in her mouth. "Down the hatch." She chased them with several big gulps of water.

Jeff settled on the sofa next to her. She'd finally gotten warm enough to leave her perch on the hearth.

"Let's discuss the sleeping arrangements."

"What?" Jessica put a hand to her cheek which grew instantly warm.

"Well, it appears you'll be here at least for tonight and maybe longer depending on the storm. You're locked out of your shop and the apartment, and there's no more room at the inn. So, let's figure out how to do this."

Jessica's mind boggled. Was he proposing that they sleep together? Did she want to sleep with Jeff? Oh my. Her brain must still be off from the accident.

"I'm suggesting that you take the bed, and I'll bunk here on the sofa."

Jessica laughed but had to grab her head when throbbing sprung from her giggles.

"What's funny?"

"Imagining your tall body draped over the sofa. You wouldn't be able to sleep here or if you did, you'd wake up with more pains than I have. You sleep in the bed, and I'll be fine here. Can we keep the fire on all night?"

"Yes. Absolutely. And if you insist, you can sleep here on the sofa. I found two extra blankets in the closet and a spare pillow."

"See, I'll be fine."

At a knock on the door, they both turned. Jeff walked over and opened the door.

"Hi, Mr. Hudson. I've brought Jessica's clothes back all warm from the dryer."

"Thanks, Penny. This is kind of you to go the extra mile for me."

"Of course. Will you both be okay in here?" She glanced at both Jessica and Jeff.

"Yes. I found extra blankets and a pillow." Jeff indicated the ones on the sofa. "We'll be fine. What are you hearing on the storm?"

"Rudy Lopez went to all the shops and stopped in here, making sure everyone was okay. He says to expect the snow to continue for the rest of the day at least. He'll come back tomorrow to make sure everyone at the inn is all right."

"Has Sheriff Halbert finished helping with the wreck on the freeway?" Jeff asked.

"Rudy expects him later tonight. Is it necessary to talk with him right away?"

"Not tonight, tomorrow will be good enough if he can make time to stop by," Jessica said.

"Okay. Good night. Don't forget to turn off all the lights." She nodded and left them alone.

Jeff clicked off the overhead light, leaving them in the dimness of the two lamps on the end tables. "Conserving is always important, but if the main power goes out and you're depending on a generator, it's vital."

Jessica nodded. "The things we take for granted."

"Yep." Jeff walked to the window and shifted the drapes to look outside. "Man, it's still coming down." He picked up his cell. "Think I'll check with Tony to find out how he and Eva are doing in Concord."

"I should check on Kathy and Lori and make sure they're all right." Jessica reached for her cell in the pocket of the warmup pants as Jeff walked into the bedroom, giving them both privacy for their calls. Jessica let out a long breath she hadn't realized she'd been holding. Why was she tense around Jeff? He'd been nothing but kind to her. She shoved away contemplation of Jeff for later, now she wanted to talk with her daughter. She tapped Kathy's name in the cell.

"Hey, sweetie," she said when her older daughter picked up.

"Mom, how are you doing? Did you get settled in a room at the inn?"

Jessica cleared her throat. "Well, to be truthful, there was no room at the inn."

"You're kidding, right? We're not that close to Christmas."

Jessica chuckled. "Two carloads of travelers got stranded, and they took the last rooms before we arrived."

"Are you sleeping in the living room of the inn?"

Jessica swallowed. Here goes. "No, I'm staying in Jeff's room. He's got the suite with the fireplace and the sofa. It's the one where the window looks out on the green."

"That's one of the best rooms in the inn." She paused. "But, Mom, where are you sleeping?"

"I'm on the sofa. Jeff offered me the bedroom, but he's much too big for the sofa."

"Okay. Mom, don't do anything you might regret."

"Kathy, my goodness. What are you suggesting?"

"I'm suggesting while Jeff Hudson may be a good person for you to sleep with someday in the future, I think you may not know him well enough yet. And when you're ready to have that kind of relationship with a man again, Lori and I are all for you."

"Tell me you haven't discussed my sex life."

"Well, we have, Mom. It's been five years, and you're still young. Too young to shut off that side of your life. Our concern is Jeff Hudson doesn't live here, and you don't really know him well."

Jessica was grateful she hadn't put the phone on audio because Jeff stepped into the main room of the suite. Good idea to change the subject. "Do you still have power, Kathy?"

"No. We lost it twenty minutes ago, but the generator kicked on. We'll probably make it an early night to conserve the power. The Jensons arrived a little while ago, and we're putting them up in the basement."

"As usual. They're lucky you have space, Kathy."

"It's the neighborly thing to do."

The lights flickered and went out in the inn. "Gosh, the power just went out here. I'll let you go. Stay warm. Love you." She disconnected and flipped on her cell phone flashlight.

"How long until the generator clicks on?" Jeff settled on the sofa with the light from his cell flashlight battling with the shadows from the fire flickering across the wall.

"I have to flip a couple of switches to make mine come on in the store and apartment. I'm guessing for the inn here it's probably more complicated and may take longer. I've never been at the inn when they lost power before."

"Rummaging around earlier, I found two flashlights in the drawers of the end tables on either side of the bed. I'll grab them. I'm sure they'll help." He walked from the main room, taking the light from his cell with him. He quickly returned. "I guess it's part of Penny's preparations for this kind of event." He handed Jessica a flashlight.

"Good. Now we don't have to run down our cell batteries."

"It's close to nine. May be best we go ahead and turn in."

"I like that idea, and besides, I'm exhausted, barely keeping my eyes open."

"Are you sure you'll be okay on this sofa?"

Jessica smiled and nodded. "Yes, and way better than you'd be. Thanks for everything. I'll use the bathroom, and then I'll be ready to settle in." She stood and groaned. "It may be a good idea to take another Ibuprofen, too."

"Smart thinking. The bottle is in the bathroom. Help yourself."

Jessica wobbled into the bedroom and then on into the bathroom. She stood the flashlight on its end on the counter. A gasp escaped at the site of her face in the mirror. Definitely worse for wear, and that included discounting for the scary shadows from the flashlight. Good grief. And

Kathy had mentioned the possibility of her sleeping with Jeff. He'd be nuts to consider the idea with the way she looked right now. And besides, she could hardly move. No telling what tomorrow would be like. She popped another pill and returned to the living room, stifling a yawn.

"Looks like someone's ready for bed."

"You're right. I'm done in. Are your friends all right?" Jessica settled on the sofa, and Jeff draped two blankets over her and tucked one up around her chin. "They're without power, too. Hoping for a return tomorrow and grateful for their generator. I'll leave open the bedroom door. You holler if you need anything, and I'll hear you."

"Thank you, Jeff. You've taken good care of me." Her lids dropped and batted open again.

He walked into the bedroom and on into the bathroom. He had taken good care of her. What might've been in store for them if they hadn't started out on opposite sides in the retirement center issue? Her eyelids drifted closed, and sleep claimed her.

JEFF WANDERED TO THE large window in his bedroom. Hard to make out much with the streetlights and the majority of the store lights off. Giant flakes continued to hit the pane. They could really be in for it. Sometimes the weather forecasters got it right, and sometimes they were way off base. Unfortunately, on this occasion, the forecasters got it exactly right. The whole state and much of New England had been buried in this snowstorm.

Was Tony right? Had he developed feelings for Jessica? If Jeff were honest, he'd say he sure had. But he didn't think those feelings were clouding his decision-making concerning the project. Tony, the numbers man, was rightfully concerned they were losing money on a project that seemed to have stalled out. The delays were unfortunate, but Jeff believed in the project. The fact he'd convinced Jessica of the wisdom of having a retirement center in town and on the green...well, he took great pride in that accomplishment. Only one stumbling block remained. Would they be able to break the contract with Worley Construction?

When he last talked with his company's attorneys, they hadn't been optimistic concerning their ability to make that happen. Guilt nagged at Jeff. Had he been too positive in his talks with Jessica about their prospects of getting out of the contract? He could find a way, couldn't he? He turned from the window, wandered to the door where his gaze fell on the beautiful woman sleeping on his sofa. He had to find a way. He wanted this project, and he suspected he wanted Jessica Allen. Blending their lives would force them to do creative thinking, but he was a problem solver. Besides, she was worth any effort he took.

"OH." JESSICA ROLLED over, blinked her eyes, and yesterday's experiences flooded her mind. What would've happened if Jeff hadn't come along? She wanted to think she'd have made it on her own, but would she? Struggling to sit up, she swung around to rest her head on the back of the sofa. She glanced around the suite. A fire burned in the fireplace, but where was Jeff? She didn't hear any stirrings from the bedroom. Was he still asleep? She flung off the blankets, groaned as she rose, tiptoed toward the other room, and peeked around the door frame.

Bed made and no sign of Jeff. Good. Scooping up her own clothes Penny had washed and dried before they lost power, Jessica slipped into the bathroom. The hot water of the shower sluiced over her aching body. To have not broken anything, her body sure ached, but the water helped relax her muscles. Because the power hadn't come back on, she decided not to wash her hair. Walking around with wet hair on such a cold day wouldn't be smart. After quickly dressing, she stepped through the bedroom door into the main room when the door of the suite opened. Jeff entered carrying two cups.

"Good morning. I've got hot tea for you and coffee for me."

"Thanks." Jessica took the cup and settled on the hearth in front of the fire.

"Fortunately, the gas stove works in the kitchen, and Penny made several old fashioned pots of coffee. Making hot water for the tea was easy. How are you feeling?"

"Sore like I expected, but lucky I didn't break anything, and thanks to you, I didn't freeze on the walk back to town."

"Does having your own clothes help?"

"Yes, they sure do."

"Can you manage going downstairs for breakfast? If not, I'll bring it up to you."

"No, I'll go down. Got to move, or I'll stiffen up and be worthless. What's the weather forecast say?"

"Better news than expected. The snow should stop soon, and they project the temps to rise. Not sure when the power company will repair all the lines."

"With the temps going up, do you think we could walk down to my shop this afternoon to see if we can make the door lock work? Maybe carry hot water to pour on it?"

"Sure. That's worth a try. We can go when the temps reach above freezing. Now, I want to head back downstairs. The aromas from Penny's kitchen have made me ravenous. Let's go find out what she's prepared."

BY MID-AFTERNOON, THE snow had indeed stopped, the sun peeked out from behind clouds, and the awful wind, instead of being twenty-five to thirty, had fallen into the five to ten miles an hour category. Manageable. After bundling up, she and Jeff stepped out on the porch of the inn. Snow piled into giant drifts everywhere. Someone from the inn had already shoveled the snow away from the door. No other folks braved the treacherous conditions.

Jessica liked the way Jeff held her arm. Besides a feeling of connection, a couple of times he saved her from falling. Jeff also carried a thermos of hot water to use on the shop's door lock. She sure hoped they made the door lock work, and she could return to her apartment. Staying longer with Jeff didn't seem to be a good idea, playing havoc with her heart the way it did.

By the time they made it to the store, both were breathing heavily. Trudging through all the snow that had blown up on the walkway made for hard work.

"We made it." Jessica couldn't stop the insane sounding giggle from bubbling out. "That was quite a trip. Can't believe only two blocks took that long and made us work so hard. Here, let's try the hot water."

Jeff unscrewed the lid of the thermos and sloshed a good amount on the door lock. "You think that's enough?"

"Guess we'll see." Jessica removed her key chain from the pocket of her big coat and inserted the store key in the lock. She twisted it, but nothing happened. "Maybe more water?"

Jeff doused the lock again. "Let me try." He took her key and slowly twisted. Click. "There we go."

"I must not have been strong enough to make it work. Let's check out how everything is." Jessica stepped into her shop and turned off the security system that operated by battery when the power went out. Dim light from outside filtered through the mullioned windows. "Flashlights are welcome."

Everything downstairs appeared fine. Jessica walked back to the ground floor office. "Oh, good, the pipes haven't burst. I worried about them. When I'm here, and we're in for this kind of storm, I always leave the cabinet doors open and let the water drip from all the faucets. The cost of the water is minimal compared to having burst pipes. Before we go up, I'll open the doors and let the faucet drip. Not telling how long this will last. Let's go upstairs."

After trudging up the stairs, Jessica stopped on the landing to catch her breath. Not something she normally had to do and must be a residual from the experience yesterday. Taking the apartment key, she inserted it in the lock and opened the front door of her apartment.

"Dark of course. I'm concerned how the fridge made out more than anything else. I'd made a recent trip to the grocery store." She stepped through to her kitchen area, opened the fridge door, and shined in the light. "Thankfully, it's all still pretty cold." She slammed the door. "That's a relief."

"Do you plan to stay here, Jessica?"

"Yes, I'll be fine once the generator is turned on, and I get a warm fire burning in the hearth. I can heat soup over the gas stove. I won't starve or freeze. We should be back to normal once the electrical workers repair the lines."

"When can you talk with Sheriff Halbert?"

"Not certain, but it's a priority." She walked over to the fire, turned on the gas, and lit the fire with a long match.

"Why don't we call him now and find out when he can stop by? I don't want to leave you until the incident is reported."

"I appreciate that, Jeff. Let me try him." She picked up her cell and tapped on the sheriff's name from her contact list. It rang for a couple of times, and then he picked up.

"Sheriff Halbert."

"Hey, Gary. This is Jessica Allen. If you have time, I'd like to report something that happened yesterday."

"Where are you Jessica? I can stop by now."

"Good. I'm at the apartment. Ring the outside bell when you arrive, and I'll let you in."

"See you soon."

And soon it was. Less than ten minutes had passed when the bell tinkled, and Jessica threw the switch to let him enter the store. She stepped out on the landing. "Come on up, Gary."

After entering, the sheriff stomped his feet on the mat and then headed through the store and up the stairs.

"Gary, you remember Jeff Hudson, don't you?" The men shook hands and exchanged pleasantries.

"I'm about to make a cup of hot tea. Can I make you coffee?"

"Thanks. Sounds great. I understand something happened on the way back to town from your daughter's. Is that right?"

"Yes. Jeff came along and rescued me." With no power to use her hot spigot, she reverted to the teapot to boil hot water for Jeff and Gary's coffees and her tea. "Well, I stupidly misjudged the timing of the storm and thought I could make it back to town before the roads became impassable. Obviously, I messed up."

"Well, that's not the only thing, Jessica," Jeff prodded and accepted a cup from her.

Jessica settled on the hearth with the men on the sofa. "That's true." She sipped her tea and held the teacup between both hands. Maybe it would warm her enough to tell the story. "I was driving cautiously and making progress when a large truck came up close behind me. I thought he wanted to pass, which was stupid, but I scooted over to the edge of the road. My tires hung almost off the roadway. I had no intention of increasing my speed in the blizzard the beautiful snowfall had become."

She sipped her tea and took a deep breath. She could tell this story. It didn't equal living through the horror. "The truck rammed me. I worried his brakes had failed or something, but he hit me again, and that's when I lost control of my SUV, four-wheel-drive, and all. I spun around 360 degrees and then careened off the opposite side of the road.

"I must've passed out because the next thing I knew I woke up in my car shivering from the cold. I opened my eyes to find a tree limb had broken through the windshield on the passenger side, glass scattered across the seat. The engine was off, and my fingers and toes were numb from the cold. I decided I couldn't stay there. Kathy had expected me to call her when I got home, but more than an hour had gone by. When I tried to open the door to climb out, I discovered it had jammed. I have one of those tools to knock out the window if you ever go in the water, you know?"

The sheriff nodded.

"I used that to break the window and crawled out that way." Jessica paused for another sip of tea. Telling felt like reliving the experience and made her shake. Jeff rose and sat next to her, draping an arm around her shoulder comforting her.

"You started walking to town instead of returning to your daughter's?"

"Yes. I'd gotten over half-way to town when the car crashed into the tree."

"What about the truck?"

"I didn't see anyone when I came to. It had snowed a bunch more, so I didn't notice tracks in the snow to indicate which way he went."

"Jessica had gotten to roughly an eighth of a mile out of town when I found her. Her daughter had called your office when Jessica didn't call her in the ordinary time. I had stopped by there and discovered you'd gone to help with the wreck on the highway, so I drove out to find her."

"Lucky for you Jeff came along when he did, Jessica."

"Yes, I was lucky."

"Oh, I have no doubt she'd have gotten back to town, but she'd been a whole lot colder." Jeff tried to downplay the importance of his rescue, but Jessica knew.

"So, Jessica, I gotta tell you I'm concerned about all the—," Gary paused, "all the incidents that have happened to you of late. You've made someone mad at you. Can you think of who it might be? Any ideas at all?"

Jessica looked at Jeff, set her cup down on the hearth, and rose. She wandered to the window that looked out over the main street and toward the green.

"Jessica?" Gary Halbert persisted.

"I hate to say this, Gary, but the only person who's angry with me, at least enough to pull one of these crazy stunts, is Tim Worley or his pal on the board, John Crowell. I've been campaigning against using Worley Construction for a couple of years now. Ever since Ed was killed really, but of late since getting elected I've been more outspoken concerning him and his business. John has given me static at meetings and Worley has threatened me. Their guy didn't win, and I think they're worried about what I can do."

"Where are you in this, Jeff? Isn't the retirement center your project?"

"Yes. Jessica and I have had several spirited discussions regarding the work—"

"But he's convinced me of its merit, and both the center and our activities can co-exist on the green together." Jessica made haste to explain. She didn't want Gary wasting his efforts looking at Jeff for any of this. At first she had suspected him, too, but then she got to know the man.

Gary stood up. "Thanks for the hot coffee. Nothing warms you up like this stuff unless it's a stiff drink."

"Wine works for me, Gary, but I avoid it during daylight hours." She grinned at the sheriff.

"Let me investigate where everyone was yesterday afternoon. At the least I can put the fear of God in them and put them on notice I've got my eye on them and nothing else better happen to you."

"Thanks, Gary. I appreciate you stopping by. Any word on when the power will be back on?"

"I'm told they've got it back in Concord now, and we should be okay by tomorrow. "What are your plans, Jessica?" Gary walked toward the door, pulling on his jacket.

"I plan to stay here. After the generator kicks on, I'll be fine. The temp dropped low enough in the apartment I didn't lose anything in the refrigerator."

"Your locks are working, but what's the situation with your security system?"

"It's operated off the battery and once I have the generator going, it will be fine."

"You can lock and unlock the front door of the shop from up here, right? Isn't that what you did when I arrived?"

"Yes, it's a special deal my security people set up. Kathy, her husband, and Lori insisted on it."

"Good plan. You stay safe and keep warm. I'll call you if I learn anything. Good to see you Jeff. I hope you can get the project off the ground. It would put a lot of people to work."

"Thanks. My partner is getting edgy over how long the process is taking, but I'm sure we'll be able to pull it off. I've got our lawyers working on getting us out of the contract with Worley Construction. If we can prove Worley had anything to do with these attacks on Jessica, that would probably make our case against them. Our using that company is the only thing standing in the way of Jessica's support."

"I'll keep you up to date." Gary left the apartment. The sounds from his boots tramping down the stairs filled the emptiness.

"Can I help you do whatever is necessary to make the generator run? I don't plan to leave not knowing if your HVAC and security system works."

"Sure, come on. It's downstairs." Pulling on their coats again, they trudged down the stairs into the colder store. The fireplace did a great job taking off the chill upstairs.

Once they got the generator started, Jeff took Jessica by the shoulders and drew her in for a hug. When he released her, he stepped back, but kept his hands on her shoulders. "I've got to head on back to Concord. I've been away too long. Tony feels like I've abandoned him and the company."

"I genuinely appreciate all you've done for me, Jeff. I hope the lawyers can find a way for you to ditch Worley Construction."

"I do too."

"When do you think you'll return?" Perhaps a tad forward, but hey, these were modern times, and she had slept with the man, so to speak. She couldn't help a smile from cracking.

"I'm not certain."

"I've told you about our wonderful Christmas Festival held on the green of course."

"Right and what were the dates again?"

"It begins the 18th of December and runs to New Year's Eve. We do all the traditional things, cookie baking, caroling, snowman building contests. To name a few."

"I'll definitely put it on my calendar. Promise me you'll be careful?"

"Absolutely. The vote is scheduled for December 17th."

"I'll be back for that for certain."

"I hope you can arrange to stay to enjoy our festival."

"Sounds like a plan."

Before she realized his intention, Jeff took her face between his hands and kissed her, a slow tender kiss. When she came up for air, Jessica couldn't catch her breath.

"I've been wanting to do that again for a long time." He whirled around and headed for the shop door. He pulled it open and glanced back once before leaving. "Make sure you lock up." He stepped through and was gone. The sound of the shop door closing, brought Jessica out of her stupor, but all she could do was stare after him.

Chapter Seventeen

Jessica trudged up the stairs to her apartment, closed the door, and leaned against it. "Oh, my goodness. Oh, my goodness." She could hardly process what had taken place. Jeff Hudson kissed her, and he kissed her like it meant something. Not a simple goodbye peck on the cheek. No, this kiss had legs, signifying it was meant for the long haul.

But they couldn't have any long haul. He lived in Concord where he had his business. Oh, he obviously traveled for business. However, her life was here in Tidbury. She'd been a member of this community for going on thirty years, for crying out loud. She hadn't been elected to the board of selectmen for long. She had an obligation. Jeff hadn't asked her to move to Concord, but even if he did, she couldn't do that.

Jessica staggered away from the door and stalked into the kitchen, giving herself a shake. Good, strong, hot tea would help clear her head. She refilled the teapot, set it on the stove, and turned on the burner. The flame glowed red, orange, and blue. She backed the knob down to medium. Earlier she'd used a teacup, but now she reached for a mug. She needed more strength than the teacup could provide.

In moments, the kettle whistled, and Jessica poured the close-to-boiling water over the tea bag. The aroma itself comforted and grounded her, and she filled her mug to the brim. Walking back into the main room, she stopped in front of the two large windows that looked out to the green. She couldn't have followed Jeff's movements back toward the inn because several stores had roofs over the sidewalk. That disappointed her. It would help bring reality to the situation. She sipped her mug of tea and wandered toward the fireplace, dropping down to the hearth to enjoy the flames better. What should she do now? The store would remain closed until the power came back on, and it wasn't like she'd drive over to visit with the girls.

Her cell phone rang, bringing her out of her reverie. Oh, perfect. She needed a good chat with her friend. "Hi, Sue. How are you and Joe holding up? Is your generator working?"

"Yes. We're toasty and warm, but how are you? I've heard rumors of you being run off the road and sleeping with Jeff Hudson at the Tidbury Inn. Are you holding out on me?"

Jessica laughed. You had to love small towns and the alive-and-well-rumor-mill. "Some of that is true, Sue."

"What? The rumors are true? You slept with Jeff Hudson? Why didn't you tell me? Did you enjoy it? What led up to what I hope was a wonderful experience?"

"Sue. Sue. We didn't sleep together-sleep together. What's gotten into you? I stayed in his room at the inn because no vacancies existed when we got there."

"So where did you sleep if I may ask?"

"On the sofa. He offered to give me the bed, but he'd never have fit on the sofa, more of a love seat. I insisted he stay in the bedroom, and I slept on the sofa. I fit fine and slept comfortably, but he'd have been miserable. That's the whole story."

"Oh." Disappointment drenched Sue's one word. "Where are you now?"

"In my apartment over the store. The generator is working, and I'm sitting here with a mug of tea trying to decide what to do with myself. Your call couldn't have been more perfectly timed."

"Why did you go to the inn in the first place, instead of to your apartment?"

"Well, you remember four years ago we had that major blizzard with temps brushing zero?"

"Yeah. Oh, my gosh. Did your lock freeze up again?"

"It sure did. So, we went to the inn, but as I said, they had no room."

Sue's chuckle came across the line. "I think you're borrowing too much from the Christmas story there. But seriously, I'm happy you're all right. One more question."

"Sure thing." Jessica sipped her tea. Guess Sue would touch on the truck business.

"I must've missed something. Why were you with Jeff in the first place? And what's that I heard about a truck running you off the road?" She laughed at herself. "I recognize that's two questions, but we have a lot of catching up to do."

Jessica sighed and told the story of her harrowing trip back to town from Kathy's. Recounting the incident this far removed still sent chills down her arms. She put her cell on speaker and scooted into her bedroom for a purple sweater which she slung around her shoulders. She returned to stare into the fire.

"Wow! That's a scary story, Jessica. I'm relieved you made it through all right. And you believe the guy ran you off the road on purpose?"

"Well, he for certain ran into me, and he didn't stop to help." Jessica walked to the kitchen to refill her teacup with hot water.

"So all the things that have happened to you, they connect somehow to you trying to block Worley Construction?"

"I don't have any proof, Sue. I'm not quite saying that, but gosh, I don't have any enemies in this town, and I got elected to the board of selectmen by a whopping 76 % of the vote. I can't help but wonder."

"That does seem to narrow down the list of suspects. What does Sheriff Halbert say?"

"Not much I'm afraid. You can't arrest someone without any proof, and Gary hasn't been able to find anything that's definitive. He hasn't had long to look into this most recent incident, but I mean unless someone confesses, I was the only one on the road in the blizzard besides the truck. We got nothing."

"Yeah, I understand, but that's so wrong. What are you planning to do next, Jessica? Will you support the plan to build the retirement center on the green?"

"Yeah, I am, Sue. I've studied Jeff's plans. He physically walked off the area on the green to show me exactly how much land was left for our festivals. He's building up three floors rather than out, which will still leave plenty of space for all our various seasonal activities."

"Well, good to hear that and thanks for doing your homework on this project. Is Jeff still planning on using Worley Construction? You've had issues with them forever. In fact, everyone is aware of how you feel. Hmm, maybe it's someone who works for the construction company who's afraid of losing their job if the company doesn't get the contract."

"Jeff is trying to find a way to break the contract but isn't terribly optimistic he'll be able to do that. If he can break the contract, construction will be delayed while he looks for someone else. But he's willing to take the financial hit from that."

"Wow."

"What? What are you wowing about?"

"He must care about you a lot to do that. Oftentimes for businesspeople, money talks and is the bottom line."

"I don't know that he does." Jessica placed her fingers on her lips. The memory of the kiss curling her toes.

"Do you have plans to meet up with each other again?"

"He's returning to town for the vote and plans to come attend part of the Christmas Festival." She sipped her tea. What could they work out between them?

"Well, next you hear he's coming to town, you let me know. Joe and I would like you both to come to supper."

"That's kind of you, Sue."

"But, Jessica, you must promise not to move away. Didn't you tell me his company's offices were in Concord?"

"Yes, but it's less than an hour and a half drive."

"Wow."

"What's with the *wow* again?"

"You've given thought to moving to Concord, haven't you?"

Jessica sighed. "More like I've given thought not to moving to Concord. This is my home, Sue. All my friends are here and my family. And I've made a commitment to the board of selectmen."

"You and Jeff have kissed, haven't you?"

"What? What makes you ask that, Sue?"

"Because you wouldn't be thinking of moving to Concord or not moving to Concord if you hadn't kissed the man."

Jessica paced into the kitchen and set her mug on the counter.

"Are you still there? Did we lose the connection?"

"Yes, I'm still here. And you're right. We kissed. And then he left to return to Concord not long ago."

"Jessica, that's lovely. I'm thrilled for you. You deserve to be happy."

"I'm not sure if we can be. If Jeff's company is stuck with their contract with Worley, Sue, I'll vote against the project, and I can convince others to join me. I will hurt Jeff's company and Jeff. There won't be any *us* after that. I'm not sure there is an us now." Jessica wandered into the main room and stared out the front windows. During the Christmas Festival they'd have a snowman building contest with the winner being the one who could build the biggest and the fastest. Always great fun, and everyone had a super time. Would Jeff be here for that?

"Listen, Jessica. I'm a firm believer in Happily Ever Afters. You two will be able to work something out if it's meant to be. Frankly, I'm more concerned for your safety. I'm worried because I can't figure out what you should do to stay safe."

Jessica frowned, figuring out what the odd sound was. Oh, she bet Sue snapped her fingers, a habit when she hit on an idea. Jessica heard it often at their various committee meetings.

"Wait a minute. What if Joe ran an article on all the attacks and what we think they are connected to? Then they'd have to back off because everyone would be aware of their shenanigans."

"Thank you, Sue, but I don't believe Joe can write an article like that without proof. Worley could sue the paper for libel or is it slander. I always mix up those two words."

"Libel if it's printed and slander if it's spoken, I believe. I'll speak with him anyway. If he writes something with a lot of questions, not stating a name, he should be okay." *Ding* "Gosh that's the timer on my stove. I made Joe my special apple pie. I swear that's one of the reasons he married me."

"I'll let you go. Tell Joe hi for me. And Sue, thanks for calling and checking on me. Don't say anything to anyone on the subject of Jeff and me, especially because there really isn't any there, there, as the saying goes."

"You can count on me being discreet. Be safe, my friend." Sue disconnected.

Jessica put her cell in the hip pocket of her jeans. What to do now? Maybe she'd whip together her homemade soup. If she wanted to open the shop tomorrow, assuming the power came back on, she'd have to head down and check over everything. She could do that while the soup simmered. Walking to the refrigerator she selected chicken breasts, onions, celery, and carrots. When she checked the freezer, the discovery of a package of frozen spinach rewarded her. Always a special flavor. And she took barley from the cupboard. She loved the texture the little pearls provided. She had everything she needed.

Lifting out a large Dutch oven, she hefted it onto the stove. After chopping up the veggies, she threw them in the pot with a couple of tablespoons of olive oil and a chopped up bud of garlic. She seared them until tender, removing them while she cooked the chicken breasts with seasoned salt and pepper while she thawed the spinach. After the chicken finished cooking, she cut it up into bitesize pieces, returned it along with all the veggies, including the spinach, and a bay leaf to the pot along with several cups of water and a can of spicey tomatoes. Soon her kitchen would smell divine. Never having learned how to cook for one, she'd be able to eat on this meal for days. Once the broth came to a boil, she lowered the fire, and added the barley. The soup could simmer away for an hour while she checked on the shop.

Jessica made her way down the stairs to the shop and flipped on a couple of lamps, not the big overhead lights that would have used up too much of the generator. She retrieved a couple hundred dollars in the till that she hadn't made a point to drop off at the bank. Most people paid with credit cards now, but a few insisted on cash, and a few rare ducks continued to use checks. At a future point in time, those would become relics of bygone days.

Maybe she could run a few sales to encourage folks to come in. Besides, it would be a reward for them getting out and an encouraging hang-in-there kind of thing. Jessica used card stock and a marker to make a few signs she set around the shop. Hopefully, they'd have power tomorrow and folks would come out. She didn't depend on the store to support her, but running the store gave her purpose over and above being a mom, gram, or a member of the board of selectmen. This was all strictly for her. And she loved the endeavor. Loved getting to chat with townspeople and visitors. She loved Thanksgiving best followed by the Christmas season. A half a dozen families already had decorations outside their homes. The town's decorations always went up on December 1 and didn't come down until Epiphany, approximately twelve days after Christmas.

The first couple of Christmases after Ed's murder, she struggled to find the spirit of the holiday. Her pastor told her sometimes you had to fake it until you made it. He was right. She now thoroughly enjoyed the holiday again, and while the memories of past Christmases with Ed and the girls brought tears, they were happy tears.

Her phone alarm beeped. Gosh, she had to go up and check on her soup. After carefully turning off all the lights, she climbed the stairs to her wonderful, cozy apartment. How in the world could she leave her girls and her life in Tidbury?

"HEY, TONY. GOOD TO see you." Jeff looked up from his desk, sitting in front of a large window from which he could see the gold dome of the State Capital. He loved that their offices were in a historic building.

Tony came around the door, Jeff hopped up, and they exchanged man hugs. "Did you have a bad trip, Jeff? Eva and I were worried." Tony settled in a chair in front of Jeff's desk.

"At the point I returned, the roads were much better. I only lost control once."

Tony laughed. "Good to know. Listen, Eva will have my head if I don't ask you to come to supper tonight. You've been gone a lot, and we'd like to catch up."

"Sounds great. I would never turn down one of Eva's meals."

"She's making her famous lasagna, using her grandfather Luigi's recipe."

"Everything she cooks is super, but that's my all-time favorite. She's good enough to open her own restaurant."

"Yeah, we've talked, but it would be quite a challenge."

"Sure, but she's up to it. I'd invest if you need help financially."

"You're a great friend. Maybe we can discuss the idea more tonight. Shifting gears," Tony leaned forward. "Where do we stand with the Tidbury project?"

"Jessica has agreed the town can use a retirement center, and the design we came up with leaves plenty of room for the town's activities."

"Well done. Worry kept me awake at night."

"Well, we're not out of the weeds yet. If we continue to use Worley Construction, she'll vote against the project. You remember she got the action item postponed at the last meeting."

"She's only one vote, though, right?"

"While she's new to the board of selectmen, she has several supporters. She's lived in the town for all of her adult life, moving there after marrying a man whose family helped settle the town. If she wants to stop the project, she can."

"Remind me when are they taking up the issue again."

"December 17th. Tidbury has an elaborate Christmas Festival that begins the next day."

"Well, I've groused because of all the time you've spent there, but it may be best if you return and use the next days to lobby the other people on the board to convince them to support our project. Leaving it to whether we can terminate the contract with Worley Construction seems iffy to me. We've already invested a lot of money in this, Jeff. It will hurt our bottom line to take a loss on the project."

Jeff rose and crossed to the window, staring out at the snow covered walkways.

"What's going on, Jeff? Is it what I suspected, you've gotten too involved with this woman to the point you'll put the project in jeopardy?"

"Listen, Tony. Hear me out. If Jessica is correct and Worley Construction cuts corners, do we want to do business with them? Especially for a facility for senior citizens?"

"Now, wait a minute."

"No, you wait a minute, Tony. Think of it. If she's right, and the company cuts corners and something bad happens to any of the residents, we'll be at fault for hiring Worley."

"But—"

"No buts, Tony. I don't want to take that chance, both with those people's lives and with our company's reputation."

"You make a good argument."

"Thanks for that."

"Well, what do we do now, Jeff?"

"We've got to find proof Worley Construction cuts corners."

"What makes you think you can find proof when Jessica hasn't in all these years?"

Jeff rose and paced behind his desk. "We're in the development business, and we have lots of contacts in the construction field. Surely someone knows something."

"Where does that leave us with our contract?"

"Our lawyers have told me if we can find proof of shoddy work, we can break the contract."

"But if we can't find the proof and still break the contract, they will sue us, and we'll take not only a financial hit but one to our reputation," Tony countered Jeff's argument.

Jeff stopped and faced Tony. "If that happens, I'll personally cover the financial hit, so it doesn't hurt our company."

Tony rose and walked toward the door where he turned. "Wow. You do have it bad for this woman. You'll have to fill in Eva and me tonight at dinner. Seven pm. Don't be late."

Jeff's partner left, heading for his own office down the hall. Jeff dropped into the swivel chair behind his desk, running a hand across his neck. Guess they were doing this. And tonight Eva wouldn't cut him any slack about Jessica. He'd have to tell her everything. But that would be kind of fun. He wanted his friends to know and like Jessica. He needed to convince her to make a trip to Concord. He'd love for her to meet Tony and Eva. How could he make that happen? Guess he needed to ask.

But first he'd do what he could to research the employees of Worley Construction and the other companies they'd done business with. While staff had checked them out, apparently, they hadn't done as much due diligence as they should have. Someone must know something. The company was convenient and reasonable. Lesson learned. Cost can't ever be the primary reason for choosing a company.

He drew his laptop closer and got to work.

Chapter Eighteen

The middle aged woman and her sister in Allen's had come for a New England winter vacation. Jessica never ceased to be surprised by the number of people who did that. Not the ones who came to ski, but people who lived where they didn't regularly have snow, and they wanted that experience. In her opinion, next to the leaves changing colors in the fall which hit the perfection button on the head, snow falling on the hills came in a close second.

"I'm sure you'll be delighted with the containers of jam. Take this card and keep it in a safe place. After you've eaten all this lusciousness, I bet you'll decide you can't wait to eat more, and we can ship it to you." Jessica smiled at the customer.

"Great idea. Thanks." The two women bustled out, intent on continuing their shopping.

Her cell chirped with her daughter's sound. "Hey, Kathy. What's going on?"

"I thought you must be about to shut down the store for the evening, and I hope I can convince you to come out and have supper with the family."

"You don't have to work hard to convince me to do that. I'd love to. What time, and can I bring anything?"

"Just yourself, and we'll sit down soon after you get here."

"Sounds fun. See you later."

Jessica took care of a few more customers and rearranged product on a couple of shelves. She looked forward to dinner with the family. She hadn't been out to the old home since the snowstorm. Lori had come in and worked a few shifts, her only connection to the family. Her younger daughter seemed much less available to work in the store these days. Probably past time when Jessica should move on hiring another person to help out. That would make

Lori more comfortable, and Jessica imagined having more occasions to do whatever she wanted. And of course, the board work added to her responsibilities now, too. Yes, she needed another helper besides Janell.

Later that evening, she steered into the long driveway leading to her daughter's house. Jessica and Ed had done a little remodeling off and on when they'd been raising the family here, but Kathy and Bob had done major redo while maintaining the charm and updating with more modern conveniences. They had one of the best generators in town, and sometimes people came and hung out with them when the town lost power. Had Jessica stayed with her daughters during the last storm, she would've been one of those along with the Jensons.

Jessica barely knocked when Lori jerked opened the door as if she'd been watching for her. "Hey, Mom, come in." Lori hugged her. "Shoppers have come into the store in such numbers, we've barely gotten to say hello to each other. We're so happy you could fit us in."

"Gram," squealed Bobby, grabbing hold of one hand.

"Gram," squealed Bonnie, grabbing the other.

Jessica laughed and boosted up one grandchild after another to kiss them on the forehead.

"Happy to see my two favorite grands."

"Gram, we're you're only grands."

"You've got me there, Bonnie. Why are you two bundled up? Can I help you take off those jackets?"

"No, thanks. We're going outside to play in the snow. Bye." The two kids tore through the door and into the front yard illuminated with a flood light.

"They have enough energy to power the lights in a house." Laughing, Jessica unwrapped her scarf, drew off her hat, and put it and her gloves in the pockets of the coat.

"I'll take those." Lori hung the coat in the closet in the front hall.

Jessica made a show of sniffing the air. "Something smells good. What are we eating?" She kissed Bob on the cheek when he entered, and she accepted the glass of Merlot he handed her.

"Your daughter hauled out the old crock pot to make pot roast with potatoes and carrots. I've tried to sample it a couple of times, but she keeps batting away my hand." Bob led the way into the large kitchen. Kathy enveloped her mother in a big hug.

"So happy you could come tonight. We've let too long go by, Mom. You should move in here with us during the winter. I wouldn't worry about you so much when the snows come."

Jessica sipped her Merlot, her eyebrows raised in a questioning glance at her son-in-law.

Bob shrugged. "Kathy has been, shall we say, uptight since your series of accidents?"

"I'm not uptight, Bob. I'm worried. Mom could've frozen to death out there." She furiously cut up tomatoes for the salad.

Jessica stepped up beside her daughter and slid an arm around her waist. "But I didn't. We had a plan. When I didn't call you when you expected me to, you called Gary."

"But Gary wasn't there, Mom. What would've happened if Jeff hadn't happened to stop by to hear my call? No one would've come for you."

"But he was, and he did. And, Kathy, I'd have made it on my own if I'd had to. I'm not ready to let go of my family, not for a long time."

Lori chimed in, "I'm sure you would have managed, Mom."

"Thanks for the vote of confidence. Now, can I do anything to help? If not, I'm perfectly content to sip my wine in front of the fire."

"Go and sit. We'll be ready in five minutes." Kathy shooed her away.

Jessica settled in front of the fireplace with her feet propped on the footstool, one of her favorite spots when she lived here. She had lots of great memories of living in this house, but contentment filled her at the sight of Kathy and her family taking over. After Ed's death, she'd been lost in the house and needed something cozier. The apartment over the shop had been the perfect answer. Being less than a quarter the size of this house, the apartment suited her, cozy and safe. The question of safety in her shop and apartment hadn't arisen past normal precautions. Until recently. In fact the only place she'd had a sense of safety lately was when she stayed at the inn with Jeff.

"Mom, are you getting too warm there? Your cheeks are flushed." Lori stood in the entryway.

Jessica hopped up. "Maybe so." What in the world must Lori think?

"Kathy says we're ready. We're in the dining room."

"Where are the twins?"

"They ate earlier, and we're leaving them outside. They will be exhausted and fall into bed without fighting."

"Okay, sounds like a plan."

"Mom, sit here at the end like you used to."

"Oh, no, Kathy. You keep insisting on that, and I keep sitting on the side. You and Bob sit at the ends of the table. This is your home now."

Kathy relented with a shrug of her shoulders. "If you pass your plate, I'll serve the pot roast. You have bowls at your place for the salad. Lori made apple pie for dessert."

"Yum. I should probably walk home after this meal." Jessica laughed at her daughter's expression. "Kidding, Kathy. Just kidding."

They ate, and they chatted comfortably. Until they didn't. An awkward silence filled the air. Jessica glanced up and caught Kathy giving Bob the eye. Had they hatched a plot of some kind?

Bob cleared his throat. "So, Jessica, we've been thinking."

"Oh? What about?"

"Well, Kathy and Lori—and I—we all think you should drop your opposition to using Worley Construction Company for the retirement center."

Jessica set her fork on her plate and gazed at the three people at the table. "You do, do you? And why would I do that?"

"Mom, we don't want anything else to happen to you." Lori's voice rose to a higher pitch than usual.

Bob reached for Jessica's hand. "We've been worried about all these incidents—better call them what they are—these attacks. Each one getting more extreme, and Gary hasn't found a way to keep them from happening or find proof of who's behind them."

"I'm not overreacting, Mom. We're all worried for you. We're worried for ourselves if, God forbid, something happened to you." Kathy brushed at a tear threatening to slide down her cheek. "It's awful that the shoddiness of the Worley Construction Company got Daddy killed. I know when we asked you before you said no, but these things keep happening to you. I hate they are still in business, but—"

Kathy rose and walked over beside Jessica, eased out the chair next to her, and sat. She took her mother's hand. "Listen, Mom. We've talked." She glanced at Bob and Lori. "We've all agreed that now you must stop this fight. We can't risk losing you, too."

Jessica studied her children and Bob, considered a son. "I—I understand where you're coming from. I appreciate that you have spoken out of love. But—" She withdrew her hand from Kathy's, rose from the table, and walked into the family room to gaze into the fire.

Her grown children followed her but didn't say more, giving her a moment to ponder the points they'd made. Finally, she stopped and faced them. "I love you and the twins more than I can say. I want to be around to see them all grown up, but I've always taught you that you have to stand up to bullies. You have to speak truth to power. Being silent in the face of evil behavior is to condone that behavior. I can't do that. I'd be a hypocrite. It would put into question everything your father and I've ever taught you."

"But, Mom, please listen. We don't want to lose you." Lori tugged her mother into a tight hug.

Jessica patted Lori on the back. "Ahh, sweetie. I promise to be careful. I can tighten up the security on the shop, and I won't go anywhere by myself. How will that work for you? Won't that relieve your worries?"

Kathy joined her mother and sister in front of the fire for a hug. "That's a step, Mom, but what we believe you should do is to let this go. Move on."

"I can't move on while Tim Worley refuses to accept responsibility and continues to cheat the public. I won't compromise on people's safety. But I do promise to be more careful." She hugged both girls and then crossed to Bob. "I love you all a great deal. It makes me warm inside to hear how much you love me. Now, don't we have Lori's pie to eat?"

Later that night, Bob insisted on following Jessica home, a part of the agreement they'd all reached. Jessica wouldn't go anywhere alone. He saw her into the store, up to her apartment, and told her he'd have the security company out the first available moment to check out how else they could increase her safety. He kissed her on the cheek and stomped down the stairs, clearly still annoyed Jessica hadn't agreed to stop fighting Worley Construction.

She hated that she couldn't make her kids happy on this issue, but she couldn't. After fixing a cup of tea, she retrieved a box of Ed's old papers and reports stored in the back of her closet. Over the years she'd tried to throw out the box, and each instance when it came right down to it, she couldn't bring herself to take that step. She'd gone through them before but hadn't been able to figure anything out. Gary had taken a look at them, but what does a sheriff know regarding such things?

She slapped her palm against her forehead. Duh. Jeff. She should ask Jeff, a man accustomed to reading this stuff. Why had she never thought of him? He told her he planned to be back for the vote by the board next week right before the Christmas Festival began. Once that happened, real work stopped, and everyone went into holiday mode, reveling in the party atmosphere.

Could she convince him to come back early? She couldn't call him tonight, but first thing tomorrow morning, she'd talk with him. She sipped her tea and gazed into the fire. Maybe this would be the answer. If Jeff found evidence to convince the lawyers, then his company could terminate the contract. She wouldn't have to vote against the project. Making everyone happy. Everyone except Tim Worley.

JESSICA ROSE EARLY and dressed before calling Jeff at eight in the morning. "Hey. I hope I'm not calling too early."

"Not at all, but I didn't expect to hear from you. Is everything okay? You haven't had any more incidents?"

"No. Thanks. I'm fine. In fact, last night, the family had an intervention of sorts and have insisted I not go any place by myself. I've agreed because I couldn't agree to drop my fight against Worley Construction, which they at first asked me."

"That must've been a difficult discussion."

"You could say that. I appreciated that they spoke out of concern and love for me, but I can't do what they asked. But it got me thinking. I have a box of Ed's old papers. I've looked through them, and Gary Halbert has, but we don't understand construction. Not the way you do." Jessica took a deep breath and then plunged ahead. "Can I convince you to come to town and look over the papers? We still have time before the meeting when we're scheduled to vote."

Jeff didn't respond for a moment. Jessica panicked a bit. "Or I can bring them to you in Concord."

"I hate to ask you to do that, but right now we're swamped with another project coming to a head. I can't take off right now for the three-hour round trip, but if you bring them, I'll look over them for you."

"Good. Thank you. Are you sure today will be all right?"

"Yes. And, Jessica, since you're coming, why don't you plan to spend the night as well? Tony has been on me to bring you to town. He and Eva are looking forward to meeting you. If we're lucky, she'll make one of her famous Italian dishes."

Jessica drew in a deep breath and pondered what his words might mean. If he asked what she suspected, was she ready to take the next step?

"My condo is large, Jessica. You can have your own room and bath."

Jeff must be a mind-reader. "Okay, thank you. I'd love to visit the condo and meet Tony and Eva. I'll leave after lunch and should arrive around two if that works for you."

"Excellent. I'll rearrange my calendar and do my best to finish off this other project before you arrive. I'll text you the condo address and meet you there." He paused. "Jessica."

"Yes?"

"I'm looking forward to having you come."

Jessica smiled. "Me too. See you this afternoon."

They disconnected, and Jessica flew into overdrive to prepare for the trip. She retrieved her overnight bag from the top shelf in the closet. What would she wear? What would her kids say? Should she tell them? Would they insist on following her to Concord? That would be terrible. Maybe she wouldn't tell them. It wouldn't exactly be dishonest, but yeah, it kind of would be. Besides, she needed to ask Lori to pick up a few more hours in the shop and arrange for Janelle to work all of tomorrow.

The sounds of knocking on the front door of the shop drew her downstairs. Who would be here this early? The shop wouldn't open for another hour and a half. Jessica peeked through the windows of the front door. Her stomach clenched. Why would two men be here at this early hour?

And then she laughed at herself. "Oh, my gosh." She unlocked and flung open the door. "Bob, is everything all right? What are you doing here?" She glanced at the other man dressed in a uniform with the logo of a security company.

"Sorry, we're hitting you at such an early hour, Jessica, and yes, everything is fine at home. Butch here only had one opening to come check out your system."

"Oh, right. Come in. I didn't understand how fast we'd act on this. Either of you like a cup of hot tea or coffee?"

"No thanks. Jessica, the family wasn't messing around."

She nodded.

"No thanks, ma'am. If you can show me where the control board is, I'll figure out a way we can make this place one of the most secure around these parts."

"Okay. It's right over here." How could she keep from filling in Bob on her trip to Concord? Darn. Would he insist on following her? She hated that. He had his own work to do. She led them to the back of the shop where the panel was.

"Don't you have one upstairs, too, Jessica?"

She nodded. "I can control the downstairs from up there."

"Maybe we should take a look at that first." Butch picked up his laptop.

"Sure. Right this way." Jessica led the two men upstairs and into her apartment. "It's right here, Butch." She gestured beside the front door.

"Are you going someplace, Jessica?" Bob stood with both hands across his chest staring pointedly at her overnight bag in the middle of the floor.

"Oh, uh. Well." Jessica literally wrung her hands then quickly thrust them behind her back. Way to look guilty. Never one for lies, she looked her son-in-law straight in the face. "To Concord this afternoon."

"Concord? Is Sue going with you?"

"No."

"Well, why not? Didn't we last night have a conversation on safety, and you agreed to be more cautious and not go places alone. How does this trip fit into those guidelines?"

Jessica walked into the kitchen. The box of Ed's papers sat in the middle of the table. "After our talk last night I got to thinking. Maybe we've had the wrong people go over Ed's papers on Worley Construction. Maybe we needed someone who understands contracts and construction documents. I want to take the box to Concord and ask Jeff to look over what's here."

"I like the idea of having Jeff look over Ed's notes, Jessica, but why can't he come here?"

"He's in the middle of a deadline and doesn't have time for the three-hour round trip plus looking at the papers."

Bob dropped into a kitchen chair, yanked off his hat, and thrust his hand through his hair. "Where are you staying? Did you plan to tell anyone you'd be gone?"

Jessica skipped over the first question, hoping her cheeks weren't blooming. "Well, Lori because I want her to come in this afternoon and plan to close up and Janelle who I need to come in for Tuesday."

"I see. Did you plan to tell Lori what your plans were, or would you imply that Sue needed you to help with the Christmas Festival?"

"Frankly, I hadn't exactly decided yet. I didn't want Lori to worry."

"What if one of us stopped by and you weren't here? That would scare the heck out of us."

"But you never stop by without calling."

"Except I just did."

"Yes. There's that."

"I bet Sue would love to go with you. If not she, maybe Kathy. And where are you staying? You didn't say."

"No, I didn't."

"Well, where are you staying?"

"I'm staying at Jeff's large condo." She rushed to add, "I'll have my own bedroom and bath."

"Okay. Huh. I'm at a loss for words, Jessica. Be safe?"

Jessica burst out laughing. "Well, this is a different scenario. I've put you in a position to have to play parent to me. Someday, you will, but it shouldn't be now."

"Okay, here's an option. I'll drive you to Concord if Jeff will bring you home. Do we have a deal?" Her son-in-law held out his hand.

Jessica took it and shook, "Deal." She pulled him in for a hug. "Love you, Bob. You're an important part of our family."

"Love you, too, Jessica. You realize it's only that we want you to be around for a whole lot longer, right?"

"I know, and I love you all the more for feeling that way."

"I can't argue with your idea. Maybe Jeff will find something we haven't. You carry on with whatever you're focused on. I'll make sure Butch here gets the security tightened up so no one can enter without you and everyone else knows something is going on."

So the morning flew by. Butch installed glass-breaking sensors on all the downstairs windows and the one by the upstairs back door. He also added motion sensors. With Jessica not having a pet, these were especially effective. If anyone got past the doors and windows, the motion detectors would alert her. Jessica had contacted Janell who'd agreed to open and close the store on Tuesday, since Jessica wasn't sure when she'd return.

The conversation with her daughter had been awkward, only made tolerable by Kathy's understanding that Bob would ferry her to Concord, and Jeff would return her home. Jessica's face warmed at the memory of Kathy telling her to make sure to take condoms. What daughter says that to her mother? Apparently, Kathy.

Because of the work on the security system, Jessica didn't leave until two. She'd texted Jeff to explain she wouldn't be arriving until three-thirty or so. She shared the address with Bob, put it into her phone's map for directions, and they set off.

She'd dithered over what clothes to bring. Jeff had said supper would be casual at the Benton's house. She decided on good wool black pants and a dark green wool sweater with her boots that reached to right below her knees. She loved the look of tall boots. And yes, she'd picked up condoms at a drugstore out of town. She'd convinced Bob to stop and let her run in on her own to buy a package of gum. Not like she could buy condoms in Tidbury. Boy, it would be all over town in twenty minutes. Even now her cheeks heated when she remembered paying for them.

They had no trouble finding Jeff's condo, and Bob had insisted on seeing her up the stairs and inside.

"Hey, Jeff. Have you met my son-in-law, Bob Shepherd?" Bob set down the box, and the two men shook hands.

Jeff looked between her and Bob and cocked his head in question.

"The family has insisted I have an escort when I go anywhere. Are you willing to drive me back to Tidbury? Otherwise Bob will have to make an extra trip to pick me up."

"Of course. Happy to." He glanced at the box sitting on the floor. "These the papers?" he cocked his head at the box.

Jessica nodded.

"Can you stay, Bob? Can I get you a drink? Coffee?"

"No thanks, Jeff. I wanted to make sure Jessica got here all right. I expect you to look after her. We don't believe there's any reason why something should happen in Concord, but we can't be too cautious."

"I agree, and I promise you I'll take good care of her."

"Guys, you're talking like I'm not standing right here." Jessica protested their treating her like a child.

"Sorry. Appreciate you checking out the papers, Jeff, and looking after her."

"You can count on it."

"Be sure to keep us posted when you decide to head back." He hugged Jessica and kissed her cheek. "Love you."

"You, too, Bob. Thank you."

And then Bob departed, and she stood in the entry hall with Jeff. Now what?

"Hang on. Let me put this on the dining table. I'll have more space to work there, then I'll show you to your room." Jeff moved into the open floor plan condo and set the box on a large dark wood dining table. Jessica liked the large open area, and the wood fire burning in the fireplace brought warmth and comfort. Jeff took her roller bag. "Follow me," and he led her down a hall.

They passed what appeared to be the master bedroom with a king bed, before stopping at the next room, tastefully decorated in soft beiges with pops of yellow. "This is a lovely room, Jeff." She crossed to the window and looked out at trees and grass and old timey streetlights. "Beautiful. How long have you been here?"

"I moved in over five years ago. The whole place needed to be remodeled, and I had a decorator help me."

"Well, I gotta say you did a great job. And look at this bathroom." Jessica oohed and ahhed over the deep soaker tub. "I didn't have room for this when we redid the apartment over the store. My shower is great, but sometimes if you've got sore muscles, the best thing is a long hot soak." What had she been thinking to go on about taking a bath?

"Hard to beat. I hope you take an opportunity to enjoy the experience." He smiled and left the suite. "Do you want a cup of tea? I bought a variety because I remember you prefer that to coffee."

She followed him into the kitchen. "How thoughtful. Yes, I'd love a cup of tea. And, Jeff, I can't tell you how much I appreciate you making an opportunity to study Ed's papers. Maybe you won't find anything there. No one else has, but you understand this stuff better than the others who've looked."

"Here's your tea, madam. We have time to take a quick looksee before heading to Tony and Eva's house. They're expecting us to arrive at six, and we'll eat around seven. Let's take this opportunity for me to scan over the documents and at least figure out how the files are organized."

Jessica stood by the large table where Jeff had earlier set the box. "Let's see what we have here." Jeff opened the box and skimmed through the file folders. "Apparently, Ed made a file or a couple on each of the buildings he inspected."

"Yes, I believe that's what he did. While the state employed him, he often worked out of our house. These were his personal files for buildings where someone hired him to investigate privately."

"So they never belonged to the state?"

"That's correct."

"They are organized by years rather than by the alphabet. So we're looking back over five years ago. And do you remember the name of the building?"

"I most certainly do. Worley Construction was building a new wing on the clinic out from town. It's kind of a regional facility named for the Ferguson Family. That's who put up the money for the addition."

"Okay, that's helpful."

While Jeff riffled through the folders, Jessica sipped her hot tea and studied the main part of his apartment, modern but warm with floor to ceiling windows. Her life had taken such an odd turn starting with Ed's death and years of pursuing Worley Construction, which made her something of an activist for safe building codes. Several months ago the death of Lonnie Melton led her to run for the board of selectmen. Not a situation she expected, but now she held a position of leadership in her town. She had the responsibility, and she enjoyed working with the other board members. The threats certainly scared her, and she hated how worried the whole thing made her family. But she couldn't stop. She wouldn't compromise on people's safety.

"Okay, I've got the right folders here." Jeff laid out three long green folders on the table in front of him and moved the box to the far end of the table. "Listen, can I get you anything? Help yourself to more tea. The hot water spigots at the sink is like you have and makes it super easy for a refill. When I dig into these things, I lose track of time. I don't want to appear to be ignoring you."

Concern for her shown from Jeff's face.

"No, I'm fine. I brought a book with me and will settle in front of the fire. It will be lovely." She paused and rested her hand on his arm. "I can't thank you enough for taking a look at the files."

"Sure. No problem. And no promises I can find anything."

"Of course."

Jeff settled in a chair at the table and didn't look up. Jessica smiled as she wandered into the room where her bag was. He did seem to dive in and lose himself. He never noticed when she walked away. Locating the e-reader she'd brought with her, she returned to the living room area and settled in front of the fire. With one last glance in Jeff's direction, she picked up the current book engrossing her, a schmaltzy Christmas story, with older characters she loved.

Chapter Nineteen

Someone gently touched her shoulder. "Hey, sleepy head. Are you hungry? We have to leave pretty soon for the Benton's."

Jessica jerked. How embarrassing. She must've dozed off. "I'm sorry, Jeff."

"Nothing to apologize for, but I thought you'd like a chance to freshen up before we head to Tony and Eva's."

Jessica picked up her e-reader that had fallen to the floor and rose. "Yes, thanks. You did say casual. I planned to wear this."

"It's perfect. You look beautiful."

"Oh." Jessica glanced away and then back to Jeff. "You're kind. I won't be a moment." She dashed to the bedroom and standing in front of the bathroom mirror, freshened her lipstick, and ran the brush through her hair. She'd never colored her, letting the silver streaks show through the soft brown. Her stylist who artfully cut her hair always said how blessed Jessica was with her thick hair. Judi called those silver streaks the wayward blondes, the color of Jessica's hair when she'd been a young girl. Guess this would have to do. When she returned, Jeff wore his jacket and had her coat in his hands. He helped her into it and picked up a briefcase.

"What's that?"

"I hope you don't mind. I want to show a couple of the files to Tony and pick his brain on what's in here."

"Of course not." She buttoned her coat, threw the hunter green scarf around her neck, and dropped the strap of her purse over her shoulder.

"Let's go." Jeff held the door for her and ushered her into the hallway and to the elevator where they rode down to the garage.

"Well, this is certainly convenient."

Jeff helped her into his four-wheel-drive vehicle. "It's one of the perks that convinced me I must buy this condo. Once you've experienced a New

Hampshire winter, you want a garage. I didn't want to have to dig out my car every morning."

"How far to the Benton's house?"

"About twenty minutes. They have a large older home outside of town. The roads are fine tonight. Not like when you were driving into town from Kathy's and got run off the road. Did Sheriff Halbert ever find any clues to who bumped into you?"

"Nope, nothing. The snow covered any tracks. And I couldn't describe the vehicle except to say maybe it was black."

It didn't take long for Jeff to pull into a long driveway that led to a stately gray clapboard two story house with black shutters.

They hadn't had a chance to knock when the door opened. "Hey, Jeff." A man with a bald head and a bit taller than Jeff greeted them. "You must be Jessica. Please come in out of this cold." Tony graciously welcomed them into his home. "Can I take your coats?" He hung them in the hall closet.

"Oh, my goodness, something smells wonderful." Jessica literally tipped her head taking a good whiff.

"What did I say. You're in for a treat." Jeff winked at her.

Tony laughed. "You've always been a sucker for Eva's lasagna, Jeff. Come on into the kitchen and let me introduce you to the chef." Tony led the way through the dining room to a giant kitchen that had what looked like a pizza oven and pot filler by the stove. Maybe they were both foodies.

"Hello, welcome. I'm Eva. You must be Jessica. I've been looking forward to meeting you. Jeff speaks highly of you."

The beautiful, slender brunette, wearing a chef's apron over her pants, held out her hand, and Jessica took it. The woman had a firm grasp. She extended her cheek for a kiss from Jeff. "I've been telling him he needed to convince you to come here so we could meet."

"Your home is lovely and from the wonderful aroma I can tell why Jeff has gone on about your cooking. Is it a family recipe?"

"Yes, my Grandpa Luigi fiddled with the lasagna recipe his father created. Grandpa passed it to his daughter, my mother, who passed it on to me. And now I cook the meal. It makes me feel close to my family's roots. I hope you enjoy the dish."

"I have no doubt. Can I do anything to help?" Jessica glanced around. "What happened to the guys?

"Oh, they've gone off to talk business. Will you take the appetizers into the living room by the fire? Is wine all right?"

"Wine is always all right." Jessica smiled at the charming woman, who she guessed to be a little younger than she, maybe in her late 40s.

Jessica carried a tray filled with yummy looking morsels into the living room.

"Just put that on the coffee table. Here are the napkins and plates. I think Jeff mentioned you prefer Merlot. Do I have that correct?" Eva had left her apron in the kitchen and wore brown pants, maybe a soft corduroy with a black turtleneck sweater and low boots.

"Yes." Had Jeff talked a lot with the Bentons about her?

In only moments, Eva had opened a bottle, poured two generous glasses, and handed one to Jessica. Eva settled on the sofa next to her. "Now, let's have us some good old fashioned girl-talk while the guys are otherwise busy." She reached for one of the canapes with a swirl of salmon on top. "I do love salmon. Yes, lobster is supposed to be the big deal in New England, but I'm a salmon person all the way. Tell me what you think."

Jessica leaned over and selected a napkin and a bite of toast with the salmon on top. Her eyes rolled back when the flavors hit her tongue. "You are quite the chef, Eva. This is wonderful."

"Thanks. I've been experimenting. I'm researching the idea of opening a catering business and having something original is important." She laughed. "But it has to be edible, too."

"Well, this is more than that. It's delicious." Jessica helped herself to another, which she followed with a sip of the Merlot.

"So tell me what you think of Jeff?"

Jessica choked on the wine, and it took her a minute to catch her breath. "Sorry. Something must've gone down wrong."

"Do you need a sip of water? Will you be all right?"

Jessica wiped at the tears threatening to roll down her face. How embarrassing, but Eva's question had totally taken her by surprise. Finally, she had herself back in control.

"You were about to tell me what you think of Jeff."

Eva was persistent. Jessica took a deep breath and jumped to pull together a response. "Well, he may have saved my life a couple of times or at least kept me from a way worse experience."

"What do you mean?"

Jessica told Eva the story of how close they'd come to being run over and him cushioning her fall. She talked about how she'd been run off the road and how Jeff came along and found her walking home in the blizzard.

"My goodness. That could've ended tragically."

"Yes, it could have, but it didn't. I'm beyond grateful, of course."

"So, Tony and Jeff have been friends since college, and he's been my friend since we married. We love him like family and don't want anything or anyone to cause him hurt."

"Hurt?" What was on Eva's mind?

"You see, we've always asked Jeff to bring women over he's dating, but he never has. Until now."

"Oh."

"Yes. After Jeff's mother died, his father buried himself with work, and Jeff got left out a little. His brother's death was a double burden on them both. Tony and his family stepped in to take up the slack. Jeff's father appreciated the assistance. When I married Tony, I brought along my large Italian family, yes, one like in the movies. Only no one is in the mafia." Eva comically wagged her eyebrows up and down. "When we all get together it is a gang, including Jeff and his father.

"Jeff's wife Beth was a shy thing, and I think our families overwhelmed her a bit, but Jeff loved her, so we did what we could to accommodate. Tragically she died after a long fight with cancer. Jeff has focused on the business with Tony ever since." Eva paused and sipped her wine and eyed Jessica over the glass.

"So we don't want Jeff to be hurt."

All of a sudden it hit Jessica. "You're afraid I might hurt him?"

"Yeah. As I said, you're the first woman he's brought over here. That has to be significant. So if you're not interested, you better let him down quickly and gently."

Jessica sat in stunned silence. What could she possibly say? She took a swallow of wine, savoring the blackberry and plum flavors, collecting her thoughts. Eva seemed content to wait in silence for Jessica to answer.

"Frankly, Eva, I'm struggling with how to respond. Let me go back to five years ago." Jessica filled in Eva on Ed's death and her commitment to making Worley Construction admit responsibility for what they did and to stop them from hurting anyone else with their shoddy work.

"Jeff and I began as adversaries of a sort. I objected to the retirement center being built on our town green, and I hated Jeff's company's plan to use Worley Construction. Over time, Jeff made me recognize how they would build the retirement center up rather than in a sprawling style. He showed me how all our activities could coexist peacefully with the center. He convinced me having the retirement center would be good for our community." Jessica rose with her wine glass in her hand and stopped in front of the fireplace staring into the flames, bursting red, orange, and yellow. She needed to be clear with Eva, finally turning to face her.

"If the company can't break the contract with Worley Construction, I will vote against the approval. And chances are, I'll be able to convince others to vote with me. While we'd like to have the retirement center for the town, that won't happen. And I recognize that will hurt Jeff and Tony and the company. And you, too. I'm sorry, but that's the way it is. My hope is they'll find something in my late husband's papers that will supply a reason for the lawyers to agree to them canceling the contract. So until we resolve this situation there's not a way I can answer your question."

"Thank you for being honest with me, Jessica." Eva raised her glass. "Here's to the guys finding something."

THE LASAGNA TURNED out to be every bit as good as promised. While they ate, Jeff and Tony brought the women up to speed on what they'd found.

"So what do you think, Tony. Do we have enough here the lawyers will let us break the contract?"

"Ed had gathered together troubling documentation, but whether it will be enough for the lawyers, I don't know. But we've worked with the Andrew

Mulligan Law Firm for many years, and we trust them. I believe it's worth sharing the documents with them."

Jessica let out a long sigh of relief. That was what she'd hoped. It still might not be enough, but now she had a chance to stop Worley Construction.

They'd all had fun together. Sharing snow stories, school experiences, and raising kid experiences, when even Jeff had taken the Benton kids on a few vacations.

What would happen between her and Jeff if he couldn't cancel the contract with Worley Construction? They had such a tenuous relationship now. She'd been upfront with him as she had with Eva. She wouldn't support the retirement center if they had to use Worley. If she didn't find the votes to stop the project, would he go ahead and build the center anyway? How would she handle that?

Jessica contemplated the evening ahead of them as Jeff helped her into her coat. His hands strong on her shoulders. Would something come of Jeff and her being together? Did she want something to happen? Heat rose in her cheeks. Apparently so. Despite this interlude maybe being all they ever had.

Jeff took her hand and led her down the porch stairs outside Tony and Eva's place, helping her navigate through the newly fallen snow, which glistened in the moonlight.

"I must've missed the latest forecast. Snow, again." Jessica said.

"That's not a job I'd ever want. They have a whole bunch of fancy new equipment, and still it's easier to be wrong than right."

"And we remember the wrong times much more easily than we do the many times when they nail the forecast." Jessica scooted into the car and Jeff followed quickly on his side.

He punched in the seat warmers for them both.

"These were a fantastic invention. Amazing how quickly the warmth hits you."

They made the trip safely home to Jeff's condo, where he parked in the garage and again took her hand to lead her to the elevator and up to his condo. He helped her off with her coat and went to start the fire.

"Would you like another glass of wine?"

"That sounds lovely." Jessica settled on the sofa in front of the fireplace, loving the crackling sound once Jeff got the fire going. She loved the gas fire in her apartment, but nothing beat the sounds, feel, and smell of the real deal.

Jeff returned with her wine and one for him. He settled next to her on the sofa and took her hand. She liked the connection and admitted she'd missed that. Oh, she routinely hugged family and friends, but this felt different.

"Jessica." Jeff took her glass and set both their glasses on the coffee table.

Jessica's heart stuttered. What happened?

Jeff took both her hands in his. "Jessica, I care for you. Whatever happens with our project is immaterial to my feelings for you."

"Thank you, Jeff." She gulped. Now was the moment if she was brave enough. "I care for you, too." She pulled a hand free and softly touched his cheek. She respected him, and yes, something else tugged at her. Something she hadn't experienced in years.

Jeff leaned into her palm and kissed her hand and then slowly drew her close to him. Jessica's heartbeat increased. Her lips parted. It had been a long time. Slowly Jeff's head descended, and their lips brushed, tentatively at first, but he quickly took charge and deepened the kiss. Jessica's tummy did flip flops like a fish out of water. Yes, a long time.

Jeff broke the connection, only to move down the side of her neck. She instinctively tipped her head, giving him more room. The blood pounded in her ears. Surely he could hear it. And his oh so expert lips were back on hers, and his hands roamed her body. And her body ached to respond. She yearned for his embrace to continue. She deep down ached for them to move to the bedroom and continue. Continue to the end when they'd both be satisfied.

As if he read her mind, Jeff stood and drew her with him. He draped an arm around her shoulders, and they proceeded to his bedroom. He drew her close, and she knew his excitement equaled hers.

"It's been a long dry spell for me, Jeff." She shivered when he slipped his hands under her sweater and gently lifted it over her head.

"You are the most beautiful woman I've ever seen, and I can go slow. I'm known for being a patient man." He knelt and drew off her boots, while she balanced with her hands on his shoulders, then he unzipped her slacks and drew them down her body. His hands skimmed her thighs, and goose bumps followed everywhere his fingertips touched. Until she stood in only her beige lace bra and matching panties. Her breaths came in pants, and she feared anticipation would cause her to hyperventilate. Ed hadn't been her first experience, but he'd been the only one for thirty years, which from this standpoint seemed like forever. And now, it had been five years since anyone had looked at her body the way Jeff did.

He drew her to him, cupping her hips and pulling her close. She got busy with the buttons of his shirt. "You're wearing entirely too many clothes, sir. You have me at a distinct disadvantage."

"Well, we can't have that. Let me assist." In moments he stood in his black briefs that he filled out exceedingly well.

Her heart sat right in her throat.

He drew down the coverlet and the sheets, but then he pulled her close again and kissed her as if he'd never let her go, and that would be all right with Jessica. She kissed him right back. Their hands all over each other, discovering each other. Jeff's kisses followed his hands and Jessica's legs gave out. He lowered her to the bed, sank down next to her, and murmured her name before showering kisses on every part of her body he could reach. Which were many.

Jessica tingled all over and struggled to catch her breath. So much better than she imagined, and she'd imagined it a lot. She stifled a giggle of pure joy. Not sure a man wanted to be laughed at when he made passionate love. And yes, that's what this felt like. Probably too soon and awkward to say that with the project between them.

But nothing lay between them now except the condom Jeff had thoughtfully provided. She needn't have worried. And oh my. Explosions rippled through her body until she saw the aurora borealis or something close to that. She and Jeff tumbled over the precipice together. Ohhhh.

Jessica snuggled next to Jeff. His hand rubbed lazy circles on her hip until they both must've dozed off in a satiated haze.

Chapter Twenty

Two days later, Jessica still floated in a hot air balloon. Stuff that normally got on her nerves didn't, and the whole world appeared brighter. Of course, maybe the bright sun reflecting off the last snow had something to do with that. She preferred to believe it was a residual feeling from the wonderful two days she'd spent with Jeff. They'd made love a couple of times after the first. Apparently all of her parts remembered how to work. Jeff had seemed happy, and she'd felt more than satisfied. They didn't discuss the change in their relationship, but a closeness had developed they didn't have before. She trusted him not to hurt her.

True to her kids' requests, Jeff had driven her home, but he hadn't stayed. He promised to keep her posted on what the lawyers decided. At the latest he'd be at the board meeting when they voted on his project this week.

Jessica had hired another woman to help in the shop, and today Jessica had trained her in how things worked. Melody Simpson had worked in a small store that closed in a nearby town and was happy to have a job she was qualified for closer to home. Janell Bacon had become a full time employee, and Jessica's daughter Lori moved into more of a back-up for the others. College kept her pretty busy. For any heavy duty lifting and an occasional shift, Jessica called in Buddy Stanley, a high school student eager to make extra cash.

If Melody worked out, and Jessica had no reason to think she wouldn't, Jessica believed Melody and Janell could manage the bulk of the store hours, giving her more options to focus on her work as a selectman. A smile spread unexpectedly across her face. And more hours she could share with Jeff.

"Hey, Mom. What are you smiling at?" Jessica had forgotten the presence of her daughter, who'd come in while Jessica trained Melody and then stayed.

"It's probably the sun, Lori. Such a beautiful cold, clear, crisp day. Doesn't it make you smile?" Jessica congratulated herself on the good save and only hoped her cheeks didn't give away the real reason for her smile. "And I'm excited that the Christmas Festival begins in a couple of days. I think the board will approve Jeff's company building the retirement center on the green."

"I'm surprised, Mom. You've been dead set against Worley Construction doing the work."

"I still am, but I don't believe they'll do the work. Jeff and Tony agreed the papers I took them raised red flags. They've passed them on to their attorneys. We're hoping to hear they agree, and Jeff and Tony can break the contract with Worley Construction."

"Great news. I'm happy for you, Mom. I looked at the plans at the mayor's office, and it looks like it will be a comfortable place."

"I think so. The project will provide lots of jobs to local folks while it's being built and afterwards when it's open. It will also offer services not only to our town but the whole area."

"Changing the subject, Mom. Did you hear that Mildred Summers had to back out of sponsoring a booth? Her first granddaughter has made an early arrival, and she's gone to help her daughter."

"No, I didn't hear that. What's Sue doing to find a replacement, or will she have to cancel that stall?"

"She's hoping to find a person who can be responsible for each day or part of a day.

A twinge of guilt hit Jessica. She'd seen Sue's name on her phone the last couple of days, and she hadn't made it a point to return her call. No way could she have done that while she stayed with Jeff and was so pleasurably occupied.

"So, Mom, couldn't you make your famous apple fritters? You wouldn't have to fill all of the slots. Could you do one day or perhaps half a day to help cover? I personally hope you will. We basically eat healthily as a general rule. Don't we deserve a splurge with those apple fritters?"

"Well, since being elected to the board of selectmen, I hadn't planned to do any work for the festival. I appreciate Sue taking over leadership. But, because you've asked nicely, and she's a really good friend, I'll find a way to add it into my schedule. Maybe a six hour shift for one day. Will that do?"

"That's great. I'll let Sue know for you. And I'll help you."

"Thanks, Lori. Appreciate that. And this is the least I can do since Sue stepped in and took over leadership on the festival when all of you convinced me to run for the board. Why don't you head on home, Lori? It's kind of slow this evening. I can manage the next hour on my own and lock up."

"Sounds good to me. I've got one last project to turn in by the end of the semester. I'm happy you've brought on Melody, too. She seems to be a friendly and competent person and looks like she has quickly gotten the hang of running the shop."

"I like her, too, Lori. I especially wanted to have enough staff to keep you from feeling an obligation to be here as much as you have been in the past. I'm assuming you'll be especially busy with your last semester of school ahead."

"It will be great to have her working during the Christmas Festival, too. Frees us both up to relax and have fun. Good night, Mom. Love you."

Jessica stood in the open door of her shop to make sure Lori got to her car safely. Probably overkill, but these days, it proved to be vigilant. She stepped back inside and went to find a sweater to cut the chill of standing in the open doorway. The bell rang as she slung the sweater around her shoulders and hurried back into the main part of the store. A tall man in a heavy winter coat and hat worn low over his eyes stopped several steps inside the door.

"Good evening. What can I do for you?"

"You can stop hassling Tim Worley."

"Oh, John. I didn't recognize you all bundled up like that." Jessica's heart tripped into her throat. Why had John Crowell, the biggest supporter of Worley Construction on the board, come to her store? She didn't want to have a discussion with him alone in her shop.

"Jessica, pay attention. You won't like the consequences if you continue on this path."

He hadn't moved farther into the shop, and yet sweat bathed Jessica's palms. She darn sure wouldn't ask what those consequences might be? She didn't want to hear the answer to that question.

The bell rang, the door opened, and two women hustled in. "I hope you're still open. Are you still open? I decided I couldn't rest until I bought the candle I found in here earlier in the day. I hope you haven't sold it yet."

Jessica's body remained frozen, but her voice found life. "Yes, of course. I remember which one you looked at. It's on the shelf to your right."

"Remember what I said." John Crowell spun on his heel and flung through the door, the bell jangling at his exit.

"We didn't interrupt anything, did we?" The other woman asked.

"No, of course not. And I've been known to keep the shop open a smidge past the regular closing hour when someone hadn't quite made a decision and needed a few more minutes to decide on a purchase."

"Thank you. I've never found a candle like this with all the cutouts. It's beautiful. It's likely I will not burn it. I can't imagine ruining the beautiful lines."

"One of our locals makes these in her basement. She lets ice melt to make the holes. A popular craft back quite a number of years ago. To my knowledge she's one of only a few still making them this way."

"Well, I love them. And I'll take two."

"Great. I'll be sure to tell the artist how much you like them. Let me wrap those for you." Jessica picked up the two candles and moved to the office at the back of the shop. Her hands had stopped trembling by the time she finished carefully wrapping the two items in tissue and boxing them up. She returned to the main area. "Here you go. These should travel well."

"Here's my credit card."

"Just tap it right here," Jessica directed her client and soon the transaction was finished. "Thank you for returning." She followed the two women to the door and locked it behind them, collapsing against it for a minute. Gosh, she'd hoped the harassment was behind her. Probably she needed to tell Gary of this latest threat. Threat is exactly what it was. Should she tell the mayor? Wasn't that a little like tattling? How would she work with John Crowell after this?

IN THE END, SHE DECIDED not to mention John Crowell's visit to the sheriff or the mayor. And certainly not to her children. They'd want him locked up. Or lock up her for safe keeping. The mayor had scheduled the vote on the retirement center project for tonight's meeting. Jeff apparently hadn't heard a final decision from the lawyers. At least he hadn't contacted her about one yet. Surely his lawyers would decide that what he and Tony had seen was sufficient for them to break the contract. Supporting the project with Worley Construction involved wasn't in her DNA. She'd never compromise on their poor management and corner cutting, convinced as she was the company had caused Ed's death.

Her cheeks heated remembering her hours with Jeff. She didn't experience a twinge of guilt. She and Ed had interesting conversations concerning the person left after either one of them died. They'd both agreed the remaining spouse needed to move on. Morbid maybe, but one of their friends died suddenly, and they found themselves discussing issues they wouldn't have normally gotten around to. Like planning for their funerals. That had certainly made it easier when she lost Ed. Everyone should make those plans before they were needed to make it easier on the remaining spouse, as well as any children. All the emotions swirling up and around the surviving spouse nearly suffocated them. The added worry of making funeral decisions added to their distress. Planning ahead alleviated some of that awfulness.

But how could she and Jeff ever have anything between them if she voted against his project? And if miraculously they were somehow able to, where would they make a home? His company's office was in Concord, and her home and her family were here in Tidbury.

"Cut it out. This is crazy thinking. You're borrowing trouble where it may not exist. And talking out loud to yourself is especially crazy." She grabbed her coat, cap, and gloves and carefully descended the stairs. Still several hours before Janell would come in to open the shop. Jessica had time to stock up on supplies to make apple fritters for the festival. A quick walk to the grocery store would accomplish that. She looped the straps of the bags she used for groceries over her hand and left her shop, remembering to set the alarm and lock the door.

The cold swatted her in the face and brought her back to real life and not a fantasy world where she and Jeff rode off into the sunset. Pulling on her gloves, she walked swiftly down the street before turning up the block to the grocery store. She'd have to make up several batches on the day she covered the booth. Too bad she couldn't freeze the batter ahead of time. It would make for a long day, but fun. Lori had agreed to help make the batter as well as work during the afternoon shift. The church had a couple of deep frying pans she usually borrowed. She'd be able to cook the apple fritters entirely on the spot. Nothing fresher than that.

"TONY, I'M WORRIED WE haven't heard back from our attorneys yet. I've got to leave soon to drive to Tidbury for the meeting this evening. If I don't hear good news, I'm certain Jessica will vote against the project."

"And you think she can convince others to go along with her?"

"I'm sure she can. But I don't know how many. I hate this." He paced his office and cocked his head right and left in an attempt to alleviate the tension. Jessica would be disappointed if the lawyers didn't agree. He would've let her down. Not a position he wanted to be in, especially after the moments they'd shared together. Could their relationship move past the issues with Worley Construction? Don't borrow trouble, maybe they'd hear good news from the attorneys.

"Jeff, if the board approves the project, we have to go through with it. We can hire a special investigator to follow along and track their every step, like you suggested, but we can't back out of the contract and the project without agreement from the attorneys. Worley would hit us with a lawsuit big enough to bankrupt us."

"Yeah, I know."

"By the way, man. Eva and I like Jessica a lot and hope things work out between you."

Jeff looked down and then met his friend and partner's gaze. "Yeah, me too. It's hard to figure how that happens if we have to keep our contract with Worley." He took a last sip of coffee and set the cup on his desk. "Okay, I'm out of here. You call me as soon as you hear anything."

"You got it." Tony slapped Jeff on the back, nodded once, and returned to his own office.

Jeff loaded his bag with several folders he figured he might need, but he'd placed everything on display at the mayor's office for more than two months. The more transparent they could be the better. He swung into his big coat and set out for the garage.

After getting on the highway, Jeff called Jessica. Better give her a heads-up it didn't look good. His call went right to voice mail. Disappointing, he'd try again later.

Half-way through the trip Tony called. "Hey man, I don't have good news."

"You've got to be kidding."

"Nope, the attorney called me a few minutes ago. Several of them perused our documents. They discussed and wrangled over them, recognizing the same red flags we did, but ultimately they concluded it's not enough for us to cancel the contract without being sued."

"I hate that."

"Yeah, me too, buddy. What do you do now?"

"I intend to tell Jessica before the meeting, so she's at least not blindsided by the news."

"Keep me posted on how the decision goes."

"Will do." Jeff disconnected. His foot getting heavier on the accelerator led to a little speeding, which got him to Tidbury in an hour and ten minutes. Unfortunately, he'd never talked with Jessica. When he entered town, he went directly to her shop. He'd be cutting it short to make it to the meeting, but he wanted to talk with her in person and tell her himself. What had she been doing all afternoon that kept her from answering his calls?

Jeff found a spot to park in front of her shop and pushed into the store. "Jessica." He paused. "You're not Jessica." He studied the middle aged woman behind the counter.

"Hello. I'm Melody. Jessica has already left for the board of selectmen meeting.

"Okay. I'll find her there. Thanks." He beat a hasty retreat and raced across the green toward the mayor's office and the town meeting room. Maybe he'd still have a chance to talk with her.

All the seats were full, and Jeff had to angle through those standing for a good view. Mayor Rudy Lopez, the chair of the board, sat in the middle a long table at the front of the room with two members to his left and right. No chance to talk to Jessica.

After the opening ceremonies, the mayor ran through parts of the agenda that didn't apply to Jeff's project. His insides tangled into snarls. He hated the information he had to share.

"All right. We're to the item on the agenda that I think has drawn this crowd." Lopez smiled at the people filling the small space. "That's the item regarding moving forward with the building of the retirement center on our Green. The motion is to move forward. Now I'll hear from selectmen who want to voice an opinion."

Stan Hinson got his hand up first.

"Ok, Stan. What say you?"

Stan Henson stood. "This will be a great project for our town and community. During the building, Worley Construction has promised to use lots of local construction people. And once it's up and running, the center will hire more of our people." Stan nodded at Crowell and then sat.

"Thanks, Stan. Anyone else?"

Jessica's hand went up.

"Yes, Jessica."

Jessica stood. Her hands twisting in front of her. She scanned the aisles of people until her gaze landed on Jeff's. He gave a slight shake of his head. The half-smile on her face faded and a crinkle formed between her eyebrows.

"Thanks, Rudy. While I agree with Stan the retirement center will be good for our community, and I'm convinced there's enough space for it and our many community activities to co-exist happily, however, I am opposed to the motion. I understand the motion as it now stands means the project will be built by Worley Construction, and I cannot support that." Her gaze locked again with Jeff's. "I'm sorry." And she sat.

John Crowell stood without waiting for a by-your-leave from the mayor. "Everyone knows Jessica has had a beef with Worley Construction Company since her husband's unfortunate death. She's let her grief blind her to the good that company can do, and this project can do for all of us. Let's not be guided by this woman's emotions. Let's vote to approve the project."

Crowell's rudeness to Jessica made red fill Jeff's vision. He wanted to punch the man. How dare he talk to her that way and in public. Nothing Jeff could do, but his thoughts triggered his fingers to form into fists.

"Anyone else?" Rudy looked to his right and left. "Yes, Ralph. I see your hand. Speak up."

Ralph McGinley stood. Jessica had told Jeff that Ralph agreed with them.

"Thanks, Rudy. Happy to have so many of you come down this evening, but I bet you have other places you'd like to be, so I'll be quick. I'm with Jessica, and I oppose going forward with the project with Worley Construction doing the work." He sat back down.

Jessica nodded at Ralph and smiled.

Rudy's gaze traveled around the people gathered in the small room until he lighted on Jeff. "Ah, Mr. Hudson. I thought you'd be here. Do you want to add anything else to your earlier presentations before we take the vote?"

Jeff made his way to the front. "Thank you, Mayor Lopez. My company understands the concerns expressed by some board of selectmen members on using the Worley Construction Company, and we're willing to hire an extra inspector at our own expense to supervise to make sure everything is done by the book and that every safety regulation is met. We hope that will be enough to satisfy the expressed concerns. We're looking forward to building the retirement center for you. While I've visited here over several months, this town," he let his gaze rest on Jessica, "has grown to mean a lot to me. My company nor I would be a part of anything that might hurt you. Thank you for listening."

Jeff moved back against the wall. Would that be enough for Jessica? Would she trust him to make sure they properly built the center? Or would she not be able to let go of her justified hatred of Worley Construction? Had he offered a good enough option to convince her to compromise? Guess he'd find out in a few moments.

Rudy Lopez looked at his fellow selectmen and took a deep breath. "If there's no more discussion, I believe we're ready to vote. All in favor say aye."

John Crowell and Stan Henson both spoke loudly, "Aye." As if the volume would make their votes count for more.

"All opposed, say No."

Jessica cast a quick look in his direction and shook her head. "No."

Ralph McGinley's voice chimed in right behind hers, "No."

"How do you vote, Rudy?" John Crowell spit out the words again louder than necessary.

"The Chair votes Aye. The motion carries. With no further business to come before us, I declare this meeting adjourned and encourage you all to enjoy our Christmas festivities beginning tomorrow."

Cheers and boos filled the room, and the people milling around made it difficult for Jeff to reach Jessica. Sheriff Gary Halbert appeared with a couple of his deputies and helped herd people out of the building and toward their homes. Jeff overheard snippets of conversation:

"Poor Jessica."

"That bully Crowell."

"So happy we're getting this retirement center."

"My Johnny will be hired to work on the construction."

"Aunt Tilly can move there instead of in with us which she didn't want to do."

As the crowd thinned out, Jeff made his way to Jessica. Still he had to wait his turn because of all the people flocking around her.

Rudy patted her shoulder. "I'm sorry, Jessica. I voted for the postponement, but I think the center will be great for the town, and I trust Jeff Hudson to see it's built properly."

She nodded. "I understand, Rudy. Thanks for giving us the extra time." Rudy ambled over to talk with other town folks.

Finally Jeff made his way up to Jessica. "I'm sorry. I tried to call you before the meeting. Where were you?"

"I'd let my phone battery die, and I had plugged it in upstairs in the apartment while I worked in the store. I'm doing extra work so I can be gone a lot during the Christmas Festival. On one afternoon I'm frying apple fritters."

"Yum. I'll be sure to stop by. When will you be there?"

"Next Tuesday afternoon from noon to 6 pm." She paused and looked at him. "What did the lawyers say?"

"We didn't hear until after I'd left to come here. The attorneys saw the same red flags we did, but they were afraid if were to renege on the contract based only on those, Worley Construction would sue us for breaking our contract without a better excuse. In fact they were surprised Worley hadn't already sued you for slander."

"Okay." She dropped her head in both hands for a moment, drew in a deep breath, and then squaring her shoulders stood straighter. "I'll have to keep working on this. I'm sorry, but I can't let it go."

"Even with our assurance of hiring an extra inspector?"

"Huh-uh. Too dangerous. I hope your inspector catches Worley doing something, but he'll probably clean up his act for this project and go back to his old ways when he takes on another project." She reached a hand and rested it on his chest, and he gripped her hand in his. "I do appreciate you going the extra mile to hire a special inspector." She picked up her purse and slung it over her shoulder. "I'm going home."

"I'll walk you there."

She nodded, but she didn't make eye contact, indicating a withdrawal. Hmm. He had his hands full winning her. But that's what he intended to do.

They were silent on the walk to her shop and apartment. "Can I come in?"

Jessica paused and faced him. "I don't think so. I'm bushed after a long day at the shop, followed by the stress of the meeting tonight. Pretty emotionally draining."

"Yeah, I can understand that. I wanted to slug John Crowell when he went off on you. What a bigoted fool."

A small smile lit her lips, not quite making it to her eyes. "He is that, but probably not a judicious act for you to have taken. Though I appreciate the sentiment. Are you staying the night?"

"No, I'm heading back. We have lots to do to make good on my promise of hiring an inspector. What if I come back during the Christmas Festival? I'm a big fan of apple fritters."

"I'd like that." She leaned up on her toes. Her lips brushed his cheek, and then she stepped away to unlock her door.

"I'm coming in to make sure everything is all right."

"Thanks." She turned off the alarm and faced him. "Okay, I'm safe. Thank you."

"I'll return in a few days. In the meantime, be safe." He pulled her in for a real kiss and then gently set her away.

"Drive carefully." Her voice had a breathy quality. Good. He wanted her to remember what they had together.

"I'll call or text. Now lock up."

When he heard the lock engage, he spun around and walked to his car. Backing out, he called Tony. "Hey, man. We got the project."

"Even with Worley doing the Construction?"

"Yes. We won on a three to two vote. Jessica and another member voted no, and two members and Mayor Lopez voted yes. I did promise the extra inspector like we discussed. Despite Jessica's not supporting us, I want to be true to that promise."

"Of course. I don't want us associated with shoddy work. You're staying with Jessica tonight?"

"Nope. Driving home now."

"Sorry."

"I'll return next week for the Christmas Festival. It's a big deal in Tidbury. Jessica is working one afternoon making homemade apple fritters. You should come."

"Sounds great. Let me talk with Eva. I bet she'd like to attend."

"Check right away for a place to stay. The inn books up fast during their festivals."

"And where do you plan to stay, my friend?"

"Hopefully, at Jessica's. If I have to drive back and forth between Tidbury and Concord, I'm determined to find ways to spend time with her."

"Good luck. See you tomorrow."

They disconnected. Luck. That's exactly what he'd need with Jessica. He had to convince her that he didn't hold her vote against him. She had to learn to trust him with the project. They had a few hurdles to cross, but his motto was never give up.

Chapter Twenty-One

Tuesday dawned sunny and bright, and Jessica rose early. The Christmas Festival had already been in full swing for several days and more visitors than usual made their way into her shop. Melody was a welcome addition to Jessica's staff. Not being tied to the shop the way Jessica had been for the last five years proved to be a positive change in her life. Particularly needed now with the requirements of serving on the board.

Lots of folks had reached out to her about the building of the retirement center on the Green. Many understood her concern and appreciated Jeff Hudson's company would institute extra precautions to make sure the building met or exceeded code. Others were mad at her for not supporting growth in the community, and still others were glad she worked to protect the green. It seemed everyone acted like they had a piece of her.

She'd heard no more from John Crowell or Tim Worley, which suited her fine. Besides now they wanted to celebrate the Christmas season and focus on the Tidbury Christmas Festival, the highlight of the celebration. Working this afternoon selling her apple fritters would be fun, even if exhausting. Jessica appreciated Lori's offer to help, and after their shift, the whole family would troop over to the Christmas Tree Lighting.

Would Jeff come? He'd said he would, but he must be mad at her for voting against his project even when he went out of the way to hire an extra inspector. She'd wanted to trust him, but she couldn't bring herself to make that compromise. She couldn't let go of her five-year crusade. Maybe her family was correct, and the time had come to move past her distrust of Tim Worley and his company. But the slam of guilt that hit her whenever anyone told her to stop her fight, suggested otherwise.

Two forks of the same river. Her personal relationship with Jeff. And her crusade against Worley Construction. Couldn't she have them both?

Were they mutually exclusive? The idea of giving up the fight made her want to throw up. Giving up any possibility with Jeff...that made her ill, too. Apparently a crack had appeared in her heart. Would that crack allow love in again?

STANDING OVER THE FRY pans making apple fritters warmed Jessica's face and the rest of her, too. Jessica and her daughter both worked two pans and still had trouble keeping up with the demand. The line outside their booth never got any shorter. No sooner than they seemed to catch up when more folks got in the line.

"How are you doing, Mom?" Lori glanced at her.

"Hanging in. Thankful my boots are warm and comfy. Otherwise, my feet would be causing real grief." She glanced down at the black fuzzy topped boots as close to house shoes as possible. "What about this long line?"

"It's your own fault. Since you skipped making them for the Fall festival, it's been a full year. Folks have missed your special apple fritters." Lori slid a piping hot fritter into a paper napkin and handed it to a man and his daughter. "Be careful. You don't want to burn your tongue."

"Well, I'm probably up for doing it every year if I can sign up for a half-day booth like this. Working an entire week or two is just two much anymore. Here you go, Millie. Enjoy." She handed a fritter to Millie Melton, pleased the widow had decided to come to the celebration. When Jessica had last visited with her, Millie wasn't sure she could come.

"That's great news and will be a big draw for the community. I thought we'd freeze without a small heater in here, but I'm staying warm hanging over these pans."

"It helps the wind is gentle."

"Hey, Jessica. You're doing a box office business here." Her friend Sue scooted through the back canvas. "Everyone is thrilled you agreed to make these again. Promise you'll do them next year?"

Jessica shot her a quick glance flipping one after another of the fritters. "I can do the half day thing, Sue. We should offer this as an option. Maybe more folks would take part if they didn't think they had to sign up for an entire week or two."

"Like your idea. More involvement is always better. And a larger variety of crafts, activities, and foods will bring folks back day after day to discover what's new. I don't want to keep you from your work. We could have a small riot on our hands."

Jessica laughed and shook her head.

"Don't forget the Christmas Tree Lighting at seven." Sue slipped out the way she'd come.

Finally the little hand spun toward six pm. Jessica and Lori had cooked almost the last of their batter, saving a dozen apple fritters in reserve for the family breakfast.

"Hi there."

Jessica didn't have to look up to recognize Jeff's deep voice. "Hi yourself. Wasn't sure you'd make it tonight. It's getting pretty late." She glanced up, admitting how happy seeing him made her.

"Am I too late for one of those world famous apple fritters?"

Jessica smiled and popped the last bit of batter in the pan. "I'll have a fresh one for you in a couple of minutes."

"Hello, Lori. Have you made many of these?"

"I've lost count. We each have two pans and fry three of the tasty morsels at a time, and it takes right at five minutes from the moment they hit the oil. My mind boggles at the math. Let's say it's been a bunch." She focused on the people in line. "I'm sorry. We're shutting down now. We only have enough for the next two in line. Thanks for stopping by. I think you can find frosted sugar cookies two booths over."

All but the two people behind Jeff nodded and moved on. Quickly, Lori handed out her last fritters. "Enjoy." She smiled and waved. "Whew. I'll start cleaning up, Mom. We're supposed to meet the rest of the family at 6:45 to find a good spot for the Christmas Tree Lighting."

"Can I tag along?" Jeff shifted from one foot to the other and fiddled with the plaid scarf at his neck.

"Of course. Here you go." She handed him the fritter in a napkin. "Remember you better blow on it, or you'll burn your tongue."

Jeff juggled the pastry in his hands. "Wow, it is hot, but it's also light and fluffy and smells great." He tore off a chunk and popped it in his mouth. His eyes rolled back in his head, and he let out a long sigh, reminding her of other times he'd sighed. Oh my.

"This is sinfully delicious. It's a good thing you only had one left, or I'd scarf down more than would be good for me."

"Well, we do have more. We're saving them for breakfast with the family tomorrow morning."

"Are you inviting me?" He polished off his apple fritter.

She ducked her head and stuffed supplies into boxes. "If you'd like to come." She cut a glance at him, and then she went back to the work of packing up.

"Yes, I would. Thanks. Can I help you in there?"

"Wouldn't hurt. You'd help to ensure we make it to the Christmas Tree Lighting on time."

Jeff stepped in, and Jessica gave him succinct instructions. Between the three of them they'd boxed up everything in little time and carted it to Jessica's shop for a temporary resting place before they returned the pans to the church.

"Mom, I'm heading on out to find the fam. I'll keep an eye out for you."

"Thanks, Lori."

Jeff's hands rested on her shoulders. "How thoughtful of her to scoot off that way." He took her face in both his hands and placed a soft kiss on her lips. "I've missed you."

"I wasn't sure you'd still be interested after I voted against your project." Her fingers fiddled with the lapels of his coat.

"You didn't vote against our project. You voted against Worley Construction."

"Will it cost you a lot more to add the extra inspector?"

"Yes it will run up our costs, but it will be worth every penny to prevent him from building a shoddy product. I want to convince people they have a safe, not only a pretty place to live."

"Thank you, Jeff. That does help me a lot. Let's go to the Christmas Tree Lighting. It's quite spectacular."

In moments, Jessica and Jeff found themselves surrounded by what looked like everyone in Tidbury plus visitors who'd all gathered for the event. The twenty-foot Douglas Fir stood majestically to the left of the gazebo.

"Mom," Lori hollered. Jessica and Jeff made their way to the front next to the family. Introductions were hastily made during the singing of *Oh Christmas Tree* by the church choir. The twins seemed particularly interested in Jeff.

Jeff kept his arm around her waist and Jessica liked the feel. She only blushed a little at her daughters' glances and raised eyebrows at each other and at her and Jeff.

Mayor Rudy Lopez used a microphone to ask for everyone's attention. "Good evening. Is everyone having a wonderful time?" Cheers from the crowd answered his question. "I hope many of you got to eat one of Jessica Allen's apple fritters. I consider myself lucky to have snagged one. You gotta keep that up every year, Jessica. We've missed them."

Jessica laughed and waved in acknowledgment.

"You're famous." Jeff whispered in her ear, sending lovely tingles down her side.

"Okay, let's get this started." Rudy's deep voice blared through the mic.

"I can't see, Dad." Bonnie held up her arms asking to be lifted, and Bob did.

"Lift me, too." Bobby waved his arms above his head.

Jeff removed his hand from around her waist and faced Kathy and Bob. "I can boost him up if you don't mind."

"Thanks, Jeff." Bob nodded at him.

"Here you go, pal." Jeff boosted Bobby up, so the boy sat on his shoulders.

"Yea! This is great."

Jessica put a hand on Jeff's arm and squeezed her thanks.

"Everyone, join me," Rudy's voice bellowed. "Five, four, three, two, one." The crowd's voices got louder with each number. Rudy pushed the lever, and the tree burst into glorious colored lights twinkling red, green, yellow, blue, and white to the cheers and claps of the crowd.

"Thanks to the church youth group for handling the decorations this year. There's another hour left tonight, and we still have over a week until

Christmas to enjoy the festival which runs through New Year's. Be safe, stay warm, and buy a lot." The audience laughed and clapped more. Maybe to help keep their hands warm.

The church choir separated into two groups and wandered through the crowd singing carols.

Bob and Jeff lowered the twins. "Hold on to someone so you don't get lost out here," Kathy cautioned.

As the crowd thinned out, Jessica's family focused their attention on her and Jeff. "Would you like to come over to the house for hot chocolate?" Kathy smiled her most welcoming smile. She probably planned to give Jeff the third degree. If they were to have any kind of a longer term relationship, they had to face this official meet and greet with the family.

Jessica glanced at Jeff, and he smiled at her and spoke for them. "Thanks, Kathy. We'd love to drink a cup of hot chocolate with you."

At the end of the evening with her family, who all seemed to hit it off with Jeff and he with them, Jessica carried their mugs to the kitchen where she found her older daughter.

"A fun evening, Kathy. Thanks for having us over."

"Mom." Kathy stood with her arms crossed over her chest.

"What is it?" Jessica had thought the evening went great. What had she missed?"

"Mom, I like him. He's a good guy. If you love him, we're all okay with that. We want you to be happy."

Jessica swiped at pools of moisture in her eyes, stopping them from trickling down her face. She swallowed several times to speak around the lump in her throat. "Thank you. That means a lot. I'm not sure how he feels."

Kathy huffed a short chuckle. "Well, I am. All you have to notice is how he looks at you and how he listens to you. We'd hate for you to move to Concord full time, but bottom line, Mom, we want you to be happy."

Jessica hugged her older daughter. "Thank you. We'll see."

Jeff appeared in the kitchen. "I've got your coat." He helped her into it. "Kathy, your home is beautiful. Thanks for letting me crash the family tradition."

"You're more than welcome, Jeff. Come any time."

After good nights to everyone, Jessica followed Jeff out into the cold night. With the roads cleared, they made the trip in no time, and Jeff parked in front of her store. He helped her out of the car and walked her to the door. After unlocking it and entering, she turned off the security system. She faced him. "Well, uh, did you make a reservation at the inn?"

"Nope. I was kind of hoping I could bunk with you." His hand eased away from her face a few strands of hair that had come out of her hat. She leaned her face into his palm and kissed it.

"Come upstairs with me. I have plenty of room." Jessica took him by the hand and led him upstairs, unlocked her door, took off the extra alarm, and reset it and the downstairs one. "Do you want something to drink?"

"I only want you." He drew her to him and drank from her lips until she had not a breath left in her, and her knees grew weak. Jeff removed his coat and hers, and then he scooped her up and carried her to the bedroom where he lay her on the bed. Sitting down beside her, Jeff took her hand and drew it to his lips, kissing each finger and the palm. "In case you can't tell, I love you, Jessica Allen. I hope you love me too. But I'm a patient man, and I can wait until you love me."

Jessica sat up and rested her arms around Jeff's neck. "My kids have urged me not to keep fighting with Worley and to move on with my life. Maybe I'm at a place where I can do that." She drew in a deep breath and let it out. "I love you, Jeff. I'm not sure what this means for us, but I wanted to tell you what's in my heart."

"Let me show you what's in mine."

Chapter Twenty-Two

Jessica walked into her bedroom, carrying a tray with refills of Jeff's coffee and her hot tea.

Jeff sat up in bed. "I could become used to this kind of service." He took his cup.

She laughed, set the tray on the bedside table, and climbed in next to him. "I think we'll save it for special times."

"Maybe we take turns."

"I warmed up the apple fritters. Would you like one?"

"I thought you left a bunch at Kathy's house."

"Well, I did, but I kept out a large one for you and a medium sized one for me."

"Planning ahead, huh?"

"Hopeful is more accurate."

He picked up the offered pastry. "So, how often do you make these, Jessica?" He patted one hand on his flat stomach. "Keeping in shape could become a challenge if you make them very often."

"Well, you're in luck. I only make them twice a year, for the fall festival and for the Christmas festival. Except this year because of the campaign, I didn't have time to make them for the fall festival."

"Okay, I think I can handle that much temptation." He took a large bite of his fritter. "Umm. So good."

"Thank you. Glad you enjoy them."

"Jessica, I hate we couldn't break our contract with Worley. Can you forgive me?"

She dropped her head on his shoulder for a moment. "There's nothing to forgive, Jeff. You did the best you could. You're going the extra mile to hire a special investigator to keep an eye on things. I do appreciate that. I hate it will cut into your profits."

He nodded. "Yeah, but I'll sleep better at night, knowing we're making the place safe for the staff and the residents who will make it their home."

Jessica finished her fritter and then snuggled closer to him. "And that's one of the reasons I love you."

Jeff kissed her forehead.

"So what's the next move?" Jessica sipped her tea. She hoped he didn't think she asked about the two of them, though that question had occupied a chunk of her time. "I mean how soon will you begin work on the center?"

"Probably not until the ground begins to thaw. And it may take longer than we'd like for the project to be built properly and have it up and running. That's part of construction, and weather always plays a role in the timing. It may not be until late May. I'm hoping for earlier, but hard to count on the weather. We'll have to see."

"I've heard talk of several families who are looking forward to having a safe place for their family members. Their home is too small, or the parents still want to be on their own, giving them a sense of independence."

"I don't think we'll have trouble filling the facility. Last bite of this yummy apple fritter." He licked his fingers and wiped them on a napkin. "Thanks for saving me an extra-large one. What's the plan for today?"

"I don't have to work in the store. If you'd like to experience all of the Christmas Festival, we can do that."

"I like that idea. We can take notes to help with rearranging the kiosks after the center is built. Tony texted me he and Eva do plan to come down for the festival. They'd intended to yesterday and Eva got hung up at work."

"Great. I enjoyed meeting them and spending the evening at their place. It will be fun to return their hospitality. Okay, buster, let's get a move on. There's lots to do and enjoy today." Jessica jumped from the bed. "I'm showering first."

"We'll save time and water if we shower together." Jeff's grin spread across his entire face.

Warmth tinted her cheeks, but Jessica nodded. "Okay."

JESSICA AND JEFF WALKED all around the festival area fairly fast to give him a better lay of the land than he'd had time for last night, and then they started back through. They hadn't gone far when Jeff got a text from Tony saying they'd arrived and asking where they should meet. Jeff directed them to Jessica's store. By the time she and Jeff got there, Tony and Eva walked up.

"Great timing," Jeff said. He and Tony bumped fists, and Jeff gave Eva a hug.

"Good to see you both." Jessica held out her hand, but Tony stepped in close for a brief hug.

"I think we're on hugging terms now."

"Well, of course." Jessica laughed, then turned to Eva, and they hugged, too.

"So this is your store, Jessica? Can we go in?"

"Of course. It's not big but let me show you around." She pushed open the door. "Hey, Janell, I've brought friends." After quick introductions, Eva browsed the items.

"You have several unique things. And look at the jams and relishes."

"Everything is local or at the least made in New England."

"And you live above the store, like in the olden days, right?" Eva picked up one of the hollowed out candles. "I love these. Haven't seen anything like them in ages."

"Back in the day, many of us tried our hand at making them, but the hobby sort of faded away the way things sometimes do. We have a local woman who still makes them, and I have trouble keeping them stocked. And yes, I live above the store." Jessica explained how after her husband died, she'd rattled around in the big house on the edge of town. The apartment above the store provided the perfect solution.

"Am I being too bold? May we go up?"

"Of course, Eva." Jessica mentally congratulated herself on picking up before she and Jeff had left. Fortunately, they'd gone the extra steps to make the bed.

Eva, Tony, and Jeff followed her up the stairs and Jessica let them in. "It's pretty small, right at 1300 square feet, but it's been perfect for me."

Eva glanced around. "Nice. I love the open concept set up with your kitchen."

"I have a large owner suite and a smaller bedroom I use as an office."

Eva crossed to the window. "Look, Tony. Jessica's got this great view of the green."

"Good set up," Tony agreed. "But my stomach is about to growl. Let's head down and find us this festival food you've been talking about."

Eva smiled at Jessica. "Thanks for showing us around."

"Happy to."

"But can we go sample the foods before my husband here passes out from hunger?"

They all laughed in agreement and trekked back downstairs and outside.

"I've heard the corn on the cob and hot dogs are something special," Jeff said.

The four enjoyed sampling a variety of foods. Each ate a corn on the cob, and they all shared two bowls of the fireman's chili.

"Hey, let's try the hotdogs," Jeff suggested.

"I love these New England buns that are split on the top. We didn't have them in Texas. The split was on the side, and everything always fell out. These are much easier to eat."

Jessica bit into her dog with extra pickle, relish, and mustard. "Umm." She wiped her mouth with a napkin. "I've always been messy with these. Nothing falls out, but I still get the mustard all over." Everyone laughed as they walked along.

Then they focused their interest on the different activities, including a snowman building contest to determine who could build the tallest one in the allotted time. A contest they did not win because they got carried away with a snowball fight, which started as next to nothing but sent them wandering off from their task of building the snowmen. Laughter bubbled up all around them when they finally stopped to find snow covering them all. As a result, a couple in their late twenties won who'd been much more focused on the competition than the four of them had been.

"Gosh, they win almost every year." Jessica dusted the snow off her gloves and coat. "They've been together since high school, and this is their deal."

With the cold air and snow freezing them almost to death, Jessica suggested they sample the hot chocolate at one booth over.

"This is good, Jessica. I can't believe I'm saying this, but this is as good as what your daughter made if that's possible?" Jeff reached forward and wiped at her upper lip which must've acquired a streak of whipped cream. "You needed a bit of help there."

Jessica's stomach tumbled at the look in his eyes. She quickly glanced away. "I'll be sure to tell her. Eva, how much longer can you two stay?"

"We're staying the night."

"Oh, that's wonderful."

"We lucked into a cancellation at the Tidbury Inn." Eva sipped her hot cocoa. "This is yummy. I've never had it with whipped cream. I may like it better than with marshmallows. Of course, the marshmallows are easier."

"I'm delighted it worked out you can stay there. The inn is such a warm, welcoming place."

Tony yawned. "Gosh, between the effort making the snowman, the snowball fight, and this warm hot chocolate, I think I'm turning into a zombie. What say we meet up with you at the inn for supper?"

"Sounds good to me, Tony. You okay with that, Jessica?"

She nodded, pleased he included her in the decision making.

"Okay, that's the plan. Tony, you better make a reservation for us for supper when you get back. The times I've stayed there, the restaurant kept busy, and in the middle of the Christmas Festival with lots of visitors in town, they may be busier than usual. Despite all the good food out here."

"Any time work better for you?" Tony swallowed the last of his hot chocolate.

"We'll probably have to take what's available. We'll be flexible. Text me when you find out. See you later." Jeff waved as Tony and Eva walked away toward the inn.

SITTING IN THE COFFEE shop in the nearby town waiting for Tim Worley to arrive, John Crowell sipped his coffee. In John's mind, arriving first indicated who was in charge. He'd called the meeting. He was in charge. Tim came through the front door, stopped to order coffee, and made his way to the table where he slumped into a chair.

"So what do we do, John?" Tim's fingers tapped on the turquoise Formica table.

"That's the reason for the meeting, Tim. To decide what to do. Here's how I figure it. Number one, we continue with our regular way of doing business and run the risk of this independent inspector catching us. Number two, we take out the independent inspector. They'll spend time finding someone else for the position, and we can slide a couple of things by, we'll make a little money, but probably not what we're used to."

"You got a third way?"

"Number three is you walk from the contract and find work far away from Jessica Allen. Business won't be the same. You'd have to find someone on another board of selectmen to work with."

Tim rubbed his chin with one hand. John could imagine the wheels turning in his head.

"Where does the last plan leave you? If I don't need the approval of the Tidbury Board of Selectmen, how does any of the money reach your pocket?"

"I appreciate your concern for me, my friend. We'd have to have an agreement between the two of us, one specifying I'm included in the revenue."

"And why would I do that?"

"To keep me from ratting you out." John sipped his coffee. He figured Tim would take the last option.

Tim grinned at him, but John didn't like the kind of grin it was.

"I've listened to your proposition, but I don't find a reason to cut you in on the profits, John. Make no mistake. The same thing that happened to Ed Allen can happen to you. It's in your best interests to keep quiet. You've made a pretty penny on the side over the years. Take the money you've made and keep your mouth shut."

"Here's the coffee, sir." The waitress set a cup in front of Tim. "Sorry it took a while. I had to make a fresh pot." She moved on to other customers.

John took a sip from his cup. "You may be right, Tim. We've had a good run, and I've invested the bulk of my earnings, and I'll be more than comfortable. More would've been better, but neither jail nor death look appealing."

"Excellent. Then we've reached an understanding. I'll cancel the contract with Hudson, to keep things neat and tidy." Tim rose. "I'd say I'll be seeing you, but I don't expect that to happen. You enjoy your coffee."

John nodded. "Sure." He picked up his cup and sipped while Tim walked from the coffee shop.

That didn't go quite the way he'd expected. John clasped his hands around the mug. He loved their fresh hot coffee, and he'd miss this little shop, but it was smart to know when to fold'em. And this game had played itself out. And all because of Jessica Allen. Maybe he should stop by for a visit. Pay her back for screwing with his plans. He'd give that more thought. Man he hated to let Jessica win with Tim canceling the contract, but it was probably the wisest course of action.

After finishing his coffee, John stood, left money on the table, nodded to the waitress, and walked from the coffee shop determined to find a way to revenge himself with Jessica. She managed to ruin a great deal. He climbed in his truck and started down the road. Hmm, looked like Tim's truck up ahead. He should've been farther along. Maybe he stopped for gas. John slowed at the corner a couple of cars behind Tim's truck. Worley started across the intersection, getting only halfway when a large truck blasted through, his horn blaring, but not stopping. The large truck broadsided Worley's smaller one, pushing it along several hundred feet, before finally both vehicles came to a stop. People left their cars and trucks and ran toward the wreck. All of a sudden Worley's truck exploded, the sound deafening. John scrubbed a hand down his faced. Damn, not how he'd expected all this would end.

JEFF HAD RETURNED TO Concord for business. He made the drive back and forth every other day. Jessica hated that for him but loved all the occasions to be with him. The Christmas Festival continued. All the businesses were doing great, including her own. Every night Jessica restocked the shelves. Sometimes she ran out to her suppliers for more product.

The bells over the door chimed and Jessica looked up. The mayor stepped into her shop. "Hey, Rudy. This festival is one of the best ever."

"Yes, it is. Thanks to you and Sue and all the other hard workers. It's one of my favorite times of the year, and all because we come together and work closely to make it happen."

Jessica chuckled. "Isn't that a little like all our festivals? St. Patrick's Day, Fourth of July, and, Labor Day, and Fall to name several."

Rudy joined her laugh. "You may be right. It's what's great about a small town."

"What brings you in? Looking for something for your wife?"

"No, I've heard news I need to share with you."

"You look serious. What is it? You're not sick, are you?"

"Sheriff Halbert called and told me Tim Worley was killed in an accident two days ago."

"What? How?" Jessica leaned back against the counter, her legs refusing to do their job of supporting her.

"He'd been having coffee with John Crowell in a coffee shop the next town over. Apparently, they met there regularly according to the waitress who served them. Gary reported according to the police, Tim left the coffee shop followed later by John. At an intersection, a truck broadsided Tim's truck, which then burst into flames. Officials pronounced him dead at the scene."

"Wow. That's just...well, I'm shocked. He wasn't a man I liked, him or his business practices, but I'm sorry to hear he's dead. Did the driver who hit Tim's stop to render aid?"

"The truck's brakes failed and hitting Tim's truck helped stop him. No telling what might have happened if he'd kept on going. All the witnesses commented about the horror and suddenness. Officials are continuing to investigate, but at this point, it looks like a tragic accident."

"The horror of that must've been stunning." Jessica straightened her fingers which had tightened into fists, the nails cutting into her palms.

"I'll report it at the next board meeting, but I thought you'd want to know. Can you tell Jeff Hudson? That will impact his work on the retirement center."

"Wow. Gosh, I don't seem to be able to find any other words." Jessica shook her head to brush away the cobwebs that made it hard for her to think. "And of course, I'll let Jeff know."

"You should continue to be cautious, Jessica. We don't know that Worley carried out all the assaults against you."

"Of course. I'm not driving much anyway. Jeff comes here. The kids pick me up and carry me back and forth to the big house. But thanks for telling me. I'll be careful, and I'll call Jeff."

"See you around." Rudy pivoted and let himself out of the shop as visitors entered.

"I told you. Isn't this the perfect little shop?" An older woman spoke to her younger companion. Maybe a mother/daughter duo.

Business kept up until she closed and locked the door. Jessica set the alarm and went upstairs. She wanted off her feet in the worst way, to sip a cup of hot tea, and to call Jeff. She hadn't had a second to do it earlier because of all the people coming in and out. She kicked off her boots and put on comfy slippers. After setting the cup under the hot water spigot, she carried her tea into the main room and lit the fire. With the cup in her hand and her feet propped on the hearth, she tapped the button to call Jeff. Doing that caused her heart to beat a little faster. He meant everything to her. No telling how they'd work out their lives, but they'd be together, though perhaps not in the traditional way.

"Hi, pretty lady." Jeff's low tones stroked a place in her middle, making her almost giddy.

"Ahh, Jeff. Listen, I have news to share." Best to get straight to the point.

"What's up?"

"Tim Worley was killed in a wreck two days ago. Mayor Lopez stopped by earlier this evening to tell me. Sheriff Halbert told Rudy and wanted him to let me know."

"That's unexpected, and that could change things with the building of the retirement center. Did he have heirs or someone else to take over the firm?"

"I really don't know much about his family or if there's anyone he might have left the business to. What does this do to your contract with the company?"

"Might make it null and void if he didn't have someone set up to carry on in his absence. Most CEOs do, though. I'll talk with our lawyers. They may be able to find out about a will. How are you feeling, Jessica?"

"Shocked. A shaft of guilt struck when I heard the news. I never liked the guy or how he ran his company. I didn't want him dead, but I gotta admit to a feeling of relief."

"Probably normal. I'll be there tomorrow, but it will be late. I can't leave until four-thirty or later."

"I'll hold supper for you. Promise you'll be careful, okay?"

"Of course. Love you."

"Me too, you." She disconnected and stared into the flickering flames. She'd learned not to take things or people for granted. They could be snatched from you without a moment's notice. Hard to believe she'd gotten a second chance at love. She and Jeff had started as adversaries but became partners to find a way to stop Worley from getting the contract to build the retirement center. And now? Worley's death shocked her and made her count her blessings. And Jeff was one of those blessings.

JESSICA HADN'T SCHEDULED herself to work in the store the next morning, and now regretted it wasn't one of her days. She had too many hours to wait for Jeff to arrive. Those would drag without something productive to do. Maybe someone at one of the booths needed a break. In fact, she could go from booth to booth helping out. The organizing committee scheduled folks to do that, but no one would complain about extra help. Standing all day on your feet took its toll. Not like walking and moving around like she did in her shop, but working in the booths, a person mostly stood around. The booths were approximately five feet wide by four feet deep. Not much pacing room.

The weather cooperated, presenting them clear, cold days with plenty of sun and little wind. The wind made low temps brutal. Jessica shivered, remembering how cold she'd gotten trudging home after the truck rammed her, putting her vehicle out of commission. She liked to think she'd have made it back to town on her own but was grateful Jeff found her, and she didn't have to. She drew her teal wool scarf tighter around her neck to block the memory.

By late afternoon, exhaustion drained her muscles, and she gave it up, glad she'd been able to lend a hand. Everyone seemed pleased at the larger than usual number of visitors. A few people spoke about Worley's death. Jessica managed to avoid getting caught up in one of those conversations. She never crossed paths with John Crowell, though she overheard several people mention they'd seen him. She'd heard he'd made a point about what a loss to the community Worley's death was. Frankly, Jessica was gratified she hadn't run into Crowell.

At five, she set out toward her shop and home to prepare for Jeff's arrival. She'd had enough presence of mind to put chicken breasts with green beans, new potatoes, and garlic in the crock pot. She hoped Jeff liked the meal.

Jessica entered the shop to the friendly sound of the bell. "Hello, Janell. How's the day been? Are you holding up?"

"The day has flown by because people have stopped by continuously. And I'm doing fine. I gulped a quick supper during a short lull, and I'm good for the evening."

"Thanks. Jeff will be here soon. Tell him to come on up."

"Will do. I'm going to do a bit of reshelving. You have a good evening."

"See you tomorrow, Janell." Jessica took off her coat and climbed the stairs to her apartment, excitement growing with each step at the idea of seeing Jeff again. She unlocked the door, went in, hung up her coat and scarf, and went straight to the kitchen. The aroma from the crock pot made her stomach growl. It had been a busy day, and she hadn't taken a break to grab lunch.

What were she and Jeff going to do with each other? They could keep dating a couple of times a week. But she wanted to drive to Concord herself. It wouldn't be fair to expect Jeff to make the trip all the time. Could she convince her children the threat was behind her now with Tim Worley's death?

Jessica went to work preparing the salad to accompany the chicken. She believed in her heart Worley and Crowell were behind all the incidents, though who carried out what she didn't know. Since hearing of Worley's death, she walked with a lighter step, not looking over her shoulder or sensing someone staring at her, even though Crowell was still around.

What would happen to her and Jeff? What did their future hold? Marriage? Did she want to marry, Jeff? Wasn't she being presumptuous? Maybe he didn't want to marry her. She loved being with him. She loved sleeping in bed next to him, not to mention making love with him. But did she want to be married again? Life would be complicated with his business centered in Concord and her family here in Tidbury. Of course, Lori only had another semester of college, and afterwards who knew where she'd end up. But Bobby and Bonnie were in Tidbury. She'd be hard pressed to move away from them. Maybe no marriage, but friends with benefits?

Warmth flooded her cheeks. What had gotten into her? Friends with benefits like she starred in one of those old 90s TV shows. She laughed at herself while setting the small table in front of the window overlooking the green. The sound of footsteps pounding up the stairs drew her to the front door, and she flung it open. Jeff stood on the landing.

"Hi, beautiful." Jeff threw his arms around her and drew her into an embrace that lifted her feet off the floor. Then he kissed her and kissed her again.

They only broke apart at the sound of Janell's laughter from below. "Do you two need to rent a room?"

"You know, Janell, I believe we have a room." She winked. "Good night." They stepped into her apartment and closed the door. Jessica slipped her arm around Jeff's waist. His arm draped across her shoulders. "Welcome. How did the trip go? Much traffic?"

"Not bad. I made it in an hour and fifteen minutes." Jeff took off his coat and Jessica took it from him, hanging it on the coat rack next to hers. "Boy, that smells good." He put both hands on her waist. "Not as good as you do." He nuzzled her neck. "What is that scent anyway?"

"Eau de Crock Pot and Garlic."

Jeff laughed. "Well, whatever it is, I love it."

"Can you open the wine and pour while I serve up the meal?"

"Yes, ma'am." Jeff made himself at home.

He'd been in her apartment enough to know where everything was. She hadn't been to his condo as many times. Jessica put the salad in separate plates and put them on the table. She served up the chicken, potatoes, and green beans. The tender chicken fell apart when she lifted it from the pot.

Jeff set the wine glasses on the table and held Jessica's chair for her.

"Thank you, kind sir."

"You're welcome. You've done the hard work. We should toast." He raised his glass, and she picked up hers.

"What should we toast to?"

"To this wonderful meal. To the trip being easy today. To life being good."

"I'll drink to all of those." They clinked glasses and took a sip.

After several bites, Jeff put down his fork and leaned back. "You can make this anytime. Gosh, it's well, my tastebuds are saying thank you very much."

Jessica smiled at him. "I'm delighted you're enjoying the meal."

After supper they settled on the sofa in front of the fire, each with a glass of wine. Jeff put his arm around her shoulder and nestled her close. "This is the best after a long couple of days." He let out two long breaths and seemed to relax. "How do you manage to keep going for two whole weeks with the Christmas Festival? Isn't it exhausting?"

"It would be if all of us worked all day long, every single day of the two weeks, but mostly we don't. My shift this year didn't compare in length to what I've done other years, but everyone's given breaks, and everyone pitches in. It brings us all closer." She sipped her wine, the flavors of blackberry and plum her favorite. "Have you heard anything from the lawyers yet? Have they told you if you can look for another company?"

Jeff, smirked. "You know lawyers. It takes them a while. Don't hear me wrong. I love our lawyers. They've kept us from making several bad decisions over the years but so far nothing on this issue. We'll probably be okay. We wouldn't have started construction until Spring. Tony and I won't have trouble coming up with a good prospect if we're allowed to. One part of me says Worley must have set up someone to carry the company in case something happened to him."

"If so, maybe they won't be the greedy sort of person Tim Worley was."

"And we'll have our extra inspector on the job if we have to stick with Worley."

"I'm glad you intend to hire a special inspector if you have to stick with Worley's company in whatever form it may take."

Jeff sat forward, took her glass from her hand, setting the glass on the table. He grasped both of her hands and eased her around to face him.

"Are you all right?" Jessica studied his face.

"Well, maybe, depending on what you say to a question I want to ask you."

Jessica's heart rate double-timed in her chest. Did he plan to ask her to move in with him?

"We haven't known each other a long time, and we started out adversaries. But we've grown to become friends and more than that. We've both lost loved ones. We know how quickly a person's life can be shattered. Jessica, you make my life better than it has ever been before. I love you more today than I did yesterday, and I can't wait to see how much I'll love you tomorrow. Jessica, will you marry me?"

"Oh, my goodness, Jeff. Oh, my goodness." Jessica struggled for breath, much less for words.

"Too soon? I hope not. I—"

"Yes, Jeff. Yes, I'll marry you."

He drew her in for one of those passionate kisses that had she been standing would have turned her legs to cooked string beans.

Jeff finally released her. "Thank God. I didn't know what you'd say. Jessica, I haven't had a chance to buy you a ring. I couldn't wait to tell you how I feel and to learn if you shared my feelings. I can't believe I'm this lucky."

"We're both lucky to find a second love. But oh my goodness, where will we live? How will we do a together-life?"

Jeff chuckled and drew her to him. "I don't have all those answers, Jessica. But I have the most important answer. You said yes."

They snuggled on the sofa and breathed in the magic of the moment.

"Do you want to call your kids?"

"I don't know. I think I want to tell them in person. It's kind of fun to hold it between the two of us for a time. Is that selfish?"

"I don't think so."

"You're staying for a few days, right?"

"Yes, through the weekend."

"Good. We can tell them at the Saturday night family dinner."

"Perfect and that gives us an opportunity to travel to Concord tomorrow. I have a jeweler friend who I think can find you a perfect engagement ring and have it ready so you can wear it when we make the announcement."

"Oh my goodness, this is moving fast."

"It can't move too fast for me." Jeff kissed Jessica, and she drifted off into a wonderful world of possibilities with her future husband. Not something she'd ever thought she have again.

Chapter Twenty-Three

Jessica and Jeff didn't sleep in as much as Jessica had expected after their busy night full of wonderful explorations of each other's bodies, but they had plans for the day. She cooked eggs, bacon, and toast for breakfast. At nine sharp, Jeff called his jeweler friend and made them an appointment to look at rings before lunch. Jonathan Strickland carried on his father's tradition, and Jeff told her he and Jonathan had been friends since college. He promised to do his best for them.

Promptly at eleven, Jeff parked on the street in front of Strickland's Jewelry Store. They went inside and Jonathan greeted them right away, exchanging guy hugs with Jeff. Jonathan shot a quick glance at Jessica and then faced Jeff. "How'd you turn out so lucky?" He cocked his head at Jessica. "And are you sure you know what you're getting into with this guy?"

Jessica smiled and held tighter to Jeff's hand. "I think I'm the lucky one."

Jonathan kissed her on the cheek. "She's a keeper, Jeff. You two come over here, and let's find what will work for you both."

"We haven't had a chance to discuss preferences in types of rings. That's one reason I didn't buy one before I asked you to marry me."

"Frankly, that subject has been top-most in my mind since you mentioned coming here today, Jeff. Prior to that, the concept of a wedding or engagement ring had not been on my radar at all."

"You're falling down on the job, man. Never mind, Jessica. Let me show you a great variety, and you can select what seems best to you." Jonathan ushered them to cases at the back part of the store.

An hour and a half later Jessica and Jeff were on their way out of the store, having ordered what Jessica considered the perfect ring set with a matching wedding band for Jeff. Her ring had a one carat marquis diamond surrounded by five smaller diamonds that curled around the main stone making a half circle. The wedding band fit underneath making it look like one ring when worn together. Jeff's ring matched her wedding band in a brushed gold.

Jeff lifted her hand and kissed her ring finger. "You've made me a happy man."

"And you've made me a happy woman. We picked such beautiful rings. I love that your wedding band and mine match. Jonathan does amazing work."

"He's putting a special rush on the deal to have yours ready by Saturday. I'd like you to wear it when we have dinner with your family. I'll come back to Concord on Saturday to pick up the ring."

"You've got good friends, Jeff. That's a remarkable turnaround time."

"That's what friends will do for you."

JESSICA DRESSED IN her favorite black wool slacks and her low-heeled black boots. She'd chosen a purple cashmere sweater to complement the pants. Understated but classic and appropriate for the supper with her family to make the announcement of their engagement. Jeff left in the early afternoon, driving to Concord to pick up the ring. Excitement bubbled in her like a silly schoolgirl, hoping her guy would give her his high school ring. Her tummy turned cartwheels when she contemplated what her new life would become.

They'd had plenty of conversations on how to make their life work, and they'd come up with what seemed like a workable compromise. She was anxious to hear her daughters' reaction to their plan.

Her phone chirped with Jeff's signal, telling her he'd arrived. She went to open her apartment door. Jeff bounded up the stairs like a much younger man and swept her into his arms. "I missed you. I should've taken you with me."

"There'll be other times."

He took her hand, dragged her into the apartment while retrieving a package from his coat pocket. "I can't wait to see this on your hand." He twisted away putting his back to her for a moment then faced her and dropped to one knee. He took her left hand in his. "Will you marry me, Jessica?"

"Yes." She chuckled. "Did you think I'd changed my mind?"

"Just wanted to hear it again."

He eased the ring on her finger. "And make it official."

Jessica's gaze fastened on the ring. "It is beautiful."

"Just like its owner." He drew her in for a passionate kiss, one of those that turned her knees to gelatin.

"Oh, my goodness, if you kiss me like that again, we won't make it to Kathy's house." Jessica laughed. "I'm bursting with happiness, and I can't wait any longer to share us with them."

"Well, let's go. It fits all right?" Jeff lifted her hand again.

"It's perfect. Like you are. Let's go talk to the family." They bundled up and after a quick drive Jessica remembered little of, they arrived at Kathy and Bob's home.

She tapped on the door and entered. Jessica had thought to hold off making the announcement until the end of the meal, but things didn't go as she'd planned. After entering, she removed her gloves and stuffed them in the pocket of her coat. She opened the closet door to hang it up as Kathy greeted them at the front.

"Hey, Mom. Oh my gosh. What is that on your finger?"

Jessica handed her coat to Jeff and held up her hand, flashing her fingers back and forth. "Oh, this little thing? What is this little thing on my finger?"

"Oh my gosh, Mom. You're engaged." Kathy took her mother's hands and swung her around and around. "Lori come out here. Mom's getting married." Kathy released Jessica and hugged Jeff. "You will take good care of her, right?"

"Absolutely."

"Why are you hollering, Kathy? That's not like you, and I couldn't understand it all anyway." Lori came from the kitchen and immediately picked up on the festive air.

Kathy yanked Jessica's hand and held it out. "Mom and Jeff are getting married."

Lori managed to hug both her mom and Kathy at the same time. "I'm happy for you. And, Mom, the ring is a stunner with its unique design."

Bob came wandering in. "What's all the commotion? I thought we'd sit down to eat right after they arrived."

Explanations were made and Bob and Jeff shook hands. "Congratulations. It's great to have another guy in the family. Bobby and I have been outnumbered."

"I planned to tell you at dinner. I hope we haven't ruined the meal." Jessica glided her hand through Jeff's arm with her hand on top displaying her stunning ring.

"No problem. Give me a minute, and we'll be ready to sit down. Bob, go find us a bottle or two of Champagne. This is a celebration."

As they all tripped off, Bobby entered followed by his sister. "Hi, Gram. When do we eat, Mom? I'm hungry."

"Now," Kathy yelled from the kitchen. "Wash up."

Bobby headed for the bathroom, and Bonnie took Jessica's hand leading her toward the dining room. Her fingers noticed the ring first. "Oh, Gram, this is beautiful. Did you buy a new ring?"

"Well, Jeff here bought it for me. It means we're getting married."

Bonnie dropped her hold on Jessica and clapped her hands, her eyes giant in her face. "Our teacher got married last summer. I had a lot of fun. She had lots of candy. Can we come?"

"Of course, sweetheart." Goodness, they'd not even considered what the ceremony would be like.

After the family settled around the dining room table, Bob raised his glass. "To the newly engaged couple."

Everyone raised their glasses and clinked, followed by lots of laughter. The questions began after Kathy made sure everyone had good helpings of her meal of porkchops and dressing with cranberries.

"When are you getting married?" Lori asked while buttering a roll.

"We're thinking of sometime after the New Year's, maybe the first week of January." Jessica cut into the tender porkchop.

"That's in a little over two weeks? In two weeks!" Kathy's eyebrows nearly met her bangs.

"That's the plan," Jeff said.

"When you reach our age, there's no reason to wait. We'll talk to Pastor Rogers tomorrow and ask him to check his calendar to find what's available for us. We'd have already talked with him but wanted to wait until we'd told you."

"And I wanted to wait until Jessica had her ring."

"Whatever it takes, we will help you make this happen." Lori smiled with determination.

"Mom, have you told Aunt Maddie yet? Will she be able to come?" Kathy passed the basket of rolls.

"No, I haven't yet. I know it's not much notice. If she can't make it here, perhaps Jeff and I can make a trip to Texas in the Spring."

"Mr. Jeff, will you live in Gram's apartment over the store?" Bonnie's voice drew everyone's attention.

Out of the mouth of a babe had come the question Jessica dreaded more than any others.

"Sometimes we will, Bonnie. And sometimes we'll be in my condo in Concord."

"Oh. Okay." The innocence of youth.

"Can we come visit you there?" Bobby wanted to know.

"You bet. We have a spare bedroom that will work great for you." Jeff tousled Bobby's hair.

Jessica's daughters looked at each other in a sort of secret communication. Lori nodded to her sister. Kathy took a sip of champagne and set down the glass. "All of us are okay with that. This has ended up better than we hoped. We were afraid you'd live in Concord full time. That would've been harder, but we were prepared to accept that because we want you to be happy, Mom. And if Jeff makes you happy, we're all on board."

"So let me understand. You have discussed this?" Jessica eyed her daughters.

"Of course. We aren't blind. We didn't miss the way you two look at each other. And it's sweet. Concord is under an hour and a half away. And we can shop." The sisters giggled and high-fived each other.

"See why I'm relieved to have another man in the family?" Bob raised his Champagne glass toward Jeff who met his across the table, a grin covering his face.

LATER THAT NIGHT JEFF and Jessica headed for her apartment. A bright moon spotlighted the road and surrounding trees. Quite a spectacular night in many ways. Nothing like the times Jessica drove through storms to get home. Jessica glanced at Jeff. "I think that went quite well, don't you?"

"Of course, but what did you expect? They're your family. They love you more than anything, and they want you to be happy. What did Kathy say? If I make you happy, they're on board. Or something like that. Do I make you happy, Jessica?" He dropped his right hand onto her left and brought it to his lips for a kiss."

Jessica sighed. "Yes, you certainly do, Jeff. More than I have any right to experience."

"You deserve everything, Jessica. It's not original, but if I could give you that moon, I would."

"I think that's Jimmy Stewart in "It's a Wonderful Life.""

"Well, there you go. We'll have a wonderful life." He eased the SUV into a driveway of a house at the edge of town.

"Why are we stopping? What are you doing?"

"I have to kiss you." Jeff pulled her into his arms, and the kiss opened soft and gentle then roared into a flaming inferno. Finally, he set her away. "Okay, we're going home before I act like a teenager in this car, and the sheriff arrests us for making out in someone's driveway." He got the car back on the road. "You know we never made that trip to the Mount Washington Resort. What would you think about going there for our honeymoon?"

Jessica laughed as she settled back into her seat. "I'd like that a lot. Maybe after a few days there, we can fly to Fort Worth to see my sister Maddy if she can't make it here for the wedding."

Jeff nodded and kissed her hand. "Sounds like a winner."

A smile covered her face as she marveled at how wonderful Jeff's love made her feel. She thanked God for this second chance at love with such a good man as Jeff Hudson. And to think they'd started as adversaries.

Epilogue

Jessica was in awe at how her daughters came together to help her pull off this rushed but oh, so desired wedding. With fewer winter weddings than any other season, Pastor Rogers scheduled their ceremony for January 5th. Jessica stared at herself in the mirror in the bride's room of the church. Reflected behind her were Kathy, Lori, and her sister Maddy who'd made herculean efforts to arrive to be her matron of honor.

"You look beautiful, Jessica. The long, purple velvet sheath is exquisite."

"Ah, thanks, sis. I'm so grateful you could make it.

"Of course, I wasn't about to miss my little sister's wedding." She leaned forward and kissed Jessica on the cheek. "Happy for you, sweetie."

Jessica pivoted right into Kathy's hug. "She's right, Mom. You look radiant."

"We're so happy for you, Mom," Lori chimed in.

A knock was followed by Bob sticking his head around the door. "It's about time, ladies. Kathy and Lori, you need to take your places in the pew. I've got a nervous bridegroom checking his watch every couple of seconds.

One more kiss and hug from each of her daughters, and they left. Bob extended his elbow. "Are you sure about all of this, Jessica?"

Jessica smiled at Maddy and Bob before taking her son-in-law's arm. "I sure am. Thanks for walking me down the aisle. Let's go do this. After you, Maddy."

Maddy handed Jessica a bouquet of daisies and lavender hydrangeas, kissed her once more, and set off, wearing a short black wool sheath.

Jessica stopped in the narthex. The doors opened for Maddy, who stepped down the maroon runner past the fifty gathered guests, including Jeff's father. Jessica liked him a lot and was glad he'd been able to come.

When Maddy reached the front, Bob gave Jessica a nod, and they set off after her sister toward where Jeff stood with Tony next to him as best man. When Jessica's gaze connected with Jeff's, her heart swelled within. It was hard to breathe. The love flowing from his eyes to her made her feel like she could float down the aisle. But indeed she walked on Bob's arm to the chancel area. Bob kissed her on the cheek before placing her hand in Jeff's.

Pastor Rogers began, "Dearly beloved...."

She and Jeff exchanged their vows and before you knew it, they were husband and wife, walking back down the aisle, smiling at their friends and family and on toward the rest of their life. But first the wonderful reception the girls had put together back at Kathy's house.

Maddy snagged her sister in a lull between everyone wanting to hug Jessica. "I gotta tell you, sis, I can't remember you looking so happy."

"I really am, Maddie. Your being here means so much to me. Jeff and I had talked about coming to Texas soon if you couldn't make the trip."

"Well, you still need to come. I want Jeff to meet Larry and my girls."

"Of course. I want him to, as well." Jessica took her sister's hand and squinted her eyes at her. "Is everything all right with you?"

"Of course," Maddy brushed off her sister's concerns. "Okay, I need to share you with everyone else. I'm going to check in the kitchen that we still have enough of everything." Maddy excused herself and disappeared.

"Hmm."

"How's my bride?" Jeff scooted next to her and placed a chaste kiss on her cheek. "You have a slight frown here." He brushed a finger lightly between her eyes.

"I'm worried about Maddy. She hasn't been here long, but she just doesn't seem like her usual self. We are still going to go out to Texas this Spring, aren't we?"

"Anything you want, sweetheart."

"Okay, I'm holding you to that." Jessica laughed and kissed her husband full on the lips.

"Anything about her especially bothering you?"

"I can't put my finger on it exactly, but when she doesn't think anyone is looking, I catch her with this bleak expression on her face. She keeps checking her phone, way more than she normally does. I don't know. It's probably nothing."

"Let's not worry about it now, Jessica. We can make a trip out there this Spring even if you're not still concerned. Besides, I'd like to visit the town that birthed you. But now is our time."

"You're right, Jeff. I'm sorry."

"No need to apologize, sweetheart. She's your sister. I'd hope you'd share your concern with me."

Kathy eased up beside them. "Come on you two. We need to do the toasts before we cut the cake which is super gorgeous, and I can't keep the twins away from it much longer."

They laughed and followed Kathy to the center of the room, surrounded by friends and family. The toasts brought laughter and tears, but mostly laughter. The white cake with raspberry filling was scrumptious, moist, sweet, and melted in the mouth. Eventually, the only ones left at Kathy's were Jeff's father, Tony, Eva, and the family. They pulled in a few extra chairs and settled in the great room around the fireplace.

"Kathy, Lori, thank you so much for all your hard work. To make this wedding come together the way you did in record time is amazing. We'll always be grateful for the beautiful gift of this special day." She hugged both girls and Jeff did, too. He shook Bob's hand and high-fived the twins, who had been on their best behavior, and yes, Jessica made sure her grands got candy.

"When will you return? I'm already missing you." Lori wiped at a tear before it sneaked from her eye.

"Oh, honey. That's so sweet. You'll be so busy with your last semester at college, you'll hardly notice when we're not here."

"We do love the compromise you two worked out. Here for a couple of months and in Concord for a couple of months." Kathy slipped an arm around her sister's waist.

"Neither of us wanted to give up our life in our homes. This just makes sense. Tony, I can't thank you enough for being willing to facilitate this arrangement. It complicates our work situation.

"Happy to help, Jeff." Tony smiled at his partner.

"And like any compromise, neither of us got entirely what we wanted, but we got what we wanted most, which is to be together. And, bride, speaking of our life together, it's time we set off on that adventure. The Mount Washington Resort awaits."

Jessica laughed as they threw coats on over their wedding finery. She kissed the family one more time and hugged the grands especially hard. "I'll see you soon." She took Jeff's extended hand, grateful they'd been able to find a compromise about their life together.

Grateful, too, she hadn't compromised about Worley Construction, which had been a tough call resulting in lots of negative consequences. Still, she had no regrets about the decision. Sheriff Halbert had arrested John Crowell after digging back into Lonnie Melton's death when Millie, his widow, provided a clue in the form of a restaurant bill for a meal he'd eaten just hours before his death. A meal he'd shared with Crowell. No telling when the case would go to trial, but Jessica prayed if John was responsible for Lonnie's death, the jury would find him guilty.

With Tim Worley's death, the company had passed to one of his nephews who'd been appalled to hear of the claims of mismanagement. He promised things would be different under his leadership, but Jeff and Tony decided to keep the extra inspector on the payroll to make sure the nephew kept his word. Jeff and Tony were eager to get on with building the retirement center on the green. The green, the center of Tidbury. What a difference that would make for the townspeople.

Jessica was also grateful she'd been able to convince Janell she was ready for more of a managerial position. Janell had taken over most of the responsibility for Allen's, so Jessica didn't have to worry about her shop when she was in Concord. Besides, they were only a little over an hour away, and technology would let her stay in touch.

And her decision about living arrangements with Jeff? She glanced at her handsome husband as he steered the car away from her former home.

That decision, not tough at all. Sometimes the right choice was a simple compromise.

The End

Other Books by Marsha R. West

The Second Chances Series
SECOND ACT, Book 1

Addison Jones Greer, divorced mother of two teens, is the executive director of Cowtown Theatre. When someone murders a member of the board in the costume room, suspicion rests on everyone involved with the theatre, including Addie. She has angered some board members because she wants to fire the artistic director. Although she's warned him several times, he continues to go over budget for productions.

Mike Riley, Fort Worth homicide detective, hates that he caught this case. His sister-in-law dragged him to a theatre fundraiser where he met Addison, the first woman he's wanted to pursue a relationship within a long time. Not about to happen now.

ACT OF TRUST, Book 2

A widow since 9/11 and a mother of a grown daughter, **Kate Thompson** wants to keep her and her daughter safe, but an unexpected inheritance of land in Maine pushes her out of her comfort zone in Texas and into the arms of a Maine lawyer.

Maine lawyer and environmentalist, **Jim Donovan** wants to protect Aunt Liddy's land and keep it from falling into the hands of developers, but first he must convince Kate Thompson she should hold on to the family land when she doesn't even want to go look at it. However, he's unprepared for the attraction each feels for the other but deny exists. Will they be able to settle the land deal before anyone else is murdered or they break each other's hearts?

ACT OF BETRAYAL, Book 3

A cosmetics company owner in Dallas, **Devon Moore**, wants to save her company from bankruptcy, but her ex-husband's embezzlement sends her into dangerous waters trying to pay back his clients, replace the money he stole from her company, and keep her and her daughter and her parents safe.

Private Investigator, **Brett Townsend**, wants to find who is threatening his new client and locate the missing money. He suspects the beautiful Devon hasn't been completely honest with him. A wife, even an ex-wife, has to know, doesn't she? When she is attacked twice and her daughter is kidnapped, he adjusts his thinking.

ACT OF SURVIVAL, Book 4

Encouraged by her friends to protect herself, **Kim Mason Dennison** is determined to divorce her abusive husband. **Cooper Wray**, an attorney, assures Kim that her husband, Hunter, can't keep the proceedings from moving forward because Texas is a no-fault divorce state. But why is Hunter doing everything he can to stop the divorce? And will that even include murder?

STAND-ALONE BOOKS
VERMONT ESCAPE

Jill Barlow has lost everyone she cared about except her grown children. Caught in her father's fight to keep casino gambling out of Texas, her husband and dad are murdered. She'll do what it takes to ensure her kids safety even if it means leaving Texas and moving to Vermont.

Jerrod Phillips has come a long way in the twenty-odd years since his wife abandoned him and their two children. With no room in his heart for love, he'll do anything to keep his family from being hurt again, especially when the threats come packaged in the form of the attractive Jill Barlow who he suspects is involved in murder.

Forced to trust each other when trouble follows her, they'll battle, not only killers intent on ending her life, but the attraction drawing them together.

TRUTH BE TOLD

Looking forward to a peaceful Christmas visit with her Fort Worth family, **Meg Bourland** is shocked to discover someone is blackmailing her father. When he rebuffs her offer to help, the Atlanta SWAT team member enlists her LA police officer brother and his former partner to uncover the truth. She fights her attraction for **Scott McClaine** and the immediate tug to her heart caused by his sacrifice. Her life is in Atlanta, and his is in California.

Scott McClaine, medically retired homicide detective, came to Fort Worth to recuperate from life-threatening bullet wounds he received saving the life of Meg's brother. Hard enough to accept his new physical limitations, but they make him unacceptable for strong Meg. Regardless, he commits himself to helping her stop the blackmailer. Working closely with her, a bond forms. Could she feel the same?

In the search for truth, they uncover pieces of the puzzle, which threaten to ruin her father's career as mayor and destroy the family she holds dear. Will Meg and Scott find their way through the maze of family secretes? Will they find the strength to make the sacrifices required for real love before the blackmailer makes good on threats to kill?

THE THEATRE

Forty-year-old, never been married stage and TV actress **Kelly Lawson** returns to her Texas home to choreograph and star in the Glenview Theatre summer season. Kelly's mother has made a hobby of trailing out every new man in town for Kelly's inspection, hoping she'll fall in love and use Glenview as her home base, especially now that Kelly's father has entered the beginning stages of Alzheimer's. Two years ago, Kelly broke off an engagement shortly before she discovered her former fiancé dead, a gun in his hand and a hole in his head. Reason enough to guard her heart.

When Kelly accuses a Glenview police officer of harassing two of the theatre's gay actors, Police Chief **Josh Kincaid**, her mother's candidate for this trip, becomes involved in the investigation. Incidents pile up, making it clear someone has it in, not only for the theatre, but for Kelly as well. Josh searches for clues to the person behind the attacks and the reason for them, all the while trying to ignore his developing feelings. How could he trust his heart to a New York actress?

TAINTED

Socialite and philanthropist **Elizabeth Hartman** needs to start a new life after divorcing her husband Gerry Richardson who's in federal prison for money laundering, a crime the Feds suspected her of being involved in.

Her mother's family vacation home in Red River, New Mexico offers just the respite she needs. Or does it?

One too many deaths sends retired Dallas homicide detective and now **Marshall Matt Thornton** to Red River to seek a less dangerous place to serve. The New Mexico mountains promises to be that refuge until his high school sweetheart Liz Hartman arrives, bringing with her danger to his town and his heart.

<u>NEXT BOOK</u>

Follow up with Jessica's sister Maddy. Why was she upset at Jessica's wedding? And learn about what happened to the heroine's brother David in TRUTH BE TOLD.

Don't miss out!

Visit the website below and you can sign up to receive emails whenever Marsha R West publishes a new book. There's no charge and no obligation.

https://books2read.com/r/B-A-HZRF-HIASB

BOOKS 2 READ

Connecting independent readers to independent writers.

About the Author

A retired elementary school principal, a former school board member, and theatre arts teacher, Marsha R. West writes Romance, Suspense, and Second Chances. Experience Required. She lives in Texas with her supportive lawyer husband and Charley, a deaf, Chihuahua/Jack Russell Terrier. Their two daughters presented them with three delightful grandchildren all who live nearby.

The theme of Marsha's eight books is always second chances, and she even has a four-part series titled The Second Chances Series. She believes in Happily Ever Afters. Her husband picked up a plaque for her on one of their several trips to Maine that states her philosophy exactly. *Everything will be all right in the end. If it's not all right, it's not the end.* The Heroines and Heroes in her books are in their 40s and 50s with their parents and children often playing supporting roles.

She's a member of Romance Writers of America, the North Texas local chapter, NTRWA, Authors Marketing Guild LLC, & the WORD BY WORD Blog. She has her own weekly blog and monthly newsletter. Marsha loves making presentations to groups and has twice taught a Silver Frogs class on Indie Publishing for Texas Christian University. Her books can be found on AMAZON, B & N, KOBO, and iTunes and other sites. Print books are also at Draft 2 Digital, Indie Lector Stores, and Amazon. Blurbs for each of her books with links can be found on her website https://authormarsharwest.wordpress.com/ Where you can also sign up for her blog and her **NEWSLETTER** MRW Press LLC (list-manage.com)

Contact her at marsha@marsharwest.com_,_and follow her on... https://www.facebook.com/?ref=tn_tnmn

https://www.twitter.com/Marsharwest @Marsharwest

https://wordbyword.net/category/blog/

https://www.pinterest.com/marsharwest/

https://www.instagram.com/marsharwest

Amazon.com: Marsha R. West: Books, Biography, Blog, Audiobooks, Kindle

Marsha R. West (Author of Vermont Escape) | Goodreads

If you enjoyed COMPROMISE, I'd appreciate a review. They are so important. Thanks. Marsha

Read more at https://www.authormarsharwest.wordpress.com.